THE SEX LIFE OF THE AMOEBA

BARRY HEALEY

MiroLand
publishers

MIROLAND (GUERNICA)
TORONTO • BUFFALO • LANCASTER (U.K.)
2014

Michael Mirolla, general editor
Connie McParland, series editor
David Moratto, book designer
Guernica Editions Inc.
1569 Heritage Way, Oakville, ON L6M 2Z7
2250 Military Road, Tonawanda, N.Y. 14150-6000 U.S.A.

Distributors:
University of Toronto Press Distribution,
5201 Dufferin Street, Toronto (ON), Canada M3H 5T8
Gazelle Book Services, White Cross Mills, High Town, Lancaster LA1 4XS U.K.

First edition.
Printed in Canada.

Legal Deposit — First Quarter
Library of Congress Catalog Card Number: 2014934823
Library and Archives Canada Cataloguing in Publication

Healey, Barry, author
The sex life of the amoeba / Barry Healey. -- First edition.

(MiroLand ; no. 4)
Issued in print and electronic formats.
ISBN 978-1-77183-005-8 (pbk.).--ISBN 978-1-77183-006-5 (epub).--
ISBN 978-1-77183-007-2 (mobi)

I. Title.

PS8615.E252S49 2014   C813'.6   C2014-901613-1   C2014-901614-X

For Carson

The characters and events in this book, of course, are not intended to resemble any incidents or persons living or dead. I myself am a fictional character and, as the reader knows, a fictional character can only write about other fictional characters. That is to say, the characters of a work of fiction by a fictional character are only figments of a vivid (and possibly disturbed) imagination. Whereas, this is not true of settings. By depicting actual locales, I'd hoped to add realism to my story so that these fictional characters could, for a few hundred pages, come to life and seem a little less fictitious.

I hope this is clear.

— SARAH FIELDING, JUNE 2014

I ONCE TOLD Vlad I thought I was asexual.

"A sexual what?" he asked.

"Not 'a sexual,' 'asexual'."

"What is asexual?"

"Without sex, at least, not involving sex."

"An asexual is someone who is not having sex?"

"Yes."

"Like us?"

"I can't speak for you, but yes, on my side."

1

Vlad looked at me with pity, the Russian kind that flows from deep within the soul. "Sarah, I don't want to pry but you are young woman having life with no sex?"

"Sort of, I mean, it's not like I planned it or anything, it just happened, and it's habit now, sort of."

"Like marriage," Vlad said wistfully.

"I wouldn't know."

"So asexuals, are they in favour of some-sex marriage?"

Vlad's quips defuse your concerns only fleetingly. I had felt asexual since puberty. It wasn't that I wasn't passionate — I thought I might be, but I didn't know. Mostly, I felt like an amoeba — sexless.

During my university years, I'd had a somewhat relationship with Brad who, at 30, was still writing his doctoral thesis on the mating habits of sea slugs (they were more passionate than we were) and wasn't paying attention when it ended. I was articling, putting in long days at Butbung, Drucker & Warthogh, where none of the males were even remotely romantic

— none had passion potential — none. Romance is a knockdown from the right brain and lawyers (especially corporate ones) always lead with their left.

So after BD&W, I had doubts about a future in law. I wanted time to think and to travel but I had no money. So I went job hunting, which is how I met László.

"My movies," he explained during the interview, "are sexy, but for sophisticate audience." Like all Hungarians I've known (two), László is compact and stocky, has a vault full of charm, wears impeccably-tailored suits (without a tie), and smells like the cologne mart of a department store. Glancing at his watch, he nodded. "Come," he said and, driving off in his ancient Mercedes, I wondered if this was a test.

"So tell me why you want to be secretary."

"I don't ... necessarily. I need to make money."

"What you want money for?"

"To go to London."

"London?"

"I want to see English theatre."

"Ah, theatre," he muttered. "When I go to theatre, I fall asleep. Actors talk too much. Not like movies which are vibrations of life. In movies, everything is possible." Even though László immigrated here 17 years ago, his English remains in the experimental stage.

After a few blocks, he pulled into the parking lot attached to Willington Heights High School, stopping near a group of movie trucks. Zombies, vampires, witches and princesses stood near a catering table, eating buns, drinking coffee, smoking, gossiping, and peering at their cells. László strode past them into the gym, through the 'Halloween dance' set, and down a hall to one of the classrooms, inside which movie lights, a camera and crew were focused on the teacher's desk. Behind the desk sat a young, brown-skinned actor, French-kissing an older woman on his lap.

A rodent-like man yelled "Cut" when he saw László and everyone stopped.

"Good morning, everybody," said László pleasantly, taking the rodent-like man aside. "I am looking at footage," he said quietly, "and not seeing passion, so I show you what I want." He took a paper from his pocket and, glancing at it, walked to where the actors were waiting.

"Good morning, Gloria, Jesus."

"*Heysus*," the actor said.

László peered at him.

"It's pronounced *Heysus*."

László glanced at the paper again and smiled at the woman. "This morning, we are shooting most important scene in movie. 'Miss Jensen' is teacher who is bored because students are deadheads except 'Raoul' who is excited by you — older sophisticated woman. In class he is looking sideways always to you and making trouble so you will look to him. He is sending vibrations to you, and you are thinking maybe you would like to feel young man's passion. It is forbidden by school, but you think maybe he needs older woman. You are watching him. And you, 'Raoul,' are always looking at 'Miss Jensen.' She is most beautiful teacher in school, and you are most handsome student, so you are wanting each other, badly. Now we do take."

László glanced at the Assistant Director.

"Lock it up, please," the A.D. called out.

The actress sat at the desk, the actor standing a few feet away.

"Picture up." As the camera rolled, László nodded at the rodent-like man who yelled: "Action."

'Raoul' ambled up to the desk. "Ms. Jensen?"

The actress looked up.

"Why do I have to stay after class?"

"I thought we should have a talk."

"About what?"

"Your lessons."

"What about them?"

"You haven't learned them."

"Which ones?"

"Any of them. You've learned no geography this year. You don't even know where the equator is."

"I don't need to know that."

'Ms. Jensen' glanced at her report book. "You don't like school, do you?"

"I like some school."

"The young girls?"

"Nah. They don't know nothing."

"They don't know *anything*."

"Yeah, they're not like you."

"Like me?"

"Yeah, you know everything. This is like my favourite class."

"It doesn't show."

"Yeah, well, that's 'cause I only like some kinds of geography."

"What kinds?"

"Well ... I like *your* geography."

"*My* geography?" 'Ms. Jensen' stared at him.

"Yeah, I'd like to study that."

Now she was gazing at him, curiously. "Would you?"

"Yeah. I could be like one of those explorers."

"Explorers?"

"You know, like those guys looking for the equator. I could look for your equator."

She removed her glasses. "Do you think you could find my equator?"

"You betcha."

"And what do you think you'd see there?"

"A big fiery volcano."

"Really?"

"Really."

"Now," said László urgently.

'Raoul' pulled the older actress from the chair and, as their limbs clutched and grabbed each other, they clamped their mouths together.

"Pull her to desk. Push everything off. Lay her on top."

Flailing out one arm, 'Raoul' swept the teacher's desk clean and pushed 'Miss Jensen' onto her back.

"Now you are wanting her beautiful breasts."

The actor fumbled with the top button of her dress.

"No, no, no. *Tear* it. You are crazy with desire."

The actor ripped the dress open.

"Now you caress her breasts. You want her so much. And you, Ms. Jensen, want him so much you are undoing trousers."

Awkwardly, as the actress fumbled with the actor's pants, 'Raoul' began kissing her breasts. Both actors began to moan, pant and gasp, and simulate intercourse.

I was dumbfounded. I didn't know where to look. I mean, I was embarrassed. I'd been taught by nuns, and it was ten o'clock in the morning. I was gaping at László who was focused intently on the scene. I looked at the crew who were casually watching and waiting for the actors to finish — the groping and moaning seemed to take forever. What were they thinking?

At that moment, I knew I didn't want the job.

Finally, László nodded at the director who yelled: "Cut and print."

"Good," pronounced László, nodding at the actors. Taking the director aside, he said quietly: "In close-ups I need to see passion and breasts. Make them go for it."

Back in the Mercedes, he seemed ebullient. "So, Sarah, what you think?"

"It was interesting," I said politely, still dazed. "Where do you sell these ... movies?"

"Everywhere."

"People *buy* them?"

"Of course, I can afford to pay top salary to executive secretary with degree in law. You will come work for me."

"I'm sorry. I can't."

"No?"

"I'm a feminist," I said pointedly.

"I am feminist too," László said. "I know many women who are friends."

I was stunned. "Do *they* watch your movies?"

"Of course."

"And they *like* them?"

"Everyone wants to see people wanting each other. It is only natural; but in this country when you make movie of this they think it is 'porno-graffe'. They do not understand it is healthy to see sex in movie. You are intelligent woman, I can tell. This is crazy business, and I need smart woman to tell me what women think, and what they desire, and to make ideas for women's movies. I think you would be good for this."

"What do you mean 'what women think'?"

"What they want. Career ... husband ... lover? How they can see who they want to be. How they can live. What kind of movie they are watching. I need smart feminist woman to tell me this."

László's flattery always sounds sincere, and probably is — no doubt he could persuade a leopard to change its spots ("you would look much sexier in stripes") — so I was conflicted. His offer was tempting, but I still hesitated. I had checked out the Felicity Pictures website, which seemed obsessed with sex — in a wide variety of positions and locales. And yet, László was against pornography, so what kind of company would I be working for?

As we neared his office, the argument was being thrashed out in my head. The nuns had said 'no' emphatically, but László was insisting that he needed me. Naturally, I was flattered (I have low self esteem), but beyond that the job, as I understood it, was less boring than corporate law (no kidding); the money was good; and I was tired of job-hunting. I liked László and he seemed to like me. And I would only have to do it until I had saved enough for London. Shouldn't I at least try it? Maybe, as a feminist, I could make a difference.

"Could I try it for a month?"

"Of course."

"I'll take it."

2

THAT MONTH WHIZZED by. After the first week, it was easy to see what could be improved to make Felicity Pictures more efficient. I put László on a schedule (at which at first he balked); set up deadlines and task lists for the staff and created a data base program for monitoring the progress on all Felicity's projects. I seemed to have a talent for this (without having an MBA), so László insisted I stay on. I did, and after completing HALLOWEEN HOODOO, he offered me the position of associate producer — in lieu of the raise I'd asked for — and gave me my own office, a former utility room (broom closet) next to the stairwell.

Now I had two jobs: associate producer *and* László's girl Friday. I had to cancel my plans for London every few months because the work load never let up. Although I was managing fine, and I knew László was pleased, by the time we'd finished shooting FIELD OF SCREAMS, nine months later, the job had begun to affect my health.

I was having trouble sleeping. I had recurring nightmares of being caught naked in a crowd, frantically trying to cover myself with my hands. I woke four or five times a night in a cold sweat, relieved to find myself under my quilt. This is an actual psychological disorder — nudophobia (I looked it up) — but I knew it was the nuns chiding me. I was paying actresses $500 a day to strip and simulate copulation. To believe that this bettered the lives of women everywhere was delusional; but of course that only caused me to smother my feminist side all the more. I had no one to talk to; and I was too busy to have a social life or a boyfriend (with Brad and László as role models, I was having difficulty seeing men as romantic objects).

László, of course, wasn't deluded — he was demented. In his world, Felicity's movies shared the screen with those acclaimed French films which also featured an abundance of nudity and love-making. He was unable to see that *his* movies lacked subtlety, irony, character and — until Vlad arrived — story. László knew how to get a picture made; he just didn't know how to make one. He was a producer, not a filmmaker. And my slow realization of this only extended my depression and sleepless nights. I realized I had to get out.

I'd decided to tell László I was quitting the day before prep on KISS MY ASP, but then he introduced me to his new director, Vladimir Pudovkin. Meeting Vlad, an intelligent, witty, six foot three, meaty Euro-Russian, saved me. It was like finding a long-lost brother.

Shaking my hand firmly, and eyeing me (an earnest, naïve 25-year-old), he said, "László tells me you are finest associate producer he has worked with."

"I know, he says that to everyone."

"I don't know if you are finest," he said without the flicker of a smile, "but you must be wackiest to work with Hungarian lunatic."

It was instant simpatico. We knew why we were there — money. As the associate producer, I made sure László's pay cheques were never late, a rarity in the picture business, or so Vlad assured me. We also shared the same work ethic (on set, I often heard him mutter, "Maybe we can make this shit smell little sweeter.").

So making those two pictures with Vlad was revelatory. From him, I learned about movies, art and life; and, for a time, the nuns' voices were muted, even though I still hadn't resolved my moral dilemma. Meanwhile, Vlad fought ceaselessly with László (art versus commerce) to give the actors dignity and to raise the tone of our pictures, trying to show him a more sophisticated and intelligent method of making movies. During many of those twelve-hour days, it seemed like a losing battle. Halfway through KISS MY ASP, I noticed Vlad looking morose. "What's up?" I asked.

"I think László is winning. I was just working out how to make slow dolly shot close-up on breasts."

Vlad understood the war between business and integrity, and he did the best he could with what he had. Our pictures were well directed — still exploitative — but less offensive, even artful in places. Even so, during those two years, Vlad and I continually urged László to aim higher; and as a result, four months previously, he surprised us by putting me in charge of a new department. I became Head of Quality Development (Hungarians have a sly lack of wit) with no increase in salary, authority or perks (my desk remained in the broom closet); and although I still had to function as László's associate producer *and* girl Friday, Vlad and I felt we had established a beachhead.

As HQD (as Vlad now referred to me), once a week I had to present László with ideas for 'quality' movies. I saw new plays, read stories, novels, and the unsolicited scripts that arrived daily in the mail; but whatever I presented, he rejected.

Vlad smiled when I complained. "How difficult can it be," he said, "to find quality screenplay with excessive copulation?"

László's constant rejection left me discouraged and angry. I told him it was a waste of my time, but he was adamant I continue — his way, I suppose, of pretending that we weren't going to go on making schlock. So I kept searching, relentlessly, for a worthy story he would want to produce, but was still unable to stifle the nuns' voices in my head. Vlad, meanwhile, was fed up with making (what he called) 'flicky-flicky-bang-bang movies'. Those were tense days.

What follows is the story of finding Honor's novel; and the subsequent making — or rather, unmaking — of the picture. I know this account won't be entirely accurate but by using all available sources (emails, cell records, my journal, script notes, and interviews with those involved — in some cases having to assume what was said and who said it), I think it's as close as I can come to explaining what happened — and how. Some of those moments I found embarrassing to relive — behaviour under stress can result in the farcical rather than the tragic — but it is intended as a cautionary tale, so I sincerely hope the reader will find the story not only engaging but morally instructive.

3

IT IS SAID that *The Smoke Pickers,* Honor Lamprey's period love story set on a tobacco farm in southwestern Ontario, is likely her most Canadian novel. I'd read a glowing review ("an exquisitely passionate tale") and, thinking it might have potential as a quality picture, I drove across town to Goode's Booke Emporium one warm August evening where Honor was giving a reading. Squeezing into the shop, its tall replica-Victorian shelves crammed with new and pre-owned books, I was immediately besieged by a pack of expensively-dressed, middle-aged women — each one clutching a copy of Honor's book, all blitzed on white wine, and all loudly gabbing. The kind of woman I imagine who parks her SUV next to the mall planter just before the shrubs disappear.

Through a gap in the crowd, I spotted Honor sitting next to the makeshift podium, calmly sipping tea and flashing her acclaimed-author's smile about the room like a beacon. She resembled an ageing (fiftyish?) cherub, her lined, seraphic pink face under a mound of dyed burgundy hair, both of which complemented her dark green designer suit. She was unfazed by the noise which didn't lessen when Emerson Goode, in crumpled black suit and tie, tried to address the crowd.

"Attention," he said hesitantly. "Could I have your attention, please? We're about to begin.

Tonight is a special night for us. It's a great privilege for Goode's to be able to welcome internationally-celebrated author Honor Lamprey whose depiction of Canadians and life in this great country is always rendered with a deft touch. I know we're all proud of her many achievements, but I think *The Smoke Pickers* might be her most important work yet. Please welcome Honor Lamprey."

Honor stepped up to the podium, gazing calmly out at the audience silently atwitter as, at the back, a few young cyber-fans twittered silently.

"*The Smoke Pickers*," she announced, her acrid voice deadening the remaining chatter, "takes place in 1968. The tragic story of the love affair between Maddie, the young wife of a middle-aged tobacco farmer, and Miguel, a Guatemalan migrant worker, it's set in that corner of my memory where I came of age, the flat, fertile farmland of Southwestern Ontario — an endless chasm of long, hot summer days, sweating in fields redolent of leafy green tobacco, or lazing in the shade of a brick Victorian farmhouse porch, sipping lemonade — and sometimes something stronger. It was evocative for me to write and I hope it will be as vivid for you to read."

She put on her glasses, opened the book and began:

> "The day broke like a fresh farm egg, the sun bursting like some giant yolk pouring onto toast, soaking its buttery rays into the secret burnt corners that had been stove-black an hour before. And, like an industrious ant colony, the migrant workers emerged from the squalid bunkhouses preparing for the long, arduous day ahead; some washing from the trough; some holding bowls and chewing the stiff, tasteless porridge that old Matthews served; and some, like Miguel, squatting against the bunkhouse walls, smoking and staring out at the still, verdant fields.
>
> "His eyes flickered when Maddie stepped out onto the farmhouse porch. She ignored the workers, not daring to glance in their direction for fear of seeing Miguel and being overcome with that same hot quivering that had made her

tremble before him the night before. He also tried to avoid looking at her, but found his eyes fastened on her tied-back flaxen hair and her long, shapely legs as she strode across the yard to the old Ford.

"He glanced away, sniffing the air, stiff with the stench of the workers' cigarettes, the scent of fresh tobacco and now with the exhaust of the old truck, which had coughed to life and was slowly driving past Miguel. His eyes sought hers. Seeing him, she quickly averted her gaze; and the Ford, an industrial-age relic relying more on good faith than technical proficiency, sputtered forward, carrying her down the long elm-lined driveway."

At this point, Emerson had leaned back and knocked Honor's teacup to the floor. She read on, ignoring the clatter, finishing to great applause. Emerson hurriedly rang in sales of the book, and a line formed in front of the signing table, behind which Honor — reminding me of Sister Fiona — sat imperiously. The line finally dwindled to the girl in front of me. "Ms. Lamprey, you're like my favourite writer, and *The Smoke Pickers* is like so beautiful, I want to like get one for my sister. Can you like sign it 'to Kathleen'?"

"Of course."

"Is it like based on a true story?"

"I made it up." Honor smiled. "It's what we writers do."

"It was like so real."

"Thank you."

"When Maddie went off with like Miguel, it was like that girl on TV who eloped with that guy from like Guatemala."

Watching the girl walk off, Honor grimaced slightly then automatically smiled up at me as I stepped forward to hand her my copy of the book. "Could you sign it 'for László, please, L-a-s-z-l-o. You read so elegantly."

She smiled modestly and began to write the inscription.

"Can you tell me," I asked, "if the movie rights are available?"

Her eyes darted up, flashing me a look I'd seen once before when László had offered a writer cash for his screenplay, and the writer's face had gone from surprise to joy to disbelief in a fraction of a second. Then, quickly, she affected to be uninterested. "I'm sorry, your name is Laz ...?" she asked, trying to focus on the inscription.

"No, I'm Sarah Fielding. Mr. Kovac's associate." I gave her my business card which she took carefully, holding it delicately between the tips of her fingers.

"Yes, I believe, the rights are *still* available," she said casually, as though it were of no importance, but staring at my card as if it might hold some hidden meaning. "My agent has had a number of inquiries of course ... but I believe ... they are ... still available." She smiled hopefully, to welcome any offer that might be forthcoming.

"Good, well, I hope to be in touch with you soon. Thank you," I said, clutching the book. "I shall look forward to reading it." As I walked away, I glanced back. She was still staring at my card.

EAGER — NO, DRIVEN — to make a movie with substance, I read *The Smoke Pickers* twice in three days. I knew right away that Honor's protagonist, Maddie, who falls in love with Miguel and fights for worker's rights, would touch audiences. After letting Vlad skim it, I gave it to László hoping that, when he picked me up, he would be just as enthused as I was.

We had wrapped SORORITY PLAYGIRLS (László took pride in titling all Felicity's pictures) two weeks before, but he'd scheduled today for pickup shots. SORORITY had tons of juvenile movie charm — teenagers faking nooky, college girls exposing their breasts, frat boys performing fart jokes, a hackneyed plot about a 'fixed' college football game, even a 'naughty' locker-room scene — but I knew László felt something was missing. I didn't. I thought there was too much already.

"Did you read it?" I asked him, as soon as I got in the car.

"I glimpsed it."

"And ...?"

"It's not so good."

"No? A love affair between a tobacco farmer's wife and a migrant worker?"

"No sex."

"Not explicit sex, no, but it is a love story. And it has a kind of permeating charm."

"'Permeating' is not box office."

"With a tight script and good actors, Vlad could make a wonderful picture. I'm sure it'll make a profit. It might even win some awards."

"Sarah, there is no sex."

"When you interviewed me you told me you wanted 'ideas for women's movies'. So I'm giving you one. *The Smoke Pickers* would make a great woman's movie."

"No sex no box office."

"Do you want me to cancel the meeting?"

He must have heard the frustration in my voice. "No, it would be impolite. We will meet with her."

Arriving at the location, I was shocked. I'd had to beg the University for permission to be allowed to film in the stadium, and had promised the grounds crew that we wouldn't 'deform, deface, degrade, defile or disfigure' the playing field in any way. So I was stunned, as László and I crossed the field, to see the crew huddled near a fresh pile of earth on the 35-yard line. Beside the pile gaped a large hole from which the camera peeked, the lens pointing up at the bleachers. Vlad lay on the ground behind it, peering through the viewfinder. I didn't know whether to be sick or angry. I had no doubt that Vlad would have a valid cinematic reason for digging up the field, but *I* would be the one facing the wrath of the University.

Five actresses dressed as cheerleaders stood waiting in front of the camera, their pom-poms poised high. Behind them four beefy young men in football gear (actual players) lounged on a bench, and in the bleachers thirty extras huddled in the early morning chill. We had shot the real game two weeks before but László, unhappy with the cheerleading scenes, was determined to re-shoot them. He'd had Hardy re-write them, adding 'more spice', and now, seeing Vlad about to shoot, he quickened his pace.

"Action," Vlad shouted. Promptly, the cheerleaders jumped up, waved their pom-poms in unison, and chanted:

> "Rah, rah, boomty-bye.
> We're the girls for Fairmount High.

We love our Studs, we love their spore,
We love it when they try to score."
Go, go, go. Yay!"

At that point, a young actor rushed into frame, spritzing the girls' T-shirts with club soda from a champagne bottle. The cheerleaders giggled — their breasts now outlined against their wet jerseys — and set off again:

"Rah, rah, boomty-bye.
We're the girls for Fairmount High.
We love to yell. We love to scream,
And putting out for all the team.
Go, go, go. Yay!"

"Cut!"

Our costumer, Nadia, rushed in to hand out towels, blankets and dry T-shirts. The dampened cheerleaders, huddling against the morning chill, towelled off, watching Vlad warily, hoping he wouldn't ask for another take.

"What are you doing?" demanded László, now standing over Vlad.

Vlad twinkled as he stood up. "That was great shot," he said. "When you see it on screen you will say: 'Vlad, you are one fuck director.'"

"What are you shooting? Toes?"

"On CITIZEN KANE," Vlad explained, "Orson had to dig hole *in studio floor* to get the camera low enough, but it was only way to get great depth in shot."

As I wondered how to explain 'great depth in shot' to the grounds crew, László spoke calmly and quietly. "Vlad, let me tell you what we do here. We are not making picture of girls' toes. No. If I send this to Jeremy, he will punch my lights off. What we want you to do, Vlad, is to shoot cheerleaders' tits. You cannot shoot tits with camera in hole in ground. Even I know this, and I did not go to Leningrad Film School. To shoot cheerleaders' tits, you must to put camera … here …" He placed his hand at chest level. "Where tits are …"

Vlad never directly contradicts László, so he responded with silence, gazing at him, his eyebrows tectonically converging. Then, as László focused his attention on the cheerleaders, Vlad gestured to Teddy Wong, our cameraman, to raise the camera — and waited.

"We need more," mused László.

"We need great shot, is what we need," muttered Vlad.

"Sshhhhh," chided László, stepping forward to address the cheerleaders. "Beautiful young women," he said, amiably. "You are so gorgeous and you are making fantastic scene, but why you look so sad?"

This is one of László's techniques: he offers a compliment then poses an oblique question to get your attention. It puzzled the cheerleaders.

"You know what I think? I think you know that cheering will not make the young men win. And I think this is what makes you sad. So you ask to yourself, what can I do to inspire the young men to touch their balls down?"

Some find László's mangled English charming. but having tried to correct him many times, I know now he does it deliberately to get people's attention. The cheerleaders waited — Candy, a demure blonde, listened attentively, while next to her, Vicki, a lanky redhead, regarded László as you might a previously-unknown reptile.

"You know what all young men respect? Woman. Woman is the sun and moon. Men know this and they are inspired by … what?"

Candy hesitated then tentatively offered, "Love?"

"Yes, love … love of woman's beauty. Her body is mother earth. It is life. So when you see young men are not winning, you cry out to yourself what can I do to inspire?"

I could see Candy silently mouthing: "What can I do to inspire?"

László waited. The cheerleaders, wrapped in towels and shivering, gaped at him.

He spoke softly, admiringly. "I know what you do. You show to them your beauty; your beautiful legs, *and* your beautiful breasts. And then, then they will be so, so ..."

Smiling now, Candy didn't hesitate. "Brave."

"Yes, brave," cried László, "like gladiators, and they will touch all their balls down to win."

Usually, László can hypnotize people into doing what he wants, so he slowly raised his hands, as though willing the cheerleaders to pull up their jerseys. Mesmerized, Candy started to lift hers, but Vicki took hold of her hand and pulled it down.

Seeing where his opposition lay, László addressed Vicki directly. "I know what you are thinking — and you are right. Movie will be sexy, but most important, it is story of brave men ..."

" ... and women," I added.

" ... *and* women, fighting to win game for school, but you, brave beautiful cheerleaders, must inspire the young men. I am from Hungary, a country where all men worship the beauty of woman, so I know where I speak from. In Hungary, to see a woman's breasts is holy, so this is how you inspire the young men. Am I right?"

László looked to Candy for confirmation and she nodded. I never nod, if I can avoid it. I need to appear neutral — to be able to sort out the messes once László's finished making them.

"And the other team will not touch their balls down because they do not have the beautiful women to show them their breasts. So everyone," he said, indicating the extras freezing in the bleachers, "will see that your beauty was winning the game."

Except for Candy, I could see that the Cheerleaders weren't buying it, especially Vicki.

"László?"

"So, brave, beautiful women, only you can win game for school, only ..."

"László?"

"Excuse me," he said to the cheerleaders, and turning to me. "What?"

"They don't want to," I said, gently manoeuvring him out of earshot.

"What?"

"If you want the shot, we'll have to offer more."

"How much?"

"At least triple scale."

"What we pay them now?"

"Double."

"They want to. I can tell."

"I don't think they do."

"They didn't want to wet T-shirts," said Vlad, pointedly.

"No? It could be most beautiful scene. Vlad, do you know why this is great country?"

Vlad sighed. "Because it's got lakes and beavers and mooses?"

"No. This is great country because you can have whatever you want, but ... you have to go for it. I want *you* to go for it, Vlad. What other movie has cheerleaders showing us their beautiful breasts?"

"A porno movie?"

"No, no, no, no. What *great* movie has beautiful women's breasts? None."

"You don't need breasts to make great movie."

"What?"

"Orson didn't show breasts in CITIZEN KANE. Why?" Vlad waited for the answer, but László just stared at him. "Because he had a fuck of a script. What we need is a fuck of a script."

"Vlad, CITIZEN KANE did not do box office. Do you know why? It was not beautiful. People go to movies to see beautiful people, doing beautiful things ..."

I couldn't resist. "Like showing us their beautiful breasts."

"Yes. Sarah?"

I knew I would pay for that. I followed László to where the cheerleaders waited.

"This is my associate Sarah Fielding. She is thinking also that your beautiful breasts will inspire the young men to win the touchdown balls." He looked at me, waiting for my confirmation.

"It could ...," I said, slightly embarrassed as I faced the cheerleaders, "be a very provocative, and unusual scene. If I were a young man... I think I would be inspired."

"What's your offer?" asked Vicki, staring at me as though I had betrayed my entire sex.

I glanced at László. "Triple scale."

"No."

László's tone was brisk. "So you won't show your beautiful breasts to inspire the young men?"

"We will," said Vicki, "if they show us their pee-pees."

To his credit, László knows when to quit. I followed him back to the Mercedes.

***

On the road to Honor's, László was talking on his cell *and* driving. "Yes, Jeremy, SORORITY is looking good ..."

"László ..."

"I am happy with footage, picture is sexy and funny. I will send you ..."

"László!"

"What?"

"You're going to get us killed."

"You talk to Jeremy," he said, thrusting the cell at me.

"Hello? Jeremy? László can't talk now. He's driving and I don't want to die. Can he call you tomorrow? Good. Bye."

"So, tell me why you want I should buy *Smoke Picking*."

"*The Smoke Pickers*. I don't *want* you to do anything. I just think it would make a wonderful movie, and a bigger budget would increase our cash flow — but if you don't like it, don't do it."

"I liked older woman and young man. Made me think when I was young. But it's nothing special."

I could see he wanted to be convinced. "The book has already sold thirty thousand copies here in Canada; it's a beautiful love story; Honor is internationally-known; but mostly we need to grow. It wouldn't hurt to increase our cash flow."

"How can I sell movie with no sex?"

"It has passion — turn here — but if *you* can't see the passion, there's no point."

"Maybe you are right. It would be good to have more cash flow."

Honor's farmhouse was just outside Toronto, nestled beside a small forest near Uxbridge, a village sustained by wealthy, nature-loving commuters. As László pulled to a stop in the driveway, I caught sight of Honor in her attached greenhouse office, staring at a computer. The red-brick, Victorian farmhouse, with its grounds submerged in plant life, was large and well-cared for. Clearly, her books sold.

In her sitting room, perched on an antique sofa, László gazed at the room appreciatively — a high-ceiling space neatly adorned with expensive, impersonal copies of antique furniture, neatly crammed bookshelves, and large, abstract, original paintings (chosen, it seemed, for their bold beigeness).

Honor poured tea into three fragile cups, handed two to us, and sipped hers delicately.

"This is very elegant. It is kind of house," László announced, "I am thinking to buy." I knew he was flattering Honor, but telling her, not so subtly, that he was just as successful as she. He may have actually believed at that moment that he wanted to move to the country — the sly salesman buying his own pitch, but I couldn't imagine this Budapest-raised cosmopolitan giving up his downtown, lake-view condo to sit in the woods and commune with nature.

"Thank you," said Honor.

"I like your book very much. It has much passion."

"Thank you."

"It will make fabulous movie."

"Do you think so?"

"Yes. I am certain of this. It is beautiful love story, it is, ah ... permeating."

"Thank you." Regarding him, Honor hesitated. "I've researched your company on the internet."

László waited attentively.

"You seem," she said finally, "to have a reputation for making movies which are ... ah ...

"Sexy," he said.

"Well, I wouldn't ..."

"I know what you will say, but people in this country do not agree. They do not like sex even though it is beautiful — part of every day. You know this. You cannot ... cannot forbid it. It is everywhere — right now in your garden insects are having sex, dogs and cats are having sex in bushes, people are having sex in ... Uxbridge. Everywhere everyone is making love, but in this country when you try to make movie of this, people ... are ..."

"... offended?" said Honor, gazing at him.

"Yes, I try to make beautiful movies, but sometimes director is not right, or star is miscast, or script is not so good ... and I am human, I make mistakes. But I tell you this, I love your book. Story is beautiful. It will make audience cry."

"I saw," said Honor, tenaciously, "a clip of one your movies. It was ... ah ..."

"Sexy."

"No. Pardon me for saying so. Unpleasant."

László appeared surprised. "Sarah, you think my movies are 'unpleasant'?"

Honor Lamprey was now staring at me with a look I'd endured many times before, a look that stated: "What're you doing with a sex pervert?"

"Sometimes," I said.

Looking at Honor, László said, sighing, "You see, I have very smart associates but sometimes they are out-speaking too much."

In the time we've worked together, László and I have fallen into our respective roles: he, the opportunist producer; and I, the prim idealist, shocked by what he says, but conveying the impression that, in spite of his arrant behaviour, he's a decent man who wouldn't hurt a fly — or in this case an author.

"So you don't think Honor should let me make movie of her beautiful book?"

I could see Honor was conflicted. Every author wants their book made into a movie, but fears it being done by carpetbaggers, so I had to reassure her. "I think Honor could consider an offer if we were able to address all her concerns in the contract." I had never pushed this hard for a project before.

"You see, Honor, already I struggle to make movie of your beautiful book. Come to my screening room. I show you movie we make now and you meet director. Then you can decide."

He had inserted the hook but knew, like a seasoned fisherman, that he couldn't yet pull on the line. Honor's expression contained hope, avarice and apprehension. "When?" she asked.

Driving back, László was quiet. I knew he'd been stung by her remarks. He was not accustomed to begging writers to sell him the rights to their work.

"Do you want me to look for another story?" I asked.

"No."

"She's not going to go for it, László."

"Ms. Lamprey knows about books. I know about movies. We will show Ms. Lamprey how we make quality movie."

5

I WAS TAUGHT by the nuns my first three years of school and, although I remember very little Catholicism, their influence on me was indelible. Every fibre of my being was infused with the Golden Rule — 'Do unto others as you would have them do unto you' — with the result that I am compelled always: to let the queue go ahead of me; to worry about what others might think; and to put the concerns of everyone else first — in short, to erase my personality. While this might seem excessively noble or selfless, it isn't, for if everyone were to follow the Golden Rule, there'd be no wars, and excessive politeness would slow our accelerating lives immeasurably ("oh *no*, after *you*"). And ultimately, wouldn't the world be better off?

The second thing the nuns bestowed on me was the gift of theatre. By casting me as the lead in the Grade Three play, they gave me a love of acting that captivated me at once. I was shy as a child until I played Rebecca, the little girl who wouldn't eat her vegetables. Being able to over-dramatize Rebecca's dilemma somehow freed me. During the dramatic denouement, when my schoolmates — dressed as carrots, turnips and broccoli — explained how much nutrition they contained, I overplayed the part shamelessly.

"Eat me," they said.

"I will, I will, I will. I promise, I promise, I promise," I said, ad-libbing the last two 'I wills' and 'I promises' ardently and tearfully, and hugging my stage mother, Yvonne Lynnquist, a year younger than I.

Sister Fiona and the nuns applauded my performance and so, until age fifteen, I envisioned my future as an actress. Then I played Sophie in the high school drama club's four-hour production of *War & Peace*, and realized that I might lack genuine talent, which my parents noted, quickly persuading me to take up law. I still loved going to the theatre, and was thrilled, as Felicity's HQD, to be able to charge my tickets to the company.

Nathan, on the other hand, was a natural, having discovered his gift at age sixteen in a summer camp show. By seventeen, he had read all Shakespeare's plays (and understood them); by twenty-one, he'd dropped out of theatre school and was auditioning for every theatre in town; and by twenty-four, he'd performed in Ibsen, Brecht, Molière, and had worked in summer stock (Coward, Ayckbourn, Rattigan, etc.) two years running.

His acting baffled the critics: 'electrifying,' 'mesmerizing,' along with 'ostentatious' and 'bombastic' being words used to describe his performances. Having studied the films of the greats (Olivier, Burton, Finney, O'Toole, Day-Lewis, Branagh, McKellen and Fiennes), in interviews Nathan spoke of aiming for the gods, which for him had a double meaning: the illustrious actors he admired, and the cheap seats in the topmost balconies of Britain's classic theatres which he dreamed of performing in one day.

That season, he was the lead actor with the Madbrain Theatre Company, a group of respected Fringe actors, running three plays in rep entitled *The Essential Shakespeare* (pared-down versions of *Hamlet*, *Romeo & Juliet*, and *Twelfth Night*). Their performances took place in a dingy, high-ceilinged, ramshackle warehouse space (formerly Walter's Mattress Depot), an auditorium so small that some of the audience — totalling 127 — had to sit beside the actors on stage.

During rehearsals for *Hamlet*, Nathan was so committed to the 'truth' of the play, so focused on inhabiting Hamlet's dark side — a pain in the ass, according to Nancy — that he left his fellow cast members anxious and edgy. I would never have had the courage to attempt a role like Hamlet. But neither would I have broken, as Nathan did, the first rule of theatre — the show must go on.

On the second night, when Nathan began the "Get thee to a nunnery" scene, he was inside Hamlet completely. The acid revulsion the Danish prince felt for his Uncle (Claudius) and Mother (Gertrude) who, with the collusion of Ophelia's father (Polonius), had murdered his father the King, "flooded my mouth, like dank regurgitation." Seeing the production later, I realized that Nathan forced us to experience the same revulsion. His ability to conceal Hamlet's cunning, while exposing his inner conflict — loving Ophelia so much he was attempting to repulse her in order to protect her from *his* rage against her father — was breathtaking.

Offstage, you might wonder at his power as an actor — he was only 5'8" — but onstage his intensity overwhelmed you, as when he bore down on Ophelia.

"You should not have believed me; for virtue cannot so inoculate our old stock but we shall relish of it: I loved you not."

Nancy, a fellow theatre-school student of Nathan's, keenly felt his dislike for Ophelia that night.

"I was the more deceived," she cried.

"Get thee to a nunnery: why wouldst thou be a breeder of sinners? I am myself indifferent honest; but yet I could accuse me of such things that it were better my mother had not borne me. I am very proud, revengeful, ambitious; with more offences at my beck than I have thoughts to put them in, imagination to give them shape, or time to act them in. What should such fellows as I do crawling between heaven and earth? We are arrant knaves, all; believe none of us. Go thy ways to a nunnery. Where's your father?"

"At home, my lord."

"Let the doors be shut upon him, that he may play the fool nowhere but in's own house. Farewell."

"O! help him, you sweet heaven!"

"If thou dost marry, I'll give thee this plague for thy dowry: be thou as chaste as ice, as pure as snow, thou shalt not escape

calumny, get thee to a nunnery, go; farewell. Or, if thou wilt
needs marry, marry a fool; for wise men know well enough
what monsters you make of them. To a nunnery go; and
quickly too. Farewell."

For the first time in the play, Hamlet's hostility — his hatred of Polonius — is directed at Ophelia; and it singed Nancy, who was terrified, Nathan railing at her with an intensity she hadn't seen before.

"O! heavenly powers, restore him!" she cried.

Nathan was on her like a dog, growling, snapping.

"I have heard of your paintings too, well enough; God hath
given you one face, and you make yourselves another: you jig,
you amble, and you lisp, and nickname God's creatures, and
make your wantonness your ignorance ..."

At that moment, a cell phone blared out the theme from ROCKY, shattering the hush like a gunshot. Nathan, so savagely wreaking destruction on Ophelia's love for Hamlet, seemed not to have heard it.

"... go to, I'll no more on't; it hath made me mad. I say, we will
have no more ..."

But no, he was thrown; his frenzy hesitant now; his bond with the audience — no longer inside Hamlet's pain — broken. In the audience, he saw a man jump up in the third row, pull a cell from his pocket — now blaring out ROCKY again — push past his companion (sitting frozen with embarrassment), and rush from the auditorium.

Nathan's struggle to keep Hamlet's rage alive sputtered.

"I'll no more on't; it hath made me mad. I say, we will have no
more marriages; those that are married ... already, all are ..."

The fury faltered. Hamlet's too, too solid flesh vaporized and abruptly Nathan exited the stage a line early.

Dumbstruck, Nancy watched him disappear into the wings then realized, after interminable seconds, that the audience wasn't aware that he hadn't finished, and hurried into her closing speech.

"O! what a noble mind is here o'erthrown: the courtier's,

soldier's, scholar's eye, tongue, sword; the expectancy and
rose of the fair state, the glass of fashion and the mould of
form, the observ'd of all observers, quite, quite down! And I,
of ladies most deject and wretched that suck'd the honey of
his music vows, now see that noble and most sovereign reason, like sweet bells jangled ..."

Glancing again at the wings, she worried he'd been taken ill.

"... out of tune and harsh; that unmatch'd form and feature of
blown youth blasted with ecstasy: O woe is me, to have seen
what I have seen, see what I see!"

She rushed from the stage and, as the King and Polonius entered to
finish Scene 1 (Act III), searched backstage for him. When she and the
others realized that Nathan had left the theatre, Blake, the actor playing Polonius, came out to tell the audience that Nathan had been
taken ill, abruptly apologized on behalf of the Company and offered to
exchange their tickets for another night.

Meanwhile, Nathan — dazed, beyond angry, walking aimlessly
around the block — found himself in front of the Monacle Bar & Grill.
He has no memory of how he got there, what he was thinking, of entering or walking up to the bar. Having seen him come in, the bartender, Barney, poured him a draft.

"Triple vodka, Barney," he said, downing the beer.

Puzzled, Barney poured him a triple vodka which Nathan downed
in a gulp. "Another, Barney."

"Show out early?"

Nathan, staring off, muttered: "Umh?"

"Show out early?"

"Triple vodka," he repeated, blankly.

He downed the second vodka and, as the alcohol started to
soothe — for the enormity of what he had done had begun to pene-
trate — dismissed any thought of returning. There was no point. He
had lost Hamlet.

He sat gazing at the room without seeing it, not noticing two men enter, look for a table, spot him and saunter up, until they were standing dead in front of him. The taller one said: "Can I buy you a drink?"

With the vodka blunting his senses, Nathan looked up. The man seemed familiar. "What?"

"Can I buy you a drink? I feel bad about ... what happened — my cell."

Slowly recognizing him, Nathan was disoriented. Was it a full moon?

"What're you drinking?" The man waved at Barney down the bar, and pointed to Nathan's glass. "One more here, please," he said, then sat on the stool beside him. "My name's Arthur. This is Robert, my associate. I'd like to invite you to have dinner with us ... by way of apology."

Nathan gazed at his blue eyes, set close together. He couldn't speak.

"I *am* sorry, very sorry," said Arthur, holding the phone in his palm. "But someone always needs to contact me. Your performance, by the way, was awesome."

Nathan didn't intend to be rude, but couldn't help staring. He had nothing to say to Arthur. Barney set the third vodka on the bar and, sensing tension, stayed to wipe it down.

Waiting, Arthur said sharply: "I did say I was sorry."

The first vodka was now coursing through Nathan's brain, easing all anxiety. He had felt almost amiable until he realized that Arthur was irritated with *him* — was he offended because Nathan hadn't acknowledged his apology?

"Yes, you did," muttered Nathan, "yes, yes, yes, you did ... But what about Hamlet?"

Arthur gaped at him.

"What about Hamlet, ah ...?"

"Arthur."

"Arthur. Did you apologize to him?"

"What?"

The alcohol was releasing Nathan's id. "You know why Hamlet's a great play, don't you, Arthur — not a 'good' one — a great one. Oh, it's not perfect, there are problems — it's too long, too disjointed, sloppy in places and there're too many holes in the story. But it's a great play, Arthur, a great play because it's a rite of passage — an Eiger, a Terra del Fuego, an exploration of Antarctica — an actor's trial. Every actor — *every* actor, Arthur — dreams of being Hamlet. Why? Because of the inner turmoil — how do you play that, Arthur? Most can't. Most actors don't know how, and most never get the opportunity, but we all want to crawl inside Hamlet's madness. All actors want to see what Hamlet's made of, what Shakespeare was telling us — if he was telling us anything. What was he telling us, Arthur? There's never been a play like it. Never — and I've been lucky. I have twenty-three nights to live inside Hamlet's madness, to explore it. And tonight, tonight Arthur, I was beginning to glimpse something, something I hadn't seen before — a hint, a hint of what? — what was Shakespeare showing me? A glimpse of Ophelia's fragility? Had I made a discovery? Had I found the key to Hamlet's madness? I almost had it. Yes, I almost had it ... and then your phone rang. Your phone rang. *Your...* phone... rang, and it was gone."

Nathan slipped from the bar stool, held himself erect, downed the vodka in one swallow, held up his hand to silence Arthur and, wobbling slightly, made for the door.

When Nancy realized that Nathan had left the theatre and wasn't ill, she was disturbed. Knowing his temperament, she guessed he'd left because of the cell, and that made her angry. She changed hurriedly and, wondering if he might've gone to the Monacle, dashed around the corner, almost bumping into him as he weaved his way down the sidewalk. "Nathan?"

"Get thee to a nunnery..."

She realized he was drunk. "You bastard."

"Sshhhhhh ..."

"How could you?"

"Yes ... how *could* I? *How* could I? How could *I*?"

"Are you drunk?"

"... to a nunneryyyy ... get thee." Nathan was not a drinker and the vodka was now releasing voices in his head. "How could I *what*?"

"What were you thinking?"

He stared dumbly at her, making no response.

"What did you think we'd do, Nathan? Cover for you?"

Nathan gazed blankly at her.

"'Oh, I wonder where's Hamlet gone? Maybe he had to take a shit. Well, let's carry on, shall we? Who's going to kill Polonius? I don't know, shall we draw straws?'" Watching him, she knew the sarcasm wasn't getting through. "Were you thinking at all about your fellow actors, Nathan, staring at a hole on the stage where Hamlet had been standing seconds before? Where's your fucking integrity now?"

She thought she might've detected a flicker of remorse behind his blotted gaze.

"I have none," he said quickly.

"Why are you drinking?"

"'What should such fellows as I do crawling between heaven and earth?'"

"Oh, shut up."

"To a nunnery go, and quickly to, farewell."

"Why ... are ... you ... drinking?"

"So I can throw up."

"Are you going to?"

"Did I not promise?"

"Do it in the street."

Nathan leaned over and tried to vomit. Nothing came up. Wearily, Nancy watched him.

"O, oh, oh, oh, oooohhh ... puke, puke ... sir puke ... my horse for a puke … funny word, puke. Speak the speech I puke you … speak the puke, I speech you …"

"Nathan, shut up."

Nathan peered into the gutter, then, deciding that he hadn't thrown up, stood up and started to amble off.

"I'm not finished, Nathan. Where are you going?"

"Frailty, thy name is woman," he said, stopping and peering at her.

"Fine," she muttered angrily, and left him balancing on the curb.

When Nathan arrived at the theatre the next night his fellow actors were silent about his abandoned performance, but he felt a distinct chill backstage. He knew then that never again would he leave a stage in mid-performance, unless he, or the theatre, was on fire.

***

Most people think the movie industry is an endless party — a smash-up — producers squandering millions (of what Vlad calls "Canadian Tire money") in search of grand illusions on screen and off. This is true. Flinging wads of investors' cash at feckless ideas, producers spend all their time exuding confidence, pushing everyone to work harder, hoping that the actors, script and director will magically coalesce to create — often against the producer's will — à series of emotionally-charged images, reaping hundreds of thousands in profit. Failing that, it's always an excuse to party — the investors insist on it.

Our five main investors were harmless enough as individuals, but as a group they resembled a frat house debauch. They loved owning a piece of a Felicity movie, and showing clips of sex scenes on their cell phones to friends and associates — but they also wanted profit.

We'd gone into production on SORORITY PLAYGIRLS to keep our cash flow fluid, and because László had bought the script for a pittance. But even though our investors had done well on KISS MY ASP, they were anxious because SORORITY had no name actors, no real violence, and no deeply explicit sex. So László was showing them a fine cut, hoping the sight of all that young flesh on the large screen might distract them. I was surprised he'd invited Honor to the screening, and wondered if he thought that seeing his movie on a big screen would impress her.

She arrived after the screening had started but remained at the door, transfixed, peering into the room at the naked bodies on screen and at our backers lounging in the front row. Lowering herself into a seat, she watched as our five investors raptly ogled the 'schoolgirls' bare breasts, cheered the 'teenagers making out,' laughed uproariously at the 'boys discharging fart noises,' and snickered at the 'nude jocks' prancing about in the locker room slapping each other with wet towels. I could see that even László, seated behind them, was unsettled by their behaviour, although he took care not to show it.

László was proud of SORORITY PLAYGIRLS. The idea of making a football picture had been inspired by his ex-wife, Felicity, a former runner-up to Miss Winnipeg Blue Bombers, who had starred in his first picture, ATHENA'S REVENGE, the only one of his movies to lose money and the unspoken cause of his divorce. After that he avoided Classical Greek names in titles, and dating 'actresses', seeking 'companionship' from successful businesswomen (middle-aged divorcées) on an ad hoc basis.

I watched for Honor's reaction to the movie. SORORITY ends in victory for the home team and Vlad, on a tiny budget, had managed to dramatically heighten the climax with a tight montage — our team scoring the winning goal in the final few seconds, the crowd yelling, cheerleaders bouncing up and down, hurrahing in their 'champagne'-doused jerseys; until finally, in a long swooping shot, a tall, meaty football player embraces Candy, crushing her with a lusty, penetrating kiss as the fans go wild in the bleachers. I was hoping that Honor would bypass the picture's content, and note how well the movie was directed.

To impress the investors, László had asked 'the director' to attend so Vlad, along with Teddy Wong, our talented cameraman, sat in the back row, staring grimly at the "fratboys". Teddy always kept things light on set, usually by spoofing the bigoted view of Chinese with his Charlie Chan impression. That night he was irrepressible, whispering to Vlad: "Confucius say: 'Fratboys immutable when not inscrutable."

When the house lights went up, László noticed Honor rising hurriedly. He signalled her to wait, then turned his attention to the investors.

"Gentlemen, that is fine cut, but we are still tweaking. We have some nibbling from foreign distributors and cable, so I think we will have profit in six months. Next week, I will make announcement of exciting new project. Sarah will arrange lunch and let you know."

"When can we download it?" asked one.

"As soon as we freeze picture. Sarah will arrange."

At the door, each shook hands with László, and offered the macho equivalent of social chit-chat.

"Looks great, László. I wouldn't mind doing a little cheering with those babes."

"Keep us posted, Laz. Tell the girls there's always champagne and dry T-shirts at my apartment. Yuk, yuk."

"Call me for lunch, and don't fart in the huddle, ha, ha."

"I liked the blonde, and the brunette, and the redhead and ... all of them. Are you gonna introduce me?"

"Watch out for those wet towels. Ouch! Heh, heh."

We'd managed to distract them yet again and, chuckling, they wandered past Honor out into the night. László now turned his charm on her. "So, Ms. Lamprey, you will let me make beautiful movie of your wonderful book?"

"Call me Honor. And no, I won't let you make the movie of my book."

"No?"

"You're very charming, László, but I wouldn't let you anywhere near my novel."

He seemed puzzled, almost hurt. "Why?"

"I bought a copy of KISS MY ASP. I watched the naked girls and snakes for about five minutes until I realized it was crap; and what I've just seen isn't any better. How could you imagine that I would allow *The Smoke Pickers* to be turned into a sex romp?"

"You think I don't know how to make beautiful movie of your book?"

"No, honestly, I can't imagine how you would."

"Some pictures I make for money, to pay for ones I make for love. I want to make movie of your book because I must."

Saying nothing, Honor gazed at him.

"Story of Maddie and Miguel is movie I have been wanting to make all my life. It *is* my life, and story of Canada. I know this after reading first page. We will work well together. I will pay you two hundred thousand for rights, plus 10% of profits."

I was stunned by his sudden offer, and the amount. I could see Honor was too, but trying not to show it. "How can I be sure Maddie won't end up in a wet T-shirt?"

László looked at me and winked impishly. "That is good idea. Sarah, write it down."

"I will not," said Honor sharply, "allow my story to be turned into porno."

László gaped at her. She had used the 'P' word. To suggest that his pictures were "porno-graffe" was an affront, and I could see that he was containing his anger.

"We understand perfectly," I said quickly. "You need to feel your work will be protected, and respected. Instruct your lawyer on what you want — and don't want. Have him or her write up the clauses, and we'll put them in the contract."

"But," added László, adamantly, "you must think how we show Maddie's passion for Miguel."

Honor gazed at him. "If I left it up to you, László, you'd have Maddie stroking Miguel's private parts in the first scene."

László was barely able to restrain himself. "You insult me."

"Oh, I don't think so. You know exactly what you're doing. I don't blame you for trying, but I'd rather you did it with someone else's novel."

László sighed, pausing to reassemble his charming demeanour. "I want you to meet my director. Vlad, come meet Honor. Honor, this is Vladimir Pudovkin. Vladimir is internationally-known director who studied at Leningrad Film School with Sergei Melencofski."

"Melokovski," corrected Vlad.

"Vlad, should we get other book to make movie?" László asked pointedly.

Vlad, comfy in the role of charming, artistic émigré, centred his deep brown eyes on Honor. "No László, this is one fuck of a story. Let me advise you, Ms. Lamprey, you are right not to trust László Kovacs. He is Hungarian — he cannot help himself — but I am Russian, and it would be privilege for me to make beautiful film from your book."

"Let us agree," said László, "to make movie; and you can have lawyer make agreement as you wish." He took Honor's hand, clasping it tightly. "I promise you. THE SMOKE PICKERS will be great picture."

Deliberately, she pulled her hand free, her eyes searching his. "I'll think about it," she said, backing cautiously from the room and closing the door behind her.

Vlad looked at László. "Why you want to buy this book?"

"You read it?"

"I skimmed it."

"So you can make beautiful movie like CITIZEN KANE."

"I need fuck of a script to do that."

"It *is* a strong story," I reminded them, glancing sharply at Vlad who winked.

"Hardy is working on screenplay," László said.

I was stunned. "She's hasn't agreed to sell us the rights yet."

"She will sign." László's boundless confidence always amazed me.

"She won't tolerate any changes."

"No?" said Vlad. "Tell her she can kiss László's asp."

A WEEK AFTER his Hamlet debacle, Nathan received a call from his agent, telling him he'd been specifically requested for a commercial audition; and that it might pay enough to get him to England.

As Nathan explained later: "I'll consider doing a commercial if *given* the part; but never — ever — will I *audition* for one. I trained as an actor. I studied Shakespeare, Chekhov and Shaw. To betray my training by auditioning for toothpaste, and then *be rejected* by an ad agency moron would be stupid."

Accustomed to shoddy theatre spaces, Nathan found the audition room palatial — comfy leather chairs and sofas under windows overlooking a garden; a digital camera standing in the middle of the room, a young techie feeding on take-out sushi at a long wooden table covered with Rosebud Margarine packets, while, beside him, an expensively-dressed, woman with dyed blonde hair sipped on a Starbucks and stared at her cell. An ageing gangly man in a designer leather jacket, baseball hat and tight-fitting jeans paced back and forth, talking intently on his cell. He glanced up as Nathan entered.

"Robert, the image needs to be much clearer. Lower the castle in relation to the Rosebud packaging, more storm grey in the sky behind the battlements, maybe a bolt of lightning striking a barren tree in the background — but mute everything; the Rosebud yellow needs to jump out at us. Have you got that? Get me something to look at ASAP." He hung up and put the cell in his pocket.

Nathan tried to place him. He seemed familiar.

"I had you come in, Nathan," said the man, smiling at him as though he knew him, "because we need a brilliant actor for this spot."

"I know you from somewhere," said Nathan.

"Arthur. Hamlet. Cell phone."

Nathan remembered. Hadn't he made his dislike of Arthur evident? "My agent told you I don't audition for commercials?"

"It's a national commercial. It'll run in all markets for at least a year. Big residuals."

"He told me that I was specifically requested. Does that mean I have the job?"

"Pretty much. I've seen you act, and you're amazing — your Hamlet was awesome — which is why I thought of you. I just need to get some sense of how you would relate to the product."

"That would be an audition and I don't audition for commercials."

"I know I can't ask you for any favours, Nathan, but I can't think of another actor who could pull this off — it's an amazing piece of writing." He picked up some pages from the table. "Dig this," he said, reading. "We fade in on Elsinore Castle. There's a storm brewing; rain is lashing at the bridge over the moat. We hear the clang of swordplay. In the immediate foreground, on an old heavy wooden table sits a packet of Rosebud Margarine on a crockery dish, next to a loaf of fresh brown bread, a knife and a large white chunk of cheese. In the background, Hamlet sword-fights with three soldiers. With one thrust of his sword, he disarms them, rushes forward to the table, sits on its edge, holds up the packet of Rosebud, looks at the camera, and says: 'To be or not to be, this is the margarine / Whether 'tis tastier to the mouth to offer / a tart and flabby sup of o'erpriced butter /or to take up the sweetness of Rosebud and by savouring, enjoy it.'" He smiled at Nathan. "Doesn't that rock your socks?"

Stunned at the audacity of someone writing a piece of doggerel reducing Shakespeare's most complex character to a margarine huckster, Nathan did remember that he was trying to find money to get to London.

"I just need you to run the lines for the camera so the client can see how stunning it'll be."

"So I have the job?"

"It's almost a foregone conclusion. Look, it's just a read-through, no big deal. I don't know what else to say."

"You could say, 'Yes, you have the job'."

"Rosebud margarine," said Arthur coldly, "is the largest selling margarine in the country. It's a big account. I wouldn't want to put it at risk because some actor 'doesn't audition for commercials'."

"No, I don't think you'd do that," agreed Nathan, his instinct telling him that Arthur was using him so that 'the client' — some brainless CEO — could vet the idea. At that point, he understood that they wouldn't give him the job *because* he'd given in; and he had no intention of 'running the lines' without a guarantee.

"So, you'll do it?"

"No. I don't audition for commercials. But I'll tell you what, you can turn the camera on and I'll talk to your client about Rosebud."

"You will?"

"Yes."

"Okay," said Arthur, curiously. "You need a minute?"

Nathan nodded, closed his eyes and tried to look meditative. After twenty seconds, he glanced at Arthur and nodded again.

"Roll it," said Arthur.

The young techie pushed a button, and Nathan stepped before the lens. "When Orson Welles made CITIZEN KANE he had Kane die at the beginning, whispering the word 'Rosebud'. As the rest of the picture unfolds, we see it's a mystery with a reporter trying to uncover the meaning of the word 'Rosebud'. It turns out that Kane was remembering his sleigh which to him represented his happy boyhood. But what Welles and only a few people knew was that 'Rosebud' was the word William

Randolph Hearst, the real-life Citizen Kane, used to refer to his mistress' clitoris. And that's what I think of when I hear the word 'Rosebud'."

Nathan walked out of shot and to the door as, ironically, Arthur's cell phone rang out the theme from ROCKY. "I was trying to do you a favour," he said angrily, pulling it out.

"You did. I enjoyed myself," said Nathan, closing the door behind him.

***

I had no illusions about 'getting ahead' in the movie business — or God forbid, emulating László. I still had the urge to see Europe, but wanted to be part of making one good picture before I left Felicity (I probably thought I could show László how it should be done). It's not that I wouldn't mind being a producer — making key decisions on script, casting and director (hiring Vlad to direct every film) — but then, like László, I would need to be the money muscle (MM). Every picture has an MM because no picture gets made unless somebody finds the money to make it. Sometimes it's the star, or the executive producer, or the producer, or the director, but almost never the writer, or associate producer. It's the MM (no matter how inept) who determines what the picture will look and sound like by deciding who will make it. The MM operates under the Golden Rule of Business (not the one the nuns taught me) — 'whoever has the gold makes the rules'. So László — because he raised all the money — made all the important creative decisions, hiring 'yes-men' directors (until Vlad).

Having watched him struggle daily, I respected his ability to hustle. Being the MM is tiresome, tedious, relentless and thankless. The MM is constantly negotiating, dealing, begging, and wheedling financing and services to get the movie made. Which, says Vlad, is how the industry begets more producers. In exchange for money — but more importantly a producer credit — wannabe producers cluster around the MM who in turn attempts to pick the brightest and best (a contradiction, says Vlad) to service his picture.

So all wannabe producers work unceasingly to cram their resumes with movie credits, which is why you see so many listed — executive producers (one movie I saw had *twelve*), co-executive producers, producers, line producers, co-producers, associate producers, assistant producers, post-production producers, supervising producers, etc. Like a pot-luck dinner, they all bring something to the table, and when you see a mob of them uncomfortably decked out in ill-fitting tuxedos on stage, clutching their Oscars for Best Picture, you can be sure they're all producers, but only one is the MM. And it's a safe bet that none are associate producers.

So, even though I was Felicity's Associate Producer and Head of Quality Development, I knew I was just László's girl Friday, the person who kept the office humming, and oversaw Josie (the bookkeeper), Simone (the receptionist), and Jared, the withdrawn young man to whom László paid a meagre wage to run errands and do odd jobs.

Supervising these three, keeping track of László's paperwork, overseeing the building's maintenance, running László's schedule, coordinating pre-prep on whatever picture we were about to make (dealing with contracts, hiring picture crew, casting directors, etc.), and arranging post-post-production on whatever picture we had just made (marketing, promo, PR, etc.) — plus being HQD — took long hours. I was a Jill of all trades and master of none. I worked hard and, although I knew I wouldn't be receiving any awards, I did want desperately to make a movie that Vlad and I could be proud of.

Honor's novel was artless — a simple, intimate and evocative story. With the right actors and a tight script, Vlad could have made an inexpensive, eloquent and touching film. The problems on THE SMOKE PICKERS came about because László didn't understand the strength of that simplicity. *He* was the producer; and *he* knew what his investors — and the audience — wanted.

Two evenings after the investors' screening, he and Simon Lauth — our connection to the wacky world of finance — sat over their monthly dinner, working out future strategies for relieving the brokers of their excess cash. László liked working with Simon, a tall, taciturn, balding, pear-shaped man who didn't ruffle easily, and who knew the money players and how to pry the cash from their grasp.

"So?" asked László.

"I read it."

"And?"

"No sex," Simon stated flatly.

"Investors did good on Kiss. They want to invest again."

"Maybe, but they're already nervous about Sorority Playgirls. A love story about a tobacco farmer's wife and a migrant worker isn't going to turn their cranks without some raunchy sex and a name or two."

"It's award-winning, prestidigious book."

"They don't care about that; they want sex and a profit."

"Lamprey's putting no sex in contract."

"Whose idea was that?"

"Lamprey didn't want to sell. Sarah was quick to think."

"Why do you want to make it?"

"We need to make quality picture, and have more cash flow."

"But why this book?"

"It sold thirty, forty thousand copies ... I don't know, I like it. Sarah likes it. It's permeating."

"Permeating?"

"Older married woman, young man; it's got appeal."

"And how do I sell investors on a movie with no sex?"

"What if we have revolution?"

"In Canada?"

"No, no, South America."

"Do you know how much that would cost?"

"Of course. We shoot here."

"In the snow? It won't look like South America."

"They have no snow in South America?"

Simon thought about it. "Maybe in Chile."

"Chile?"

"They got mountains, there must be snow."

"Ah." László nodded. "They have revolution in Chile?"

Simon thought. "Pinochet."

"You want more wine?"

"What? No, no, Pinochet was a dictator."

"Ah, that's good. Dictators always cause revolutions. Maybe Miguel fights Pinochet."

"He's dead now."

"So he fights son of Pinochet."

Simon was sceptical, but he'd made a number of pictures with László, and had profited by them. "Five million's a big budget. Can Jeremy sell it?"

"Jeremy can pre-sell up to five million if he has names."

"Who?"

"There are one or two possibilities. In few days I go to LA to sign stars."

I had never seen László excited, nor had Vlad — his demeanour wouldn't allow it — but Simon told me later that László gave him the impression of someone who appeared as though he'd finally arrived. There was no smile or boasting, but he exuded confidence.

ALL THAT WEEK, László was either constantly on the phone or bustling in and out of the office. By the end of the following week, Hardy Bingham had spent ten days feverishly working on a rough draft screenplay; we'd received the clauses from Honor's lawyer (although, technically, she hadn't as yet agreed to sell László the rights); our lawyer had quickly prepared the contract, and sent copies to Honor and her lawyer; and László had invited Honor to come in to 'discuss contract,' placing a half bottle of champagne with three glasses on his desk. I was there as a witness — and as the instigator.

László was his most 'sincere' self. He clutched the novel. "I love this book," he said.

Warily, Honor watched him from across the desk.

"You are happy with contract?"

"I seem to be giving you a lot of rights."

"Yes, this is always problem. Writer wants all rights, but producer has to protect investors. You and me, we will agree not to disagree. We will make beautiful movie together."

"My lawyer tells me you can make whatever changes you want to the story."

"When you make movie of book you need to make changes so it will look like movie and not like book."

"Who's going to write the screenplay?"

"Hardy Bingham. He is best writer I have worked with. I have spoken to him. He likes your book."

"Would I have seen one of his movies?"

"He wrote screenplay of YELLOW-BELLIED MARMOT." Honor nodded; she had heard of it. It had some notoriety. The rodent movie, as it was referred to, was based on the true story of a old, deranged mountain man who comes out of the wilderness, falls in love with a suffragette, kills two men in a bar brawl in a small town, is jailed, and — after a struggle — escapes with the woman to live in the wild. It was considered a 'quality' picture (beautiful cinematography). It had won awards, and had a Hollywood 'look,' but didn't, as László would say, do box office. He didn't bother telling Honor that Hardy (using an alias) was also the original screenwriter on Kiss My Asp and had written a 'polish' on Sorority Playgirls.

I could see she was still apprehensive. "László, I want your word that you won't turn *The Smoke Pickers* into a sex romp."

"This is most important. How do we show love of Maddie and Miguel if we don't show their passions? Don't they have connubial relations?"

"They do, but we don't need to see them."

"It's unhealthy not to see them."

"I've made some inquiries, László," Honor said after a pause. "Do you know what they call you?"

László hesitated. "What?"

"Show-me-your-tits Kovacs."

For a fraction of a second, he looked vulnerable — like a small boy who'd wet his pants. Then he forged on. "I know that. Is that why you do not trust me? I feel you do not trust me."

"I don't."

"Why?"

"Because you're Hungarian."

"Now you are making racial slur."

"Yes. I was married to one."

"Ah, so you like Hungarians."

"I did until I married one. The point, László, is that the only thing Hungarians understand is violence. So, I promise you, if you do anything to fuck up my book, I will rip your heart out with my bare hands."

He held up his hands. "Trust me. I know who it is not to pick the fight with. *The Smoke Pickers* is story of this great country. It is my gift to Canada to make this picture."

Honor regarded him silently, her instincts clearly conflicted.

"In every life there is moment when you must make trust of someone. Yes?"

She hesitated, as if trying to gauge whether or not he had a heart and if she *could* rip it out with her bare hands, then picked up his pen and signed. While I witnessed the contract, László popped open the champagne and filled the glasses.

"Tomorrow I fly to Los Angeles."

"Los Angeles?"

"We need big star to play Miguel."

"Who?"

"There are some possibilities but I won't like to disappoint you. I will tell you this: This is most important picture I have made in my life." László raised his glass. "To THE SMOKE PICKERS." Honor silently raised hers. In spite of her reservations, she seemed genuinely moved. Even I was touched.

As soon as Honor left, I followed László down the hall to the meeting room where Hardy Bingham was stabbing at the keys of his Underwood portable with a great velocity, his mouth vigorously punishing a large wad of gum.

Thin, fiftyish, Hardy stubbornly insisted on writing on a portable typewriter just as he drove the rest of his life — with absolute certainty. A copy of an Eames chair in front of his TV dominated his bachelor condo. He drank vodka martinis, wore aviator sunglasses at all hours, and had pre-fixed ideas about what to do with actresses. László liked hiring Hardy because he worked fast, knew how to insert plots, and was adept at 'improving' a movie's narrative by replacing thought-provoking ideas with explicit sex and violence.

László placed the book beside the typewriter. "Where are you?"

"Page 97," Hardy said, not looking up. He *was* fast. Most screenplays (at roughly 120 pages) take months to work out.

"It is working?"

Hardy stopped and grinned at László. "It works great. Miguel and the revolutionaries have just surrounded the Presidential Palace. What kind of sex do you want?"

I was stunned. I'd expected that Honor's novel, at 321 pages, would have to sacrifice some of its story to work as a movie, but I didn't know that László and Hardy were deconstructing it.

László threw me a stern, don't-question-me look. He'd seen my expression — me realizing that we were betraying Honor. I knew the changes would break her heart — they were breaking mine. I again had the urge to quit, but knew that László would carry on regardless, and no doubt inflict greater pain on her, and the world, without me. Besides, I had Vlad, who was genuinely talented, and primed to make something better. Maybe between us, we could overcome what had become known as the 'Kovacs Touch.'

"Ms. Lamprey does not want to see sex," he said, pointedly not looking at me.

"No sex?" said Hardy, mystified.

"No," said László, with a tone of finality I knew was for my bene-fit. He looked at me. "Hardy, it is true they call me 'show-me-some-tits Kovacs'?" I could feel him willing me to say that I knew this. I did, but would never have told him.

Hardy stopped typing and grinned at László. "Only those assholes whose pictures tank."

László nodded, reassured. "I need script by tomorrow. And you are not writing on computer."

"Laz, everyone I know who writes on a computer is writing shit. You'll have your script by noon."

On the way back to his office, I asked, as casually as possible: "You're adding a revolution?"

He looked at me sternly. "I am producer."

Clearly, no further discussion would be necessary.

LOS ANGELES, I discovered, isn't a city that beckons to me, but for those three days the ersatz charm of the endless 'boulevards of broken dreams,' the low-rise, faux architecture (Spanish, English, Colonial, Cape Cod, French Chateau, Ancient Greek & Roman, Japanese, and American Neo-Cartoon), and the hot smoggy air perfumed with the scent of swimming pool chlorine did have its own reeky allure.

László was conflicted about the value of taking me along: (flight and hotel) expense versus utility (the many services of his Girl Friday). In meetings, I run interference, taking up the slack when he gets tired of keeping the conversation going (he can fake interest in actors only for short periods); and so he instructed me to book two rooms at the Beverly Wilshire, one of the posher hotels in Beverly Hills.

Normally László is thrifty, but on his first visit to the City of Angels, he stayed at the Holiday Inn Beverly Hills to save money, and discovered that his meetings were either unproductive or cancelled. Vlad suggested he'd been staying at the wrong hotel — impressing no one. Producers aren't expected to 'save' money, but to 'spend' it. So on his next trip, I booked him into the Wilshire, and magically he returned with a major TV star for KISS MY ASP. Staying at the Wilshire made him feel important, and as soon as we arrived he grew expansive and, to my surprise, was actually fun to be with.

At our lunch meeting with Matt Couch — the agent for the young star we were hoping to cast as

Miguel — László was having difficulty concentrating on his sales pitch, surrounded by seven or eight dazzling blondes at the adjacent tables, chatting on their cells. He was like the kid in the proverbial candy store. As he later told Vlad, he'd been encircled by "*twenty* oversexed starlets".

Wanting to be taken seriously (even he was insecure), László focused on establishing the importance of our project to Couch who was peering at the menu: "Book is best seller ... it's sold forty, fifty thousand copies ... it's permeating."

Matt Couch didn't look up. "You know what's awesome here? The Chicken Cacciatore. It's to die for."

At that moment, Couch's cell rang out with the theme from TITANIC. He took it out and stared at it. "Sorry László, I need to take this. Hi." Gazing absently at the blonde at the next table, Couch listened intently. "Yeah, yeah, yeah, no, no, I know. Tell him we can go with that. Listen, I'm in a meeting here, gimme a shout later. Okay? Ciao."

László pretended their conversation hadn't stopped. "Honor Lamprey is internationally famous author."

"I know, I know. It's not that. He likes the script, he likes the part; he's just not available. He's doing a picture with Scorsese."

"So who's available?"

The waiter was hovering. I smiled at him. "We're not quite ready yet."

"There're a couple of stars who could *do* the picture, but when I read it there was only one I knew could give you that special star quality."

"Who?"

"He'd be perfect."

"Who?"

"It's the kind of role he loves."

"Are you going to tell me his name?"

"Close your eyes. When I say his name, you'll see him in the part."

"I'm not closing my eyes. I'm watching my wallet. Who is this big star?"

"Martin Gage."

"Martin Gage?" László looked puzzled.

I was stunned by Couch's audacity. "Isn't Martin Gage at least over fifty?"

"He's too old," insisted László.

"Too old?" Couch looked bewildered. "No, no ... not for the kid ... what's his name, Manuel?"

"Miguel."

"Yeah Miguel. No ... not him. For the Ambassador."

"Ambassador?"

"Yeah, you know, the guy who ... gives Miguel his papers."

"He's not an Ambassador," I said. "He's the Consul."

"Whatever. I showed him the script, and he liked it. He's never played an Ambassador before."

"Consul," I reiterated.

"Consul, right."

László looked sceptical. "Consul is two scenes. Martin Gage wants to do only two scenes?"

"László, you know what producers here do? When the opportunity to work with a big star like Martin Gage comes knocking, they jump at it. They bump up his screen time. Look at Bogart."

"Humphrey?"

"Do you know how many lines 'Rick' had in the original screenplay of CASABLANCA?"

"How many?"

Couch held up a single finger. "One. 'Play it again Sam, we'll always have Paris.' But Bogart loved the project; he loved Rick; he wanted to be Rick, he wanted to own a nightclub in Casablanca. So the producers said to the writers, whatever he wants ... you write it. And the rest is history — with a big star, you go with the flow, you know what I'm saying?"

The waiter came by again, peering at me. "I'm sorry," I said, "not yet."

"How much?"

"One point five mil."

"What you think? I know fuck nothing?" Nothing ever makes Lás-zló angrier than when he thinks someone's taking advantage of *him*.

"László, Marty just turned down a mil and a half on a Bollywood picture."

"Matt, we are not shooting in India. I don't want to insult you, but in Canada, Martin Gage is not such big star anymore."

"You don't think he's right for the Consul?"

"It's not million dollar Consul. The Consul's worth maybe two hundred thousand — if we add fifteen, twenty minutes screen time."

"Give him another thirty minutes and he'll do it for seven-five."

"Forty minutes screen time for three hundred thousand," said László adamantly.

"Thirty-five minutes at six-five ..." The theme from TITANIC was ringing again in Couch's jacket. He took out the cell and stared at it. "Just a sec, László, I need to take this. Hi, yeah ...?" Couch's eyes darted about the room, focusing on the far side of the restaurant. "No, I see you. You're at about 3 o'clock. Yeah, right. Okay. Okay. Okay. I got it. No, it looks good."

Wondering what Couch was looking at, László and I turned casually in our seats and peered across the crowded room. Against the far wall, at a table near the rear exit, seated behind a potted palm, in a tan suit and reflector sunglasses, a mature, well-groomed man spoke quietly on his cell. It was Martin Gage.

"Of course we'll be discreet," said Couch, hanging up.

"That is Martin Gage over there," said László, dumbfounded.

"I know. I thought you should meet. That was him on the phone."

"Why is he sitting there?"

"He wants us to join him. You know what stars are ... it's like his favourite table or something."

Crossing the restaurant, I caught the eye of our waiter and pointed to Martin Gage's table. The waiter nodded. As I neared the table, my eyes were on Martin who, I could see, was watching us approach with an expression I couldn't quite place. Caution?

"Martin. This is László Kovacs, and … ah…"

"Sarah Fielding," I said, watching László extend his hand, which Martin, rising, shook. When he took my hand, and offered me that famous smile, I felt almost giddy. In person, he seemed to radiate a magical life force and, as he held out a chair for me, I could feel my pulse accelerate. I hadn't seen many of his movies, but being in close proximity to this icon, I could see why he was a big star. Martin emitted what László called a "real charisma".

"This is great pleasure," said László, "I always get thrill when I meet real Hollywood star."

"You're Russian?" Martin said, surprised.

"No, no. Hungarian."

"Martin, László thinks you would be stunning as the Consul. He's gonna ask the writers to …"

"Hungarian?" repeated Martin, thoughtfully. "You guys fought the Russians, right?"

"Russians? Ah, Hungarian Revolution. Yes, Hungarians fought Russians. My uncle tried to mount Russian tank, and was shot in tuchus."

László always gets a laugh with that line, but Martin Gage didn't seem to have heard it. I noticed he was keeping a careful eye on someone approaching.

I turned and smiled at the waiter, shaking my head.

Martin glanced at László. "What's the situation there?"

"In Hungary?"

"Canada."

"Situation?"

"Somalis."

"Somalis?"

"You don't know about the Somalis?"

"What about Somalis?"

Martin glanced at Couch, then, looking directly at László and me, asked, "Can I trust you?"

"Of course," László said.

I glanced at Couch who was still concentrating on the menu, and when Martin looked at me, I nodded.

"There's a coyote on my estate. I've been watching it for the past week. Do you know why?"

"It bites?" suggested László.

"It's a spy."

"Martin," Couch said, looking up, "we're still working out the details."

László and I were nonplussed. Staring at Martin, I tried to connect the words 'coyote' and 'spy' in my mind.

"I know that sounds crazy," said Martin whose gaze seemed to take us into his confidence.

"Coyote spy," said László, assuming he was joking. "Why should it sound crazy?" He chuckled.

"You're smart. It's not crazy."

"No?" asked László.

"Animals," said Martin, "are now being used for close surveillance. They take a coyote, for example, and implant a miniature camera just above the ear, along with GPS. A former CIA operative came up with the idea so that they could run surveillance along the Mexican border. Coyotes are perfect for this, and the Chicano wetbacks haven't figured it out yet. The big fence running the border, by the way, is just a McGuffin.

"McGuffin?" I asked.

"Hitchcock ... you know, a distraction ... not the real story."

While I was trying to imagine pictures from a camera implanted in a coyote, László was staring at him. "How do you know *your* coyote has camera?"

"Good question. Abnormal behaviour. Coyotes hunt over four

square miles each day, but this coyote hasn't left my estate. I watch him from an upstairs window and do you know what I see?"

"What?"

"Him, watching me."

"Why you?" I was still trying to understand "coyote" and "spy".

"I can't tell you that. The question is, whose camera is it?"

László was spellbound. "Whose?"

"We don't know — yet. All I can say is that we have enemies." Martin's glance helicoptered around the room.

"We?"

"America."

"The Somalis?" I asked, amazed.

Martin turned his gaze on me. "You're smart. You listen. The Navy S.E.A.L. boys blew them out of the water off the coast of Africa, but they'll be coming at us from another direction."

"They will?" said László.

"Either from the sea or, most likely, across the Canadian border."

I could see László was having difficulty following what Martin was telling us — *I* was having difficulty. As I tried to connect Somalis and coyote cameras, we both glanced at Couch, who was now munching thoughtfully on a breadstick. László and I, on previous pictures, had encountered strange tales from well-known actors, but nothing like this. What Martin Gage was telling us *was* incredible.

As I shook my head again at the approaching waiter, I could see László working it out. "Look, Mr. Gage ..."

"Please, 'Marty'."

"Marty, I am just producer. I know nothing about Somalis ... or coyote spies, but it was pleasure to meet you." László started to get up.

Martin's tone was gentle but still commanding. "Please sit."

He sat.

"I know this sounds crazy," said Martin gently. "I'm asking you to trust me."

Martin seemed so vulnerable at that moment that it was hard not to believe him.

"Why would I do that?" László asked.

"For national security."

"What if you are crazy?"

"I'm not crazy."

"Marty, why would I risk five million dollar picture on movie star who's afraid of coyotes and Somalis?"

"I'm not afraid. I was in Nam."

"I have investors, Marty. What do I tell them if movie star goes crazy on set?"

"We'll give you a guarantee. You don't pay me till the picture's in the can ... something like that. You'll work it out with Matt."

We both glanced at Couch, whose eyes were closed as though he were focused on listening to the conversation.

"I can't afford to have movie star killing Somalis," László insisted.

"I won't be killing anyone. I'll be on reconnaissance only — the eyes and ears of America. Do you understand?"

"No."

"It's very simple. I'll be there for what we call a 'look-and-see.' How long would you need me?"

László looked at me.

"Ten days," I said.

Martin considered. "That's long enough. Matt, László and Sarah are on board now. They'll need a break on the price. You hear what I'm saying?"

Couch nodded. "I hear you."

Martin stood. "I like you guys. I like this project. It's important."

Martin glanced at the restaurant entrance. László and I followed his gaze. When we looked back, he'd vanished.

Befuddled, László stared at Couch. "You want to tell us now what is going on."

"I don't know. Apparently, it's hush-hush."

"He's a little crazy."

"He's not crazy. He just loves his country and he's concerned about it."

"When I make movie, I want star to think about lines, or having sex with leading lady, or what he is eating for lunch. I don't want him thinking about killing coyotes and Somalis. It's not healthy."

"László, he likes you guys. When he said you'll need a break on the price, he wasn't kidding."

Couch now had László's full attention. "What kind of break?"

Couch leaned in. "Thirty-five a day," he whispered. "That's his special, special rate for people he considers on board."

László considered this. "And we don't pay till he is finished shooting?"

"Right."

I knew that László, as a boy, had been deeply affected by LENA, a movie about a woman in the French resistance, with a young Martin Gage as her lover unable to save her from the Gestapo. Emerging from the theatre into the greyness of communist Budapest, László determined that he would go to America — to Hollywood — marry an actress and produce movies. He'd only gotten as far as Canada (marrying a cheerleader), but he *was* making movies — and romantic ones (or so he thought). Focused on the struggle to keep Felicity afloat over the years, he'd forgotten his dream, but now that he was producing a movie with Martin Gage — was that dream possible? I could see him quickly calculate how little he'd be spending on his star. "What you think, Sarah?"

I had reservations. Martin Gage was charismatic but eccentric, vulnerable but determined, charming but distant — but there was no question of his magnetic personality. "He's immensely charming," I said.

László looked pleased. "Yes, I think so too. Marty will be strong Consul."

Looking for our waiter, Couch said, "Yeah, Marty's first class all the way. Now let's order."

WHEN I WAS nine, every Wednesday evening I would rush to the TV after dinner to watch *Robin of Epping*, the Robin Hood story with Robin as a woman hiding in Epping Forest, robbing the rich and giving to the poor. It was Carey Lander's first major role and I loved her in it. The show's dated now, but over the years, I must have seen it in reruns three or four times. Her unisex Robin influenced my generation of prepubescent girls who would don tights and pretend to fight for justice. I used to climb out in my leotards on a branch of our oak tree and, having positioned our Collie, Rolf, underneath, jump down on the Sheriff of London; but Rolf always bounded off at the last minute, leaving me grass-stained and bruised.

I hadn't thought about Carey in years when I caught her being interviewed on late night TV. She'd matured quite gracefully, and I wondered if she could play Maddie.

"Have you thought about Carey Lander?" I asked Vlad the next day.

"No. Interesting. You know she is gay?"

"She is?"

"She is also very fine actress. We put her on A-list, but I don't think we need to bother László about sexual proclivities."

"Good idea."

Having asked our casting director to make inquiries, we discovered that Carey was in town for the Film Festival, and that her next picture was a no-go, which meant she was available. When it turned out that she was interested in playing Maddie, I delivered a copy of the script to her hotel, and Vlad prepped László.

"I know we can't afford Carey Lander," Vlad told him. "She is probably not available anyway, but this is stature of star we need for Maddie."

Because Vlad had suggested that Carey would most likely be unavailable to us, László started picturing her in the role. Meanwhile Carey was reading the script while Zoe Waller, our casting director, was giving László a list of possible actresses which included Carey. He chose her. Zoe quickly made an offer and, price and conditions being agreed to, Carey accepted. Initially, László was upset when he found out about the no-nudity clause in her contract, until I pointed out that it would demonstrate to Honor that we were making the picture *sans* sex.

So Carey became the second star to be cast; and it was her image that Frank Hodge was gazing at on the wide-screen TV at the Monacle as he waited for Nathan.

For months, Nathan had been urging Frank to make connections for him in England. Driven by his ambition to act with Britain's Royal Shakespeare Company, he assumed, rightly, that it would be difficult for the RSC to discover him in Toronto. So he assigned Frank, his agent and a former Londoner, to get him an acting job in London.

The Hodge Agency represented over sixty-five actors (even amateurs), but only a few (like Nathan) worked constantly, so Frank's commissions were meagre. He rarely attended the theatre, venturing out only if a theatre or actor provided him with free tickets. Attired always in the same rumpled, brown wool slacks and dark green tweed jacket, Frank conducted most of his business — gossiping with unemployed actors — at the Monacle (avoiding his cramped, shabby office next door), returning home in the evening to his wife Dilys, a former dancer.

By the time Nathan arrived, Frank was sipping his first scotch and soda of the day and watching *Eyes on Entertainment* with Barney.

"... Carey Lander," announced the TV commentator, "who dazzled festival-goers on the red carpet, has just been signed to star in THE SMOKE PICKERS, based on the book by internationally-famous Canadian author, Honor Lamprey …"

Nathan took a stool next to Frank, glancing at Carey's image on the big screen. It had nothing to do with him. He was as far from Carey Lander as the Man in the Moon. He nodded as Barney put a coffee in front of him.

"What's happening with London, Frank?"

Frank's eyes were riveted on Carey. "Just a tick."

The commentator droned on: "… Also signed is Martin Gage, and rumour has it that director Vladimir Pudovkin is conducting a nation-wide search for a young actor to play Miguel."

Rumours never 'have it.' We weren't conducting a nation-wide search (László would never have spent the money), but we'd begun looking at audition tapes, and interviewing local actors. Having cast two big stars, Vlad had suggested casting an unknown Canadian actor, and László had jumped at the opportunity to save money.

Frank looked at Nathan. "It's not cast. What do you think?"

"What?" asked Nathan.

"You could play a spic."

"*Latin American*, Frank," chided Nathan, watching shots of Carey flash by on the screen.

"… Ms. Lander, promoting THE BREME FACTOR, told us that her on-again off-again romance with Brendan Slate was quote 'non-existent'."

Frank eyed Nathan, meaningfully. "You could be the love interest, Mr. Quill, opposite Carey Lander." It was Hodge's unwavering belief in his clients' talents — any of them could play King Lear or Joan of Arc — that attracted actors to his agency, all seeking their breakout role.

Nathan had no interest in a 'breakout' role. He just wanted to perform with the finest Shakespearean actors in the world. "London, Frank."

"Shhh," said Hodge, glancing back at the screen.

"Making the move into serious drama with the five million dollar picture," a reporter announced enthusiastically, "is producer László Kovacs, whose horror sex comedy, KISS MY ASP, was the top-grossing Canadian movie last year" — the shot of László was actually flattering — "It is great privilege," said László, "for me to make picture of Ms. Lamprey's beautiful book."

Nathan sipped his coffee. "They wouldn't look at me."

"I can get you in."

"I want you to get me to London."

"Nathan, all any *English* actor wants these days is a part in a Hollywood movie — and there's one right there in front of you. Wake-up, Mr. Quill."

When he wants something, Nathan — like László — focuses his gaze on the person he thinks will give it to him. He stared at Frank.

Avoiding his gaze, Frank said quietly: "I can't get you to London, Nathan. All my contacts there have died, or moved to Miami. No one in London theatre gives a rodent's rectum about Frank Hodge because they've never heard of me."

Nathan realized he was pushing too hard, wanting something from someone who cared about him but who couldn't give him what he wanted. He reviewed his options — a major role in a movie might pay enough to keep him afloat in London for many months. "You can get me in?"

"I can get you in."

***

I was almost trembling when I dropped off the script at Carey's hotel. She had smiled at me and, two days later when I delivered her contract, I turned into the same mass of jelly. It was only when she finally agreed to do it that I relaxed, realizing that I was now the associate producer on a Carey Lander movie. And just like a real producer, I was taking her to lunch (without first having to pick her up at the airport or fetch her a coffee). Of course, we'd be meeting László there, but *I* was taking her.

When I arrived at her hotel, she was being interviewed by Rex Wittington, a local arts reporter who'd recently undergone a sex change operation and was now calling himself Sheila (photos and a poem were circulating on the Net shortly after the operation: "There was a reporter named Rex / Who reconfigured his sex / He drank some tequila / emerging as Sheila / with a libido bewildered and vexed.") I later downloaded Carey's interview to my iPod.

"You seem," said Sheila, in a husky timbre sounding, oddly, more masculine than Rex, "to select roles which suggest a kind of feminine masculinity. Would that be a fair assessment?"

"Don't you mean a masculine femininity?" asked Carey.

I could hear the hesitation in Sheila's voice. "In your movies, you always play strong women."

"It's not deliberate; I pick stories about humans struggling to survive."

"And those are the roles you're identified with."

"I'm sure you're right."

"Is it true you want to do more theatre?"

"I wouldn't say 'more'; I would say 'some.' The only play I was ever in was *Our Town* in high school."

"What sort of theatre?"

"Shakespeare."

"Isn't it a cliché that all actors want to play Shakespeare?"

"Well, he *was* a great writer."

"Which roles would be attractive to you?"

"Any of them."

"The male ones, too?"

"Just Hamlet." You could hear the smile in Carey's voice.

"*Twelfth Night*?"

"I haven't read it."

"It's a crazy play. You'd be cool as Viola, who's disguises herself as a man. Would that be the kind of role that would appeal to you?"

"It sounds intriguing."

"Is that because it's about a woman disguised as a man? Like Robin of Epping?"

It was then that I arrived. At the door, Carey, with her back to Sheila, rolled her eyes and smiled raffishly as she let me in. Turning back to Sheila, she said: "I have time for two more questions."

"What about Shakespeare's take on gender identity?"

"What about it?"

"What are your thoughts?"

"What are *your* thoughts?"

"I'd be curious to know how you see your ... your ... gender identity."

"I'm not sure what you mean."

"Well, I guess I mean, ah, how do you ... ah ... how do you feel about being gay?"

"I don't feel anything. I'm just an actress whom some people think is gay."

"So you haven't ... officially ... come out?"

"Right. And I haven't *officially* 'gone in.'"

"I don't understand."

"I'm sorry, I thought that would clarify it," she said with a smile. "Now if you'll excuse me, I really must go."

"Okay," said Sheila, shutting off her recorder, and glancing at me. I assumed she was wondering if I was anyone important, or gay. "Thank you for this, Carey. If you have some free time while you're here, I could show you some 'alternative' clubs I think you'd find amusing."

"I'm not big on clubs, I'm afraid. I need to get lots of sleep for the camera, but thank you."

Closing the door, Carey exhaled. "Why are they always so adversarial? How are you, Sarah?"

"Fine. It's good to see you again."

I had picked an upscale restaurant where I thought Carey wouldn't be bothered, but it was almost empty when we arrived, causing me to wonder if the food was inedible. László, near a couple finishing their meal on the patio, was sitting at a table by the window on his cell. "Yes, Jeremy. Presale will include prints and ads. Call me tomorrow to tell me all markets and platforms you want to buy." Seeing us, László rose and smiled at Carey. "Ms. Lander, it is great pleasure."

"Carey."

"Carey, call me László." László is never sure whether or not to hug someone, and sometimes uncertainty overcomes him mid-hug and he freezes. He played it safe with Carey, taking her hand and holding on to it just long enough to bond them forever, then pulled out a chair for her. "Is there anything you need?" he asked. "You like hotel?"

"Yes, it's fine."

The restaurant being almost empty, a waiter appeared immediately, poured three glasses of water, placed a basket of bread and menus on the table and left.

"I'm starving," said Carey, taking a piece of bread from the basket. She fingered it and grimaced. "It's stale."

"What!" said László.

"I'm sorry," I said quickly. It was the nuns speaking. I had been conditioned to take the rap whenever anything went wrong — the Golden Rule in action.

Carey laughed. "It's not your fault, Sarah."

"It is. I picked this place because I didn't think you'd be bothered here."

"And you were right," she said, indicating the empty room.

László raised his arm and snapped his fingers. "Waiter!" he said loudly.

The waiter, hovering nearby, sauntered over.

"Bread is stale," said László, pointing at the basket.

The waiter picked up the basket, sniffed the bread, then took a bit between his fingers and rolled it. We watched it crumble. After a slight pause, he said, "No, that's the texture."

"What?!" László's voice was louder now.

"The bread is stale," said Carey, firmly.

The waiter looked unmoved.

I peered at his tag. "Your name is ... Brian. Brian, here's a win-win situation. If you bring us a fresh loaf — a *fresh* one — you can feed this one to the pet mice in your kitchen."

Brian got the message and quickly removed the bread.

Carey was staring at me. "You're ballsy."

"That's why I hired her," László said. "Some day she'll be ballsy producer, and I will be working for her."

"I'm not ballsy. I just get angry when people treat me as though I'm stupid."

Carey was laughing. "It's very attractive."

"What is?"

"Your anger. I'll bet the boys liked you even more when you beat them up."

I could see that our conversation was confusing László, who has a constrained view of women. "You like the script?" he asked Carey, abruptly.

"Yes, I did."

"Because you know I'm not so sure that we have it as good as can be."

"Every script can be improved," Carey said.

"Yes," László said eagerly. "That is what I think. It needs ... I don't know ... more passion."

It wasn't obvious to László but I noticed Carey stiffen. "It reads passionate to me," she said.

"You don't think we need to show more the love of Maddie for Miguel?"

Puzzled, Carey glanced at me. I could see that she knew exactly where László was headed but, given the no-nudity clause, didn't know why. "No, I think it's there. That's why I took the role."

"I know, but I am feeling it is not enough. If we do not show Maddie and Miguel having connubial relations, how will audience know how much passion they are having?"

"What can we do?" Carey asked ingenuously. Was she curious to see how far László would go?

"Maybe," László said, reflectively, "when Miguel comes to Consulate, they are so passionate, they have to have each other."

"Hmmmm," Carey said. "I hadn't thought of that." I was surprised. She seemed to consider it, but after a moment, said: "No, Maddie wouldn't do that."

"No?" László said, startled.

"No, she still cares for Guy. She wouldn't risk having him find them together. She knows it would hurt him."

"Yes, you are right," László said. "Maybe, what we need to show is passion of Maddie for Guy."

"There's a big difference between passion and caring."

"Maybe she has caring," László said, "*and* passion for Consul."

"They've been married a long time, so I'm not sure they have any passion left, although I do believe they care for each other. Besides, it would be difficult to play both at the same time. Not to mention confusing for the audience, don't you think?"

I was admiring Carey's ability to punch her weight with László when I heard the Brahms Lullaby coming from his jacket. "Excuse me," he said, pulling out his cell and peering at it. "I have to take this. Hello? Simon? I'm at lunch, let me call you later. What? Okay, never mind, I come to your office."

He hung up and rose from the table. "I am sorry, Carey, business calls. We will talk later. I know you will be wonderful as Maddie."

When László left, Carey smiled at me. "He's pretty tenacious."

"That's why he's still in business."

"Usually when a producer wants me naked for the camera, I tell them I will if they will. I think László would."

"You must get that a lot."

"Hardly at all anymore. I'm no longer twenty-one, in a business that's predominantly anti-gay. Don't you run into this?"

I was surprised. "Me?"

"Yes."

"I'm not gay."

"No?"

Her gaze confused me. "Do ... do I look gay?"

"What does 'gay' look like?"

Was I offending her? "I don't know ... different?"

Carey grinned. "Lots of people look different. Do you have a boyfriend?"

"I used to, sort of."

"Sort of?"

"We were just together a few years, in University, but nothing ... you know ... passionate."

"How do you know you're not gay?"

"I don't. I don't think I am. I think maybe I'm asexual, like an amoeba."

She paused as though wondering who I was. "You don't look like an amoeba."

"Have you ever seen one?"

"I dated one for six weeks. He was extremely asexual, with a single-celled brain."

I laughed while Carey appraised me. I felt like a schoolgirl. Her undivided attention left no doubt as to her intentions. I couldn't imagine it was just a game, nor could I fathom why she was interested in me, although I *was* flattered. She was my girlhood hero and, even though she was older, still very attractive. What I said was true. I think of myself as an amoeba, although perhaps with something larger than a single-celled brain.

AS WE GOT closer to shooting, Vlad and I worked long days, prepping. Overriding all of our concerns was finding our Miguel; and so from the moment I got back from L.A., we viewed tapes from agents, skimmed endless movies, and begun interviewing Toronto actors. We'd interviewed 53 in three and a half weeks and, on this day, growing more desperate, we'd seen nine before lunch. By the time Nathan came in, we'd managed three, so Vlad was now in a deep Slavic brood, motionless behind the table, staring at his cell. Between actors, I was texting contract changes to our lawyer.

Nathan sat at the table without waiting to be invited. I had to check the casting sheet; the names were becoming a blur. "Thanks for coming in, ah ... Nathan ... Nathan Quill, right?" His name was familiar to me from theatrical reviews and ads, but I'd never seen him act.

His eyes on Vlad, Nathan nodded.

"I don't see any film on your resume," I said.

"No."

"Oh. Okay. This is Vladimir Pudovkin, our director." I picked up my script. "You've seen the sides?" 'Sides' were the script pages of the relevant scene.

He nodded again.

"Okay. You need a minute?"

Nathan shook his head. He hadn't taken his eyes from Vlad who now realized that Nathan was staring at him.

"Ready?"

Nathan nodded. I loved reading with the actors, which I suppose was a substitute for not being one. I nodded at Jared who was recording the auditions on a cheap digital camera.

"Miguel," I said, reading from my script, "you don't have to return. You could stay."

"*No es posible,*" Nathan said.

I glanced down at the page, even though I knew that wasn't the line, and looked back at Nathan who was still staring at Vlad. He had Vlad's attention now. Then he looked at me. It was so sudden and direct that I couldn't look away.

"We have no food," he said quietly. "The children in my village, when they are hungry, eat dirt. This morning, I watched a little girl die. She had not eaten for two weeks."

In the script, Miguel was supposed to be telling Maddie that a woman is not necessary in a revolution.

"Have you seen a child die from hunger? Her body is thin, like a stick — then lethargic. Her belly extends, she doesn't move. She grows gaunt. There is darkness under her eyes, the bones on her arms and legs stick out pushing against the skin. She cannot breathe, then ... she stops. Death lives in my village, in my country. It stalks my people. I go where I am needed. So, you see, I must say adiós." He looked like he was about to cry, then stopped, but continued to stare at me.

I didn't know where to look, aware only of an aching sadness for that little girl.

Finally Vlad broke the spell. "You studied Stanislavski?"

Nathan nodded.

"I like what you did. I do not make final decision, but you, as they say, are 'contender.' Thank you for coming in."

Nathan got up abruptly and left. I looked at Vlad, who was smiling for the first time that day, then ran to the door and caught Nathan in the hall. "Nathan," I said quietly — there were other actors present — "please have your agent let Zoe know your availability." I stepped up to him and said very softly, "You were amazing."

I wondered why those hazel eyes were staring at me sceptically. He told me later he thought that I was 'movie bullshitting' him. Ha!

***

His flight was late, but Martin Gage passed through Customs & Immigration noticeably fast. It took me a moment to realize that the man in the slouch hat, raincoat and beard pushing his luggage cart through the sliding glass doors *was* Martin Gage. What beard? I was even more astonished when I saw, close up, that the beard was obviously fake.

"Martin?" I said, approaching him.

He stopped. His eyes focused on me, apprehensively.

"Hi. Welcome to Canada."

"Who are you?"

"Sarah. I met you with László in Beverly Hills."

His eyes, scanning the small crowd waiting for relatives and loved ones, paused to examine my face. We were blocking the exit but he took no notice.

"Right."

"I'm just up here in the parkade," I said.

Pushing his cart with four old ratty suitcases precariously balanced on it, he followed me to the elevator.

"May I ask why you're wearing a beard?"

"What?"

"You're wearing a beard, which — forgive me for saying so — seems fake."

"For security."

"Security?"

"I attract too much attention."

"Didn't they notice in Customs and Immigration?"

"I don't know."

"They didn't say anything?"

"They asked for my autograph."

Crossing the pedestrian bridge into the parking garage, we came to the white Land Rover László had bought on sale. Thinking it gave the company prestige, he insisted we continue to pay the exorbitant monthly gas bills to ferry people and equipment about. As Martin approached it, he said: "Good vehicle choice, wrong colour."

"What colour should it be?"

"Sea Green. Easier to camouflage."

Just then, Martin took his cell from his pocket and glanced at the screen. I was surprised. I hadn't heard a ring tone. "Pooh Bear here," he said into the cell. "Okay, ten four." As I opened the trunk, he put the cell away and took the bag I was lifting from the cart. "I've got it," he said.

He threw it and the rest of his luggage into the back. I walked around to the driver side, unlocked all the doors and was getting in when he said: "Sarah, come unlock the door."

"It should be unlocked."

"No, come look."

I walked around the Rover, and put my hand on the door handle. Martin put his hand on mine and said quietly: "Listen carefully. The door is open. I am going to pretend to get in. I want you to drive off without me."

I glanced at his eyes. They seemed normal, but extremely alert. They were observing something in the parking garage behind me.

"Why?" I asked, turning to see a beat-up Chevy Impala slowly passing behind us, driven by a thin man in a fedora with a pencil moustache, who was pointedly ignoring us.

"Drive the Rover to the hotel and park in the garage. Wait in the lobby fifteen minutes then come to my room."

"What's going on?" I whispered.

"Just do it."

I walked back to the driver's side, got in and started the engine. Martin opened and shut the passenger door then vanished. I glanced at the passenger side mirror as I heard the Chevy Impala speed off, then looked in all the mirrors. Martin Gage had disappeared.

I was still puzzled as I drove downtown. How was he getting to the hotel? The Chevy Impala? Who was driving it? And how did whoever was driving him know where he'd be — unless they were following me?

Arriving at the hotel, I parked in the garage, went to the lobby, waited fifteen minutes, asked for Martin's room number, and gave my keys to a bellboy to fetch his luggage from the Rover. I took the elevator, knocked on his door and waited. After thirty seconds, the door was thrust open and I recognized the man from the Chevy Impala, dressed in a tight, dark blue suit with a black shirt and silver tie, hair slicked back. He had an elongated face bisected by his pencil moustache. He stared at me.

"I'm here to see Martin Gage."

"Come in, Sarah," Martin said from behind the door.

As I entered, the man with the moustache checked the hallway, nodded at Martin and left the room, closing the door behind him. A laptop sat on the desk, wires from which ran across the room to a telescope on a tripod pointed out the window at the lake. I looked at Martin, startled to see him sliding a pistol under his jacket on the sofa.

"Have you registered that?"

"What?"

"I think all handguns need to be registered with the police."

"I'm licensed."

"In Canada?"

"Anywhere."

"You probably still need a permit for Canada."

"I have clearance."

"What kind of clearance?"

"I can't tell you that."

"What's going on?"

"What do you mean?"

"How did you get to the hotel?"

"Other means. I needed a decoy."

"I don't understand."

"Don't worry about it."

I was baffled. I had experienced odd movie star behaviour before, but this was a new level of inexplicable. "Well, what do you need?"

"Need?"

"You wanted me to come to the hotel."

"My luggage."

"I have a bellboy bringing it up. That's all?"

"I'll need Wi-Fi on set at all times."

"Okay ... is that all?"

"No, I need clearance for one of my back-up people."

"Clearance?"

"Access to the set."

I was surprised. Movie stars never asked permission for their girl-friends and boyfriends to frequent the set — it's considered movie star privilege. "What's her name?"

"*His* name is Salmo but we'll need to make sure he can't be identi-fied. So, we're calling him Bruce Robinson."

"Why can't we use his real name?"

"I can't tell you that." He stated it simply, as though it were obvious.

"Okay, what does he look like?"

There was a rap-tap-tap. Martin edged his way to the door, tapped twice and, after hearing two taps back, opened it.

"He looks like 'Bruce Robinson'," Martin said, pointing at Salmo who pushed a dining cart through the door with an urn of coffee on it. Bruce/Salmo crossed the room and sat at the desk, staring at the lap-top screen, barely glancing at me. "It's vitally important that no one connects his name with my presence here."

"Which one?"

"Which one what?"

"Which name?"

"Salmo."

"Okay." I wondered if Martin Gage might be gay. If he was, he had strange taste in men. "Is there anything else you need?"

"Dossiers on all picture personnel."

"Dossiers? Why?"

"I can't tell you that."

"You're not doing anything to jeopardize the picture, are you?"

"Are you kidding? I love this project. I like László. I even like you. But I'm under a Code 5."

"What's a Code 5?"

"I can't tell you that."

"Anything else?"

"I'll need to meet the director."

"Okay. When?"

"I can't tell you that."

I stared at him. "What?"

"That's a joke," he said, without smiling. "Ask him to come Friday at nineteen hundred hours. That's all for now. We'll be in touch."

He opened the door, closing it hurriedly behind me. He didn't seem normal, but then again he *was* Martin Gage, still lustrous, and not your average, ageing American movie star.

Driving out of the hotel parking lot, I kept glancing in the rear view mirror to see if I was being tailed.

***

Vlad and I had no doubt that Nathan was our Miguel. He was the most compelling actor we'd seen, and Vlad had taken him for lunch the next day, returning to the office almost vibrating. "Nathan is not actor, he is too smart. He reads. He knows theatre, history and baseball. And he is passionate about acting."

"He told you that?"

"No, no, he has no ego, but you can tell he is smart when he talks."

We knew, however, that László wouldn't be able to see what we saw; and even though Vlad had the responsibility of ensuring that the actor playing Miguel would be able to carry the movie, László (as the MM) would insist on making the final decision. He would balk if we cast Nathan — who was striking but not handsome in a conventional sense — as a fait accompli. So we knew we'd have to guide László to the right decision, but more importantly to let him think *he* was making it. We assembled audition videos of Nathan and four other actors who, while talented in varying degrees, were nowhere as commanding; and late that afternoon, played the tapes for László. I had sat in his office with him like this many times before, watching him stare dubiously at his big screen TV, but never for something as important.

The first two actors were attractive males, the third was from Columbia, and the fourth was an actor from a hit Canadian TV series. Nathan was last, and when the auditions finished, László turned and stated, as a mild rebuke: "Actor cannot even remember lines. Well?"

"Well, what?" Vlad retorted.

"You liked first one," he said, carefully watching our expressions.

"No," Vlad said.

He looked at me then back at Vlad. "You and Sarah agree?"

"Yes."

László glanced at the names of the five actors on the paper in front of him. "You like number four."

"No," Vlad said, sighing. "Sarah and I think only number five is strong enough to carry movie."

László signalled me to run Nathan's audition again. When it finished, he frowned. "He is not saying lines."

"He is improvising," Vlad said, "and what he is saying, and way he is saying it, is better than script. Script is okay but actor is improving it."

"He is not sexy."

"I think he's very sexy," I said, jumping in, and I did. Maybe it was because he was an actor and I respected his ability, but to me he was certainly alluring.

László, baffled, stared at the blank screen. "We need extra opinion," he said, walking into reception and returning with Simone. Vlad and I looked at each other, dumbfounded. Our receptionist was an overweight, glum young woman who, in two days, would be flying south with twenty of her friends to enact her destination wedding at a Dominican Republic resort. Almost daily for the past two weeks, she had shown me sketches of the bridal gown she was having made (a long-flowing skirt with a bikini top); and for the past week she had been either on the phone with her dressmaker or travel agent, or playing solitaire on the computer. Was László asking *her* to decide which actor would carry our five million dollar movie? Vlad, containing his anger, stared at both with disdain. What László was doing, intentionally or not, was suggesting that Simone, a receptionist, might know more about acting than Vlad, a director who had graduated from the Leningrad Film Academy and had four feature length films to his credit.

"Simone," László said, "we are deciding which actor will be Miguel in movie. We would like to have opinion from you."

Surprised, Simone immediately assumed an air of authority. I ran the five auditions for her, and when they'd finished, she attempted to look thoughtful.

"So," László asked, "what you think?"

Impressed with her newly-found status, she paused, as though everything depended on her answer. "Number four," she said decisively. Number four was the actor in the hit TV series.

"You think he is sexiest?"

"Noooo ... I think number one is the sexiest but number four is a better actor."

Vlad sighed, audibly. I glanced at him. He had his hand over his face, and I knew he was working very hard to keep from yelling, or something worse.

"What about number five?" László asked.

Simone sighed, rolled her eyes and shook her head.

"Thank you, Simone," László said.

Pleased with having her talent finally recognized, Simone tripped back to her desk, closing the door behind her.

László looked at Vlad and me reprovingly. "So you want to hire actor who does not know lines, and is not sexy."

"Maybe it would be sexier," Vlad said, "to have Simone direct movie."

"You don't have to go to Leningrad Film School to know who is sexy and who is not sexy. If we do not have sexy actor, how will audience see Miguel's passions?"

"Sarah, run Nathan again."

I did, and Vlad instructed László on what Nathan was doing and why his performance was more compelling than the others. I pointed out Nathan's edginess, his danger. Major rock stars, I explained, emit the same kind of danger and that's why young girls find them exciting — and sexy. We screened Nathan's audition for him three times. At the end of the third viewing he sighed. "Stop. I have decided to cast Nathan as Miguel. I am still thinking he is not sexy enough, but you are right, he is good actor."

***

The next day, Simon and I waited with László in his office. László, doodling on a pad, appeared calm, while Simon placidly read the stock quotations in the paper. I was trying not to let my anxiety show by texting Vlad's notes on the actors to Zoe Waller. Our distributor was supposed to call at 11:00 a.m. to let us know if he was going to pre-buy the picture — the agreement we needed to guarantee financing. It was now 11:20 a.m.

Our pictures were usually shot in three weeks, cost one to two million to make, and starred some recognizable 'name' actor (usually a faded TV star) in order to be able to compete in the DVD market. As long as we kept making genre pictures (thriller, horror, comedy) cheaply enough, replete with sex and violence, we could turn a profit for our investors and for the company. This business model wasn't invented by László, but he seemed to have a talent for exploiting it. He owned the two-storey building which housed Felicity Pictures; he drove an old Mercedes sedan which he referred to as a 'classic'; and lived in (having paid cash for) a condo on the lake.

So it's understandable that producing a non-genre 'quality' picture roughly three times our normal budget would make us all apprehensive, László especially. It was a risk, and Vlad and I shared the weight of his responsibility.

When the phone rang, László held up his finger, as he always did, waited for it to ring again then motioned to me.

"Good afternoon, László Kovacs' office," I said. "Yes, Jeremy, he's expecting your call. I'll put you through. Just a moment." I pushed the hold button. László waited a few seconds and then pushed the speaker button but said nothing.

After a moment, we could hear Jeremy over the speaker, "László, you prick, are you there?"

"I'm here, Jeremy. I like to listen to you breathe to see if you are living. You are still living?"

"Considering that all my producers are trying to screw me, I'm doing fine."

"And your family? How old is little Emma now?"

"Thirteen."

"She is handsome young woman?"

"You could say that. She's screwing a 20-year-old drug addict."

"Oh. And Stephanie? She's in medical school?"

"She quit. She's playing house with a camel jockey in Morocco."

"And how is ... ah, ah ..."

"Gina," I whispered.

"Gina. How is Gina, Jeremy?"

"Gina's long gone, László — and I'm not looking for wife number four, if anyone's interested."

"Good, well, I'm glad you're good. You are good, right?"

"No, I'm not good. You were supposed to call me, you prick, and keep me posted. I want to hear your voice. I don't want emails, or god-damn twitters."

László was enjoying himself. "You don't want emails or twitters. I am writing this down, Jeremy."

"Who've you signed?"

"Ah, that's why I'm calling, to tell you the big stars we signed."

"Who?"

"He loves the project."

"Who?"

"Martin Gage."

"You kidding me? He's too old."

"Not for Miguel, for the Consul."

"The Consul? That's a nothing part. Why would he do that?"

"We are re-writing. Building it ... up." László motioned 'up' with his hand as though he were on Skype.

"Who've you signed for Maddie?"

"Only one of the most beautiful women in Hollywood."

"Who?"

"Carey Lander."

"Carey Lander? She's old. And she's a dyke."

László was surprised by this revelation. "She's still big star, Jeremy," he said, uncertain. "And she loves part."

Even though Carey had warned me, and even though I was aware of the anti-female, anti-gay, anti-age, anti-anything-except-macho-profit attitude of the industry, and even though I knew that Jeremy's gruff exterior concealed the beating heart of a genuine male jerk, I was surprised.

"Who's playing Miguel?"

"Ah-ha, Jeremy, that's why I'm calling. We discovered a new star — a young Brando. Vlad is very impressed."

"What's the little fucker's name?"

"Nathan Quill. Write it down, Jeremy. After SMOKE PICKERS, he's going to be very big. Sarah tells me he's hot."

"I thought Sarah was a dyke."

I shouldn't have been startled, but I was. I realized later that it was probably how Carey feels most of the time.

"Sarah is here in office with me, Jeremy," László said, avoiding my gaze.

"Oh. Well, *are* you gay, Sarah?"

"That's personal, Jeremy, but I can tell you that whatever I am I find Nathan very exciting. I think he'll appeal to women and to ... well, everybody."

"László, our agreement wasn't for a someday-star but for a big star-now. All you got is a couple of fading stars and an unknown — no big star, so no five mil, two mil tops, maybe."

László gets very angry when he thinks he's being crossed on a deal — some of his anger, of course, is also for effect. "Jeremy, you want out? Simon, what you think? Should we let Jeremy out of deal?"

Simon is never emotional. "If Jeremy wants out, he can get out," he said unhurriedly.

"You hear that, Jeremy, Simon says you want out, you can get out. I want you in, but if you want out, you're out."

"László, you prick, I'm not putting up five mil for two has-been stars. I need big names. Otherwise, I can't make money on the ancillaries."

"You're getting three stars, Jeremy, a new, young star, and two famous stars, in a quality movie from a beautiful, best-selling, award-winning book, directed by talented international director. That's what you're getting — for only five mil. But don't trust me, Jeremy; fly up to see footage when we shoot. If you don't think we have new Brando, you can get out."

"Alright. I'll fly up second day."

"Good."

"Don't forget my companion."

"Sarah will arrange."

More male nonsense. Every time Jeremy came to Toronto we had to engage a 'lady' from an 'escort service' (at our cost). Whenever I called the service to make the arrangements, I never got the impression that Jeremy was a favoured customer.

"Yeah, yeah, okay. Sarah?"

"Yes, Jeremy?"

"See if that Asian girl's available. What's her name?"

"Madonna?"

"That's the one, okay?"

"Right."

"Jeremy, I got picture to make."

"Bye László, bye Sarah, bye Simon."

László pushed the disconnect button, and we all sat there, dead silent, trying to believe that Felicity Pictures wasn't about to step into a large black hole.

VLAD, ENAMOURED WITH all things Hollywood — especially CITIZEN KANE, once joked that he'd thought of changing his name to 'Orson' Pudovkin.

"If you like Hollywood so much," I asked him, "why didn't you settle there?"

"When you are not lead sled dog," he said, "view is always same."

So it was to be expected that Vlad, carrying a brown paper bag, was exhilarated as he arrived at Martin Gage's hotel room door and knocked. Glancing at the peephole, he thought he saw the flash of a penetrating eye. He was about to knock again when the door opened slowly then stopped, wide enough to allow Martin Gage to peer around its edge.

Seeing him, Vlad smiled and said, "Mr. Gage."

"Who are you?"

"Your director, Vladimir Pudovkin, at your service. It is honour for me to welcome you to Canada."

"You're Hungarian?"

"Are you crazy? I'm Russian."

"Russian?" said Martin, alarmed.

"Well, now I am Canadian. Only in Canada would I have opportunity to direct Martin Gage in beautiful movie. At Leningrad Film Academy, for one week, we study RUN DANNY RUN, a great movie."

"You saw my picture in Russia?"

"It was very good in Russian. Everyone agreed, you should have Oscar."

"Thank you ... ah ..."

"Vladimir. Call me Vlad."

"Okay, Vlad. Come in."

As he entered the room, Vlad watched Martin glance up and down the hallway, quickly shut the door, and put the pistol he was holding back in his jacket pocket. Then he pushed a number on his cell. "Piglet," he said, "Pooh Bear is ready for the honey pot." He put the cell away, and gazed at Vlad, as though trying to read his thoughts. "Vlad, I need to ask you a question."

"Of course."

"You're Russian?"

"Yes."

"You ever been a Communist?"

The question was so unexpected that Vlad started to laugh. Martin stared at him, puzzled. "What's so funny?"

"I'm sorry, you are right. It is not funny. I was not Communist. My father was forced to have conversation with KGB."

"Oh. I'm sorry."

"It's alright. It is past. Now, you and I are future, Mr. Gage ..."

"Marty."

"Marty... whew. Marty, this is big thrill for me. You and I — Marty — are going to make great motion picture."

"Yes, I'm sure we will."

"Now I have question for *you*."

Martin hesitated. "Yes?"

"You like CITIZEN KANE?"

"Who? Oh, the movie. Yes. Yes, it's a great movie. Of course, it's not as good as RUN DANNY RUN."

"Ha, ha, ha. That is very good."

"Ah, Vlad, ah ... should I tell you that my right side is my good side ..."

Vlad nodded. "I know this already. I see all your movies ... even ... FLIGHT FROM DA NANG."

Vlad had thrown out the reference, curious to see how Martin would react. At the time of its making, he had heard vague stories about difficulties on set, the kind of rumours that resemble the apocryphal, so he was hoping for the truth. Martin, however, ignored the reference. Then 'Bruce' arrived, pushing a catering cart.

"Vlad, this is Bruce Robinson. He works for me."

"We have dinner here? Why don't we go out? You like Thai food?"

"I'd prefer not to."

"No?"

"I'm too visible."

"Of course." Vlad held up the brown paper bag. "It's okay, I bring genuine Russian vodka. We will drink to Russia and America working together — like old Russian saying: 'Hawk and Dove shit in same sky'."

"Jesus Vlad, that's true."

Vlad, pouring vodka into two glasses, noticed 'Bruce' — Salmo — tasting Martin's salad. "Marty, why is Bruce eating your food?"

"Some jerk tried to poison me once."

"No!"

"They said it was an accident, but my sources tell me differently."

"That is horrible."

"That's why I have Bruce to run interference."

"Those fucks. We will show them. We will not die. Let us have toast to staying alive."

"Toast?"

Vlad handed a glass of vodka to Martin, and raised his. "Old Russian saying: 'Fox is cunning but goose has wings.' Nazdrovia."

They drank and Vlad was pleased to see Martin had emptied his. Only later did he realize that Martin was putting his vodka into his water glass.

Martin had ordered a Beef Wellington for Vlad, who ate heartily, and a chicken salad for himself, which he pecked at. Vlad kept quizzing Martin about his old movies — he had seen them all — and pouring toasts which Martin presumably kept dumping into the water glass when Vlad wasn't looking. Vlad did remember seeing Martin absent-mindedly drink from his glass and almost choke, which is how he deduced what Martin was doing.

After dinner, Vlad, who, after a few glasses of vodka, will dance on a pin, samba-ed about the room, humming the theme to SATURDAY NIGHT FEVER. What I know about Vlad is that he is never not in control of his faculties when he drinks, but will sometimes exaggerate his inebriation to lull his companions into revealing more about themselves.

"A great movie. Fantastic dancing. 'Stayin alive' hnh, hnh, hnh, hnh .... Maybe Consul should dance samba with Maddie ..."

"Vlad, tell me about the KGB."

"It is not club I recommend joining. This is song you hum silently in your cell at Lubianka, KGB clubhouse: 'Stayin alive' hnh, hnh, hnh, hnh...'"

"Have you ever been there?"

"Lubianka? No. I tried to see my father when he was there, but KGB pretended not to be KGB."

"So you've never been a communist?"

Vlad looked suspiciously at Martin sitting on the sofa, and stepped closer. "You ask me that already. You do not trust me. I cannot direct actor who does not trust me."

"I trust you, Vlad. I just need to be certain."

"I tell you secret. Promise not to tell?"

Martin focused intently on Vlad. "I promise."

Vlad sat, and said confidentially, "You know why I am not communist?"

Martin shook his head.

"Because I am a Czarist; I want to bring back Czars. Under Czars Russians had great culture — incredible artists. Gogol, Turgenev, Dostoyevski — well Fyodor was depressing but still great artist — Tchaikovsky, Chekhov, Rachmaninoff, Goncharov, Tolstoy." Vlad noted that

Martin was listening to him as though the Russian names were code. "Czars were generous patrons. And that's what artists like you and I need to make great pictures. Now you tell me secret."

"Secret?"

"Yes, I tell you secret, you tell me secret. Then we will be blood brothers."

"A secret?"

"Yes."

"A secret?"

"Right."

Martin thought, and his expression grew grim. "I've never told anyone this, Vlad. And you ... must never tell anyone."

"Who would I tell?"

"When I was in Nam ... I killed somebody ... a child."

"No?"

"A little girl. In a village. I shot her. I didn't mean to. She came up from behind and surprised me. I'd been trained to shoot first and ask questions later. I shot her point blank. And I've had to live with it ever since. I can still see the stunned look on her face."

"That is incredible," said Vlad, astonished.

"I'd give anything if I could take it back. I have nightmares, seeing that innocent face transfixed in horror. Oh God." Martin's face twisted in pain. Tears flowed down his cheeks. "Oh God. Forgive me."

Vlad was speechless. Had he gone too far? Usually knowing something about an actor brings the director closer to him, but what was the point of knowing something this horrible? It wasn't something he could use to motivate the actor.

Vlad retrieved the second vodka bottle, still half full, and handed it to Martin, who poured vodka into a glass, and gave the bottle back to Vlad.

"What was it you said, Vlad? Nasa drova?"

"Nazdrovia."

"What's it mean?"

"Good health."

"Nazdrovia, Vlad," Martin said, morosely, downing the vodka in a gulp.

***

All pre-production meetings are ostensibly about ensuring that everyone on the project is on the same page, but in reality, a pre-production meeting is a signal to everyone that the picture is a 'go' ("to light fire under their tuchuses" as László was fond of saying), the co-ordination of all functions being a bonus.

Vlad and I knew that THE SMOKE PICKERS was our only chance to make a movie we could be proud of; something that wouldn't embarrass me after I left Felicity, and that would enhance his reputation. I felt no responsibility for the five million dollar investment — the investors were all grown men (supposedly), and the go-ahead had been László's — but I also knew that if any disaster occurred the Hungarian Prince wouldn't take the fall. It would most likely be shifted in my direction. I didn't care about that as long as it was recorded that we had done our best.

Which is why I was so diligent in organizing the crew. Almost from the moment Honor sold us the rights, I'd begun making up lists of potential crew, retaining many of the Felicity regulars, augmented by some of the best movie-making talents in the city. By the time I'd scheduled the pre-production meeting, I'd inadvertently created a buzz about the picture.

So the forty-three technicians and production staff were palpably excited, sitting around the four large tables, dwarfed by the interior Consulate sets under construction, which loomed in semi-darkness in the studio. All quietly observed Vlad who sat at the head table joking with the lead gaffer, a Czech émigré. I'd never seen Vlad so excited.

About to direct a picture which had, as he phrased it, 'cultural nourishment,' and surrounded by people in whom he had complete confidence, he radiated invincibility. His Slavic brood had temporary been replaced by a fleeting smile, like a boy remembering every few seconds that he has a new bicycle. He was so pumped that, at one point, he whispered in my ear: "Holy shit, Sarah, they think we are serious."

Jean-Paul Solon, our production manager, a stoical, implacable Quebecois, and David Newby, the assistant director, sat on either side of him, David chairing the meeting. I sat next to David. Sitting behind us, Beverly, our script supervisor who'd worked with Vlad on KISS and SORORITY, was reading the script. Next to her were Teddy and Eve Guiliani, our art director, a quiet, chain-smoking woman who had once worked under one of Fellini's set decorators. Middle-aged, Eve was known to have a penchant for young actors.

László, pacing in the shadows at the edge of the group, was scanning all assembled, computing the picture's cost. He knew what the budget was, but the reality of seeing such a large payroll sitting in one place was clearly unnerving him. Instead of employing two people in the costume department (as we usually did), we needed five. The art department, under Eve, had been expanded by ten: carpenters, set dressers, etc. Almost every department on the picture would double in size; we needed more vehicles, more caravans, more equipment, more shooting days, more actors, more extras, more catering, more of everything. All of this data I could see László nimbly translating into dollars as he circled the gathering. The more requirements David itemized, the quicker László paced. By the time David finished explaining the wherefores, hows and whats, two hours later, László was circumambulating the gathering every five minutes. It was then that David asked Vlad to speak.

"Seeing you all here before big battle," Vlad said, "reminds me of Stalingrad." Everyone laughed. "When I attend Leningrad Film Academy, dream of all students was to go to Hollywood to make beautiful motion picture. Because of you, today is first day of this dream come true for me; and I get to make beautiful movie in most wonderful country, with best crew in world. We will make incredible picture together. László will get rich, and finally buy new Mercedes (another big laugh). And we will all be proud to make THE SMOKE PICKERS from Ms. Lamprey's wonderful novel."

Everyone applauded, the meeting broke up and László rushed to where Vlad and I were standing. "You are happy?" he asked anxiously, nudging Vlad and I out of earshot. Vlad nodded.

"I think," László said, "we have too many crew."

"We need large crew for this size picture, so we can meet schedule."

"Then we need to cut studio to one week."

"Not if we want to shoot all scenes."

László's worried expression hadn't abated. "So we cut scenes."

"Why?"

"To stay in budget."

"Cut my salary."

"What?"

"Cut my salary too," I said.

"Cut my salary," Vlad repeated. "Are you telling me you do not have financing?"

"We are very close," László said guardedly. "But we need to make cuts, everywhere."

"Not if we intend to make Academy Award-winning motion picture."

László picked up Vlad's script from the table, and handed it to him. "I want you to cut three scenes."

As László walked off, Vlad's eyes met mine. He had a slight Cheshire cat smile, but his gaze was set, determined.

***

Vlad, knowing my obsession with all things theatrical, jokingly used to call me a 'theatre slut'. He was right. That moment in a theatre when the house lights go down and the curtain is about to go up — just before a group of brave thespians create an engaging and evocative un-reality right in front of me — is sheer magic. I know few actors person-ally, but because they're able to conjure up arresting lives on a bare stage with only a few lights and props, I have immense respect for all.

Vlad rarely, if ever, attended the theatre, preferring, when not working, spending an evening in a bar, exchanging stories with fellow imbibers. This not only relaxed him, but was the source of much of what he knew about life — and that which sustained him as a creator. Theatre was something Vlad understood and respected, but it didn't thrill him in the way film did — probably because he was a director, not an actor — although he was acutely aware of the actor's import-ance to both mediums.

On FIELD OF SCREAMS, we had hired an assistant director (A.D.) who clearly didn't like — maybe even hated — actors.

"They're layabouts," he told me scathingly, "standing around all day, horking back the food, lazily getting up to deliver a line on cam-era, incapable of any real work, like being an assistant director. They should try *organizing* a picture sometime."

This A.D. worked hard, spending 14-hour days being responsible for the running of the set. But he had no idea of the importance of an actor to a successful movie, no concept of an audience entering the emotional reality of a character, and what it took for the actor to offer up that character's interior — no understanding, in other words, of the creative process. His thinking was logical and rational — a successful motion picture had to do with scheduling, coordinating and cost — and he resented any implication that actors might be more import-ant to making a picture than the assistant director.

This A.D. finally got to direct his own movie (a witless comedy), which he brought in on schedule and under-budget. Poorly cast, acted and directed — he had no sense of comedy — the picture received negative notices from all reviewers, lasting less than a week in a theatre before vanishing forever. A year later, this paragon of efficiency became a programming executive at a TV station which, under his authority, has become progressively less creative.

This was why, on all our pictures, I took care to ensure that the actors felt needed. On Vlad's suggestion, the night before our first day of shooting, I took Carey to see Nathan perform. I had been curious about the Madbrain Theatre Company, this mysterious troupe of actors, performing Shakespeare in a seedy, once-industrial part of the city. Rents for the squalid warehouse lofts and rundown apartments in the area — already in the process of being gentrified — were cheap. This attracted artists, young professionals and pensioners, but also drug addicts and the poor. According to Nancy, it wasn't unusual to find a man passed out on the sidewalk in front of the theatre. That evening, as we approached it from the parking lot, Carey and I passed drunks, professional beggars, and the homeless.

Madbrain was performing *Twelfth Night*. Having been awed by Nathan's audition, I sensed he wouldn't disappoint on stage. Carey was aware that someone named Nathan Quill had been cast as Miguel, but I hadn't told her he was playing Orsino, the Duke of Illyria. So when she saw his name in the program she glanced at me, understanding why we had come. And from the moment he came on at the beginning of Act 1, she was engrossed; as was I.

Nathan's Orsino, a love-sick nobleman, was vain *and* vulnerable — lacking the intense compassion of Miguel, or the dysfunction of Hamlet (a performance I hadn't seen as yet). I'm not particularly attracted to 'good-looking' men, but I was attracted to Nathan. I had no idea who he was as a person, but as an actor he was electric. I ached to know him, and hoped that if I did, I wouldn't find the heart of a bore or, worse, a jerk. As the Duke, he dominated the stage:

"If music be the food of love, play on;
Give me an excess of it, that, surfeiting,
The appetite may sicken, and so die.
That strain again! It had a dying fall:
O! it came o'er my ear like the sweet sound
That breathes upon a bank of violets,
Stealing and giving odour. Enough! No more:
'Tis not so sweet now as it was before.
O spirit of love! How quick and fresh art thou,
That, not withstanding thy capacity
Receiveth as the sea, nought enters there,
Of what validity and pitch soe'er,
But falls into abatements and low price,
Even in a minute: so full of shapes is fancy,
That it alone is high fantastical."

Fascinated by Shakespeare's farcical contrivance — a young woman (Viola), masquerading in a foreign land as a man (Cesario), falls in love with the local duke (Orsino) who engages Cesario (Viola) to woo another woman (Olivia) for him who has in turn fallen in love with Cesario — Carey was leaning forward in her seat. In *Twelfth Night* — as in all Shakespeare, beyond the comedy — there is irony, and naked human frailty; and Nathan was playing on all these elements in his scenes with Nancy who, as Viola, was trying, covertly, to tell Orsino that he was a she and that she loved him. Shakespeare's message — that false love blindsides real love — was made plain in an early scene as Orsino imparts advice on love to Viola:

"Thou dost speak masterly. My life upon't, young though thou art, thine eye hath stay'd upon some favour that it loves; hath it not boy?"
"A little, by your favour."
"What kind of woman is't?"
"Of your complexion."

"She is not worth thee, then. What years, i'faith"

"About your years, my lord."

"Too old, by heaven. Let still the woman take an elder than herself, so wears she to him, so sways she level in her husband's heart: for, boy, however, we do praise ourselves, our fancies are more giddy and unfirm, more longing, wavering, sooner lost and worn, than woman's are."

"I think it well, my lord."

"Then, let thy love be younger than thyself, or thy affection cannot hold the bent; for women are as roses, whose fair flower being once display'd, doth fall that very hour."

"And so they are: alas, that they are so: to die, even when they to perfection grow!"

I felt just like Viola; for Nathan (like Orsino) didn't know me, not the real me — whoever that was.

At the end of the performance, we went backstage and I introduced Carey. It was amusing, in the cramped, dingy dressing room, to watch Nathan pretend not to be impressed by her, while the rest of the cast paid her compliments.

We invited him for a drink, and made for the Monacle. I sat across from them in a booth and, in that awkward moment when three strangers try to work out the group dynamics, we fumbled for conversation. Never having met an actor like Nathan — he seemed ego-less but intensely focused — I could see Carey was intrigued. As the conversation drew on, to my astonishment, I realized that she was quietly flirting with him. And he, after discerning the same thing, was attempting to work out which part of his personality she would find pleasing.

"It's a wonderful play," she said. "It must fun to perform."

"Some nights it just soars."

"Is that your passion, Shakespeare?" Carey asked.

"One of them."

"This is exciting," I said.

"What is?" Carey asked.

"You two, meeting — about to work together. I'd be excited."

"I'm sure we are," Nathan said, glancing curiously at me.

"All great artists," I said, "play down their greatness. I once told a guitar player in a famous blues band that they'd just played a great set, and do you know what he said?"

"What?" Nathan asked.

"'Same old soup-bone warmed over.'"

That killed the conversation; but I was determined to press on. I didn't mind being thought naïve, as long as I could get them to open up. I wanted to know how they felt about working with each other; how they went about creating believable characters; what problems they had with fellow actors; in short, I wanted to understand every-thing about them as actors. "Seriously," I asked, "what concerns do you have right now?"

"Concerns?" Nathan said, looking at me as though I were an alien.

"As actors."

"Honestly?" Carey asked.

"Honestly."

"The love scenes," Carey said.

The love scenes? What? Was she joking? "What about them?"

"I'm wondering how to prepare for them."

"Really?" I glanced at Nathan. Even he seemed nonplussed.

"Well, smooching isn't as simple as it looks, but Nathan's oddly attractive; so it might be okay."

Nathan pretended to be insulted. "What do you mean 'oddly'?"

"It's a compliment. Maybe I should have said 'striking'."

"Striking?"

"Or 'hot'? What do you think, Sarah?"

"Yes, I suppose you could say Nathan was 'hot'." Teasing him with Carey made me feel close to them.

"What's 'hot'?" Nathan said, clearly uncomfortable.

"As someone once defined jazz," Carey said. "'If you have to ask, you'll never know.' Hot is hot, that's all."

"It's a compliment?"

"I'd say so."

Was she really being this obvious? "What do you need," I asked, "to prepare for the love scenes?"

Carey thought. "I need to know who they are."

"Who they are?"

"What if you have to work with an actor you don't like?"

Nathan nodded. "Having to pretend to like someone onstage you dislike off is difficult."

"And tiring," Carey said.

"And unpleasant."

I knew acting had its drawbacks, but it didn't seem to me to be 'unpleasant' — being a garbageman was unpleasant. "It's exhausting?"

"It's not only that," Carey said. "You're hoping you don't discover that they disgust you while you're playing the love scene."

"Disgust you?"

Carey nodded. "Spitting is the worst."

Spitting? "Spitting?"

"Some actors can't control the amount of saliva they produce when they speak. If you're in a wide shot it's okay, but it's difficult to play a love scene with an actor who's spitting on you in a closeup. Anyone who can pull that off deserves an Oscar. You're not a spitter, are you, Nathan?"

"I don't think so," he said, "but sometimes I bite."

Oh my god, *he* was flirting with her now!

"Sometimes," Carey said, "they have bad breath. That's usually an actor who doesn't care anymore, and doesn't mind subjecting his fellow actors to a foul-smelling mouth. Nathan's too young not to care, but I always check. And I never hesitate to get them to do major cleansing before our mouths intersect. Would you open your mouth please?" I was surprised when Nathan abruptly opened his mouth.

Carey leaned forward, peered inside and sniffed. "That seems fine," she said. "I think the love scenes might be okay."

"Okay?" Nathan muttered. "I hope we do better than 'okay'."

I guessed Carey was putting us on, but her expression was impassive.

"You make it sound like buying a horse," I said.

By this time, she and Nathan were so busy checking each other out — discussing worst actors ever worked with, worst directors, etc. — that I don't think they heard me.

It wasn't till later that it occurred to me that Carey might have been trying to de-romanticize Nathan for my benefit; or encouraging him to find her attractive so that *I* would. I knew I was naïve, but what startled me was that I did feel jealous (and envious) of both. I was strongly attracted to him, but then again, I hardly knew him. Actually, I didn't know him at all. And I was also attracted to Carey. Was he attracted to her? I couldn't tell. They certainly enjoyed talking about acting. Was she attracted to him, even though she was gay? I didn't know her very well — actually I didn't know her at all either. I liked her, but this was a Carey I hadn't seen. Was this who she really was? *Was* she trying to get my attention? *Was* she really gay? Maybe she was bisexual. I didn't know much about bisexuals, or any other kinds of sexuals, my personal experience being limited; nor had I gained any real knowledge of relationships from making woman-thrusts-her-boobs-at-the-camera kind of movies with László. Was I expected to do something? Or nothing? I was giving myself a headache.

"Well," I said, getting up. "I've got a very early morning so I have to, ah ..."

They both glanced up at me. Carey smiled while Nathan signalled Barney for two more drinks.

"Can you catch a cab?" I asked Carey.

"I'll be fine. I'll see you tomorrow."

"Of course, good night. Good night, Nathan."

"Good night."

VLAD TRIED TO prep me for the onslaught.

"First day shooting on quality picture — picture you care about — is like French Revolution, like Dickens wrote in *Tale of Two Cities*: 'It is best of times and worst of times.' On first day, it is best of times because nothing has gone wrong — yet — so something fantastic might happen; and it is worst of times because you know in your heart your dream vision is about to get fucked."

12

I wasn't worried. I was pumped. We had a tight schedule — twenty-seven days, with the crew working flat out — but I was determined to help Vlad make something worthwhile. I had tried, through the unremitting days of sophomoric sex jokes on SORORITY PLAYGIRLS, to distract myself by imagining the movie in abstract terms — 24 frames going through the camera, times 60 seconds, times 120 minutes — 172,000 single pictures glued together. On SORORITY, imagining 172,000 frames of those scenes horrified me, so I stopped calculating. On THE SMOKE PICKERS, concentrating on story and not on nudity, Vlad could make a stunning and beautiful film, with all 172,000 frames coalescing into a moving experience. Maybe then I could sleep again at night. When I told Vlad, he cautioned me, "Do not speak too soon. Twenty-seven days is eternity to shoot movie. That is 648 hours of opportunity for anything to go wrong."

When I arrived on set that first morning at the University of Toronto, our ant colony was briskly setting up in front of Convocation Hall: Teddy was erecting lights with his gaffer and sparkies; the grips were laying dolly track and unloading equipment from the trucks; Toni and her assistants were hustling costumes onto the actors and extras; Megan and her crew were slapping on makeup; the art department was putting up signage around the 'Consulate'; and Paddy Props (Irish-born elf, his real name long forgotten after some wag renamed him) was readying the Consul's Thunderbird convertible. And, overseeing it all, David the A.D., I knew, was hoping the crew would settle quickly into an efficient rhythm.

During production, movies resemble a war zone. Everything and everyone is an enemy: equipment, sets, props, costumes, weather and the public. But you're not a army. You're a band of gypsies, attempting to fill the camera with a simple story: a troupe of actors portraying the characters, a pack of technicians defending them, and a director leading everyone forward. Always, there is the relentless urgency of the clock ticking (time is money), creating the illusion that the crew is on mission impossible — movie folk who, after trying to supplant the real world with their fake one, command you to: 'Stop your life. Can't you see we're making a movie here?'"

Jean-Paul Solon, who would have normally taken refuge in the production office to re-calculate the budget ten times a day, was standing by the camera truck, like the rest of us, curious to see the first shot. I was standing with László near the camera watching Vlad stroll back and forth in front of the massive Ionic columns. I knew László was anxious; but Vlad, brimming with energy — impossible to read in that Slavic face, visible only in his kinetic body language — gazed studiously at his set, loping over to peer through the camera every few minutes before asking Teddy to make another adjustment.

Then, the moment we'd waited for, for so long, was here. Salmo drove up in the Chevy Impala and, like royalty, Martin stepped out. As strange as the image of Martin emerging from the Impala was (he'd insisted on hiring his own car and driver), his arrival caused the needle on our glamour gauge to bounce right up. No one — Vlad,

László, nor me, nor anyone on the crew — said anything to acknowledge it, but his presence confirmed that we were about to embark on a remarkable adventure — though of course at that moment we had no idea how remarkable. Vlad and László hurried over to greet him.

"Marty, good morning," Vlad said. "It is beautiful day to make movie."

"Hotel is fine?" László asked.

Martin nodded, his eyes surveying the set and campus.

"That is some set of wheels you got," Vlad said, eyeing the Impala.

"I like to keep a low profile," Martin said, quietly.

"Of course," Vlad said, slightly baffled. "First up, simple driving shot. You drive up, stop, get out, walk into Consulate. Slice of cake." Vlad pointed at Convocation Hall, a door of which we were using as the entrance to the Consulate. "This is Consulate."

"*Walk* in?" Martin asked.

"Yes, walk in."

"What am I thinking?"

"Is too soon for thinking. Is beginning of picture, or, maybe ..." Vlad stared at him thoughtfully, "... maybe Consul is thinking it is beautiful day. Maybe he stop to look at sky."

Martin thought about it. "Look at the sky. Okay."

David the A.D., already pushing to keep on schedule, came up. "Makeup and wardrobe are waiting in your trailer, Mr. Gage."

"Thanks."

Seeing Martin cross to an old Winnebago and step into it, Vlad waved to me to join him. "Sarah, we need first class caravan for star. We can't put Marty in garbage trailer."

Panicked, László looked at me and Vlad. He was obviously calculating the cost of a First Class caravan minus the rental on our "garbage trailer".

"That's the one he wanted."

"He wanted trash trailer?"

"He requested the smallest, shabbiest trailer we could find." I was about to explain my confusion about the trailer when I spotted Honor. "László, don't look, but guess who's talking to David."

She was standing near the camera truck next to David as he consulted his clipboard. He explained something to her, then took out his cell, and my cell vibrated.

"Yes, David," I said, answering it.

"Honor Lamprey is here."

"Alright, thank you, David."

As Honor started crossing to us, László said: "I think *you* should talk to her."

"I'm sure she'd prefer to be greeted by the producer."

He grimaced. "Alright. If she is wanting to see script, tell her we will courier," he said, putting on a smile as he started towards her.

"Honor, a pleasure as always," he said charmingly.

"László, " she said, "did you forget to send me an invitation to see the movie of my book being filmed?" She was trying to sound humorous, but I could hear the vulnerability in her voice.

"I was going to invite you when we shoot sex scenes." He smiled. "Of course, I am joking. We are about to make first shot."

"Can I watch?"

"Come with me."

László took her to where the director's chairs had been set out, and made a show of seating her in his. "There, you can be producer now. Watch out you don't get headache from author."

Honor gazed expectantly at the set. "What scene are you shooting?"

"Establishing shot with Consul."

"Martin Gage?"

"Yes."

László noted that she was staring at Convocation Hall. In her novel, the Consul has two brief scenes in Guatemala, *inside* his office.

"What building is that in the movie?"

"That is Consulate. In movie you need to shoot inside *and* outside." László didn't tell her that, thanks to Hardy, her Canadian Consul was now American.

"There's something odd," said Honor, puzzled, staring at Convocation Hall. "Isn't that an American flag?"

"Yes, Consulates both in same building," László said, quickly.

"Ah, same building ...," Honor muttered.

"You are excited?"

"Yes. Aren't you?"

"Of course."

"My book, coming to life," she murmured, watching the crew practice the dolly move with the camera.

With the pictures I'd worked on with Vlad, I'd noticed that he always started with a drive-up dolly shot. "How come you always start with a dolly shot of a car?" I asked him.

"It warms up crew and actors so they are working together. You see who is not in sync and make changes before complicated shots."

Martin emerged from the trailer in an elegant suit, and we were ready to begin. Watching Vlad quietly instruct Teddy and the camera crew, I tried to imagine what could go wrong — then wondered why I was so tense.

"Lock it up, people," David said loudly. Silence fell over the set. "Picture up."

"Speed."

Mac, the camera assistant, flashed the clapper board in front of the camera and yelled: "Scene 4, take 1."

"Action," Vlad shouted. And we'd begun.

David waved, and the hulking Thunderbird roared up to Convocation Hall, stopping abruptly. As the camera dollied toward the car, Martin jumped out and started towards the door. He stopped, looked about, dashed behind a column, and peered up, as though searching the surrounding rooftops. Then, he ambled into the hall.

"Cut!" said Vlad, walking up to the building as Martin stepped out.

"Marty, that was good, but what you looking at?"

"The rooftops."

"Rooftops?"

"For snipers."

"Snipers?"

"To make sure our security hasn't been breached."

"Ah, right, yes, good," Vlad said, puzzled. "That was good for you?"

Peering about, Martin nodded.

"Okay-dokey. Print. Next shot, Consul coming out. Dolly track is now in wrong place."

We were finally shooting. I wasn't imagining it — it was real. Now I could concentrate on helping Jean-Paul, and making sure that the actors were taken care of. I intercepted Martin, retreating to his 'caravan.' "Martin, will you be having lunch in your trailer?"

"'Bruce' will deal with it."

"Okay."

As I'd observed Honor sitting in László's chair, trying not to stare at Martin, I thought it might impress her to meet him. "Martin, would you do me a favour and say hello to the author of the book?"

Martin immediately scanned the horizon. "The dyed redhead at 2:00 o'clock?"

"Yes."

"Sure."

I put on my associate producer smile and led Martin to Honor who, seeing us coming, hurriedly jumped up. "Honor, I'd like you to meet Martin Gage. Martin, this is Honor Lamprey who wrote the wonderful book on which the movie is based."

Martin beamed Honor with full star wattage. "Ms. Lamprey, it's a pleasure. What a talented writer you are."

I was certain she was blushing. "Mr. Gage … I …"

Martin chided her. "Marty."

"Marty," she said, trying to breathe. "I'm a ... a big fan. RUN DANNY RUN ... was a ... a great movie. What a ... a ... fabulous performance."

Martin's gaze was focused entirely on her, causing her legs to wobble. I noticed her hand tighten for support on the back of the director's chair.

"The Consul is an even better role."

"Really? I ... it's just ..."

"Your understanding of the situation is very perceptive."

"Situation?"

"He's very brave."

We were sliding too close to the edge. I was certain that Martin hadn't read the book, only the screenplay. "Martin, they'll be calling you for the next shot in a moment."

"Right." Martin squeezed her hand. "You keep writing, now, it's vital."

"Vital?" murmured Honor, watching him stride back to his trailer, her hand dangling in mid-air as she tried to resume breathing. "Sarah, ah, could you ... could ... could I get a copy of the script?"

"Of course. I'll have it couriered."

"It's okay if I watch?"

"Of course."

"And I can sit here in László's chair?"

"He'd be honoured." I laughed when I realized what I'd said, but Honor wasn't listening. She was watching Martin disappear into his trailer. Walking off, I noticed László, behind the prop truck, waving to attract my attention. I took my time walking over.

"What is she waiting for?"

"She wants to watch."

"Why?"

"Why? Everybody wants to watch movies being shot, especially authors."

"Don't let her see script."

"Right. Do you think she'll notice that her tobacco fields are full of revolutionaries?" It's rare that I can get one up on László. "Also, she might pick up on the sex scenes."

"Sex scenes aren't in script."

"So you are planning sex scenes."

"How did you know?"

"You talk to wardrobe, wardrobe talks to David, David talks to me." It had occurred to me that he might be planning to engage a 'body double' for Carey.

"Tell David to cut."

"She's going to figure it out, László. This is a needless risk."

"It is not 'needless,' I have to sell movie. Maybe you should be producer."

"I'm not sleazy enough," I said, unkindly.

As I walked off, I heard him mutter, "Is it 'sleazy' to want associate producer to have paycheque?"

***

Twenty minutes later, I was standing by the camera truck, as Vlad waited for the crew to settle.

"Action," he shouted.

Martin strode from the hall, passed the columns, stopped, looked up at a window on the building opposite, quickly took cover behind a column, pulled out a pistol, rushed to the Thunderbird, jumped in and roared off.

"Cut!"

Martin wheeled the car about, drove back and got out as Vlad walked up. "Marty, that was good, but why you are holding pistol?"

"The insurgents could be anywhere."

"Of course, but is too soon for pistol."

"I can't be too vigilant."

"You don't need pistol. Is only establishing shot of you and Consulate."

Martin regarded Vlad for a few seconds. "Vlad, I need to take you into my confidence. Can I trust you?"

Vlad laid his index finger against his nose. "Of course. You and I keep secrets together."

Martin walked Vlad a few paces off, his eyes darting over the set. Out of earshot, he said quietly: "Vlad."

"Yes Marty."

"I'm not who you think I am."

Vlad watched him carefully. "You are not Martin Gage?"

"I'm two people."

"Two people?" Accustomed to stars' eccentricities, Vlad thought carefully. "Would *one* of them be Martin Gage?"

"You're smart."

"Who is other?"

"Vince Brody."

Vlad thought about that. "Who is Vince Brody?"

"That's my cover name."

"Cover name?"

"I'm an operative."

"Operative?"

"Agent, spy."

Vlad noted that Martin's eyes never stopped searching the crowd. "For whom are you spy?"

"For America, who do you think?"

"CIA?"

"No. I'm more embedded than those guys."

"But why are you spy?"

"America's in danger, Vlad."

"From whom?"

"The Soviets."

"Soviets? Marty, Soviet Union is kaput."

"Not quite, Vlad."

"What you mean?"

"When the evil empire fell apart, the commies running it formed a conspiracy."

"Conspiracy?"

"Yeah. These ex-politburo a-pair-of-chicks ..."

"Apparatchiks?"

"Yeah, those guys ... came up with the idea of infiltrating countries all over the globe to incite hatred against America. So our enemies: Iran, Iraq, Somalia, Bosnia, Russia, Afghanistan, Kazakhstan — all the 'stans' — Syria, Nicaragua, Cuba, Burma, North Korea, China — just to name a few — are secretly run by ex-commies. Do you have any idea what this means?"

Dumbfounded, Vlad shook his head.

"It means the Cold War is still on."

"No shit."

"And it's heating up."

"This is incredible."

"That's why I asked if you were a communist, and that's why the Consul must be vigilant."

Vlad was having difficulty understanding how anyone could be this deluded. On the other hand, maybe Martin *was* an agent — Vlad had learned early on that life frequently resembles a paperback novel. "If you are spy why you make movies?"

"It's the perfect cover. No one expects a guy who talks to press jerks to be a secret agent. So while I play the star, I'm watching out for Uncle Sam. And I get the message out. People love movies, Vlad. It's what made America great."

Vlad nodded. "That is very clever."

"I know you know about commies. So I'll need you to work with me on this."

"Of course."

"We have to let people know that the Red Menace is still alive."

"I do what I can."

"Remember, silence is a cobra."

"A cobra?"

"Deadly."

"Ah. You can trust me, Marty."

"That's good, because if I couldn't I'd have to kill you."

"I don't think that's good idea. Can we do next take now, please?"

Coming of age in communist Russia had provided Vlad with a degree from the Leningrad Film Academy, and a valuable set of life tools. It was the source of his sly humour, and the reason he could never give you a straight answer to a question. In the USSR, he learned that a circuitously incomplete answer was always the best response to any official query. Being a young Soviet citizen instilled in him a healthy mistrust of authority, and taught him how to deal with paranoia. On KISS MY ASP, when our 'villain,' Nicolai Geldoff, a Rumanian actor who'd spent a lifetime in Hollywood playing Russians, confidentially explained to Vlad, how he, Nicolai, was constantly being stalked by warlocks and witches, Vlad had to admit that they plagued him as well.

Martin's 'revelation,' however, came as a surprise to Vlad, whose instinct told him to grab as much footage of his star as quickly as possible. He spent the morning shooting Carey and Martin entering and exiting, together and separately, Martin driving, Martin checking the Consulate security, and Carey and Martin leaving the 'Consulate' against the background of student 'demonstrators.'

"Action," Vlad shouted, leading the Steadicam operator who, walking backwards, filmed Carey and Martin as they came out the 'Consulate' door and through the crowd of yelling 'demonstrators.' Nathan, on call for the afternoon, watched as Martin and Carey hurried to the Thunderbird, got in and drove off, almost running down an old woman.

"Cut!" Vlad yelled. "Print." Vlad had noticed, as had I, that Martin had been rough with the extras and, while pleased to have the shot, he was concerned.

Carey and Nathan's first scene together was the last of the day: Miguel furtively meeting Maddie outside the Consulate at twilight — to which Vlad added a dramatic twist by including a shot of Martin sitting in the Thunderbird secretly watching them.

"Action," Vlad said, quietly.

Nathan remained motionless until the guard passed by, then slipped behind a pillar, and waited. Another guard passed. The door opened slightly and Carey emerged, held her finger to her lips and led Nathan to an alcove. She kissed him. It was Carey and Nathan's first kiss, and I could feel the pressure of that kiss on my lips and wondered what it was like for her — and for him.

"Have you changed your mind?" she asked.

Nathan shook his head.

"I have decided no matter what ...," she said, pausing.

Nathan was watching her.

"... to come with you."

Sighing, he closed his eyes and lowered his head.

"You don't want me?" Carey asked.

"What would you do?" he asked.

"I would care for you."

"Would you care for all my people?"

"Yes."

"Do you know how to wrap the dead?" Nathan said, improvising.

Carey didn't flinch. "I know how to care for the living."

"Sometimes caring is not enough."

"You don't want me."

"I cannot be with you, and help my people."

"You're pushing me away."

"It is not your life. You would not fit."

"We won't know unless we try."

Nathan gazed off, his face clouded with anguish. "It is too danger-ous. I cannot be everywhere to protect you."

Carey was still for a long time, gazing at Nathan. Then she reached up and touched his cheek. He didn't move.

"I don't have the list, Miguel."

"I know. I did not come for that."

"Oh, Miguel. Miguel." Trying not to cry, she whispered, "I can't say goodbye. Can't."

Nathan reached out and touched her cheek gently. "Adios, mi amor," he said, then turned and walked off. Carey, tears now stream-ing down her face, stared after him. I was crying as well.

"Cut, print, excellent," Vlad yelled, after a long pause. "Ms. Lander's closeup now, please."

In her closeup, Carey fought again to hold back her tears, almost making Nathan cry. When it ended, my face was wet and I was limp with heartbreak.

"Sarah?"

Nathan had slipped up beside me.

"Nathan ...?"

"You crying?"

"That was so moving."

"Yeah."

'Yeah'? What was he feeling?

"Can you have dinner with me?"

"What?"

"Can you have dinner with me?"

I wasn't sure I was hearing correctly. "Dinner?"

"Dinner."

"Dinner? Sure. I'd love to."

"Now?"

"Now? You mean, right now?"

"You can't make it?"

"No, no, I can ... of course I can ... I'll have dinner with you."

"We have to do it quickly. I have a performance. I'll just get changed."

"Right." What was going on?

Nathan doesn't drive so we motored in my ageing Toyota to the Monacle, from where, after dinner, he could dash round the corner to the theatre. In the car, I was nervous. It was the first time I had been alone with him.

"You had a good day?" I asked.

"Yeah."

"Is it fun working with Carey?"

"Yeah."

"Are you looking forward to tomorrow?"

"Yeah."

Talk about talkative. Why did he want to have dinner with me?

At the Monocle, after we ordered soups and burgers, I asked, "So, is this a social occasion, or was there something you wanted to discuss?"

"The scenes with the demonstrators."

"What about them?"

"The extras I saw today weren't ... ah, authentic. They were Canadian."

"Yes."

"I'm sure you could get some real Chileans or even Peruvians or Columbians. Real South Americans speak Spanish, and real Chileans know the problems and hardships of the Chilean people, especially if they're refugees."

"Do the extras need to know that?"

"Relevant background always adds authenticity to the scenes. What do you know about Chile?"

"Not much."

"Life in Chile is very hard; maybe only two percent of the people control all the wealth. The poor live in mouldy shacks with unsanitary water. The rich decide on the price of energy, ransack the educational system for profit, and build dams which destroy the environment. Chile's big resource is copper, but the average Chilean doesn't get to share in the mining wealth, even when it destroys their villages."

"Are you a socialist?"

"No."

"You do a good impression of one."

"You don't have to be a socialist to believe in social justice."

"Have you talked to Hardy about this?"

"He's not interested in authenticity, but if you want to make a film that affects people, you need to show how things really are. Audiences know when movies are fake."

"Aren't all movies 'fake'?"

He paused, regarding me. "Good drama is true to the idea. How can an audience believe a scene or a character if it isn't rooted in reality?"

"Good point."

He pulled out a piece of paper. "These are some organizations here that help South American refugees," he said, handing it to me.

"You've done your homework."

"They'll probably know who'd be interested in being an extra. I'm sure the refugees could use the money."

"That's very thoughtful."

"I didn't know who to mention it to."

"I'm glad you came to me. It's a good idea. I'll take it up with Vlad. I'm sure he'll think it's a good idea too."

The burgers arrived and he started in on his, his mind obviously having moved on to something else — his performance?

"If you think of anything else," I said, "don't hesitate to let me know." He nodded, silently chewing his burger. Maybe he was trying to think of something else — to impress me.

"Not a lot of actors," I said, "would put themselves out like this. You might be eligible for the Most Valuable Actor to Have On Set Award."

If he got my hopeless attempt at humour, he made no response, or expressed any curiosity about me. I felt as though I were slogging through a wetland. Maybe the four-year difference in our ages was a factor. Clearly, if there was to be a man-woman exchange of ideas, I would have to play both parts. "I don't know much about you," I said. "Were you born in Toronto?"

He glanced hurriedly at his watch. "I'm sorry," he said, signalling to Barney. "I have to go."

He got up and slurped his soup as Barney came by and put the rest of his burger and fries into a takeaway container. He'd obviously done this before. He started to fish out some money.

"It's on us," I said, "for the wonderful idea."

"Oh. Okay. Thanks."

This being the first day, there were no rushes, and although I knew I should drop by the office to see what, if any, difficulties needed attending to, I couldn't resist asking, "What're you performing tonight?"

"*Romeo and Juliet*."

"You're playing Romeo?"

He nodded again. I'd met rocks that were more talkative. But maybe when you're a lead actor carrying an entire play in your head, you don't speak much off-stage, if at all. Chill, Sarah — what you see is what you get, and isn't that enough? Especially if it's Romeo? "I'd love to see it."

"Okay, hurry and I'll take you in."

I got a container for my burger and we dashed around the corner. He took me past Blake, the actor appearing later as Friar Laurence, who was running the door, then went to prepare. I was left alone in the tiny auditorium, with 45 minutes till the curtain went up. I finished my burger, checked my cell (I always have it on 'vibrate'), and texted messages to Vlad and David to remind them to finalize the Valparaíso set with the art department. This wasn't what I'd imagined a dinner date with Nathan would be like — plus I felt guilty about enjoying myself, not knowing if I was needed back at the office. Then my cell vibrated and László's number appeared. Oh God. "Hello?"

"Sarah?"

"I'm here."

"Where? Where are you?" I tried to detect any emergency in his voice, but he sounded almost normal.

By now people had started to arrive, creating a low hum in the auditorium. "Ah, I'm in ... a mall."

"A mall?"

"I have a headache. I'm getting some pills."

"Ah."

"What do you need?"

"I want you not to send script to Honor."

"I know. You told me. What did you think of today?"

"What?"

"Were you not impressed? I thought Vlad was amazing."

"It was first day. We will see."

Don't overdo it in the excitement department, László. "Okay, I'll see you tomorrow."

"Tomorrow."

I took a deep breath. Why was I feeling guilty? I wasn't needed. It was evening, after work, when you're supposed to relax and find diversions — like going to the theatre. I flung off the guilt. At that moment, all I wanted to do was watch Nathan act. Was it infatuation? Of course, but he *was* compelling, even mysterious. I wasn't put off by his lack of interest in me over dinner — it hadn't dampened any ardour I thought I felt — but the anticipation of seeing him as Romeo was making me giddy, and he didn't let me down. I was breathless in all his scenes with Juliet (played ardently by Nancy — I, of course, imagining myself in her place). His youthful impetuosity was so personal as to be almost embarrassing. Was this the real Nathan? Or, was it the distraught young man whose grief devastated the audience in the 'banished' scene, when Friar Laurence informs Romeo of his punishment for killing Tybalt:

> "Romeo, come forth; come forth thou fearful man: Affliction is enamour'd of thy parts, and thou art wedded to calamity."

Nathan pinned us to our seats. Expecting his life to be shredded, Romeo entered meekly, approaching Friar Laurence as though anticipating torture beyond endurance.

> "Father, what news? What is the prince's doom? What sorrow craves acquaintance at my hand, that I yet know not?"
>
> "Too familiar is my dear son with such sour company: I bring thee tidings of the prince's doom."
>
> "What less than doomsday is the prince's doom?"
>
> "A gentler judgement vanish'd from his lips, not body's death, but body's banishment."
>
> "Ha! Banishment! Be merciful, say 'death'; for exile hath more terror in his look, much more than death: do not say 'banishment.'"
>
> "Hence from Verona art thou banished. Be patient, for the world is broad and wide."
>
> "There is no world without Verona walls, but purgatory, torture, hell itself. Hence banished is banish'd from the world, and world's exile is death; then 'banished' is death mis-termed. Calling death 'banished' thou cutt'st my head off with a golden axe, and smil'st upon the stroke that murders me."
>
> "O deadly sin! O rude unthankfulness! Thy fault our law calls death; but the kind prince, taking thy part, hath rush'd aside the law, and turn'd that black word death to banishment: this is dear mercy, and thou seest it not."

Nathan began weeping, pleading. I'd never seen anyone so distraught.

"'Tis torture, and not mercy: heaven is here, where Juliet lives; and every cat and dog and little mouse, every unworthy thing, live here in heaven and may look on her; but Romeo may not: more validity, more honourable state, more court- ship lives in carrion flies than Romeo: they may seize on the white wonder of dear Juliet's hand, and steal immortal bless- ing from her lips, who, even in pure and vestal modesty, still blush, as thinking their own kisses sin; flies may do this, but I from this must fly: They are free men, but I am banished. And sayst thou yet that exile is not death? Hadst thou no poi- son mix'd, no sharp-ground knife, no sudden mean of death, though ne'er so mean, but 'banished' to kill me? 'Banished!' O Friar! The damned use that word in hell; howlings attend it: how hast thou the heart, being a divine, a ghostly confes- sor, a sin-absolver, and my friend profess'd, to mangle me with that word 'banished'?"

"Thou fond mad man, hear me but speak a word."

"O! thou wilt speak again of banishment."

"I'll give thee armour to keep off that word; adversity's sweet milk, philosophy, to comfort thee, though thou are banished."

"Yet 'banished!' Hang up philosophy! Unless philosophy can make a Juliet, displant a town, reverse a prince's doom, it helps not, it prevails not: talk no more."

"O! then I see that madmen have no ears."

"How should they, when that wise men have no eyes?"

"Let me dispute with thee of thy estate."

"Thou canst not speak of that thou dost not feel: Wert thou as young as I, Juliet thy love, an hour but married, Tybalt mur- dered, doting like me, and like me banished, then mightst thou speak, then mightst thou tear thy hair, and fall upon the ground, as I do now, taking the measure of an unmade grave."

When Nathan slumped to the stage, motionless, the audience was mute. Tears were rolling down my cheeks. He had forced us suffer the unendurable pain of young love unjustly wrenched apart. Had *he* endured such pain in real life, and if so, for whom? Nancy? I could see he didn't know I was alive. Did he know I was a woman? I was attracted to him, at least to the Nathan who was Miguel, Orsino and Romeo; but who was the real Nathan?

Depleted by Shakespeare's depiction of youthful love's fragility (harsh reality destroying a tiny pure emotion), I left right after the final curtain, returning to the production office where Jean-Paul was staring at his laptop.

"Everything alright?" I was still quivering from Nathan's performance.

"Pardon," Jean-Paul said, raising his eyebrows.

"Ah, oui, excusez-moi. Tout va bien, Jean-Paul?"

"Comme si, comme ca."

"Aucun cas d'urgence?"

"Non."

"Tu voir demain."

"Bonsoir, Sarah?"

"Oui?"

"Your French gets better."

"Merci."

And that was our first day — a day of firsts: our first day of shooting a 'quality' picture; my first dinner with Nathan; and my first impression of Nathan (Romeo) as a lover — a grand, if exhausting, day. It had gone smoothly, more so than I had expected. I suspected the slaughter (Vlad assured me there would be blood) would begin on the morrow.

THE NEXT MORNING at eight, I was at the airport to pick up our beloved distributor, Jeremy Singer, here to evaluate the first day's footage to determine the size of his presale — that essential piece of paper which (along with commitments from our investors) would determine how much "Canadian Tire money" the bank would advance us to finance our illusion.

Normally, a producer has a presale in hand before shooting but, as with most of László's endeavours, our timing was askew. Because of actors' availabilities and crew schedules, we'd been forced to commence production early, and so we were, as they say, down to the wire. Our investors were also waiting for the presale to reassure themselves that their investment was safe.

If, having read the script and knowing who the stars were and liking the early footage, Jeremy decided that THE SMOKE PICKERS had commercial potential, he might commit to pre-buying the rights for up to five million; if not, he might commit to only two (or somewhere in between). Jeremy's objective was to get more picture for less money, while László's was just to get more money.

I had no idea what the budget for THE SMOKE PICKERS was — or any of Felicity's projects. Only László knew the picture cost at any given time. In the four weeks leading up to production, Jean-Paul and the accountant had calculated — and re-calculated, repeatedly — all expenditure, pre-production and production, to ensure we were within budget. Their total, however, always came in higher than the current total in László's head, which of course forced them to re-calculate it (with László's help).

No matter how many times they revised the numbers, their budget total was always higher than László's, because he was the only one who knew what was going out and what might be coming in, and was constantly shaving the 'going out' numbers. If you wanted to buy, rent or hire a prop, or extra lights or an actor, and you asked him what the budget for that item was, you would get a disparaging: "What you need it for?" which would effectively dissuade you from obtaining it — which is why Felicity's pictures cost less than everyone else's.

Jeremy and László had the same hardnosed attitude to making movies, but different personas (their colognes clashed). Jeremy, a frenetic New York Yuppie was constantly blabbing on his cell, griping about everything. He seemed always to be trying to impress — to dominate — whomever he was with. At the airport he always greeted me with: "Sarah, when are you and I going to have our dirty weekend?"

And I always replied: "You'll have to wait."

"Wait?"

"I'm booked till the end of the year."

On this visit, between calls on his cell, just for a second, he looked vulnerable, so I asked, "What're your girls up to?"

"Trouble." He startled me by snapping his fingers in rhythm and mournfully humming out lyrics, with the word 'trouble' starting with the letter 'T' rhyming with the letter 'G' which stood for 'girls'. Oddly enough, Jeremy had a pleasant singing voice and, in fact, had taken a fling as a chorus boy in off-Broadway musicals before finding his true calling as a movie distributor (a vocation, Vlad assured me, which attracts only "hardened criminals").

Driving in from the airport, Jeremy borrowed my cell to make long distance calls to producers and associates not connected to our project. He was careless with other people's money, but then again, most movie distributors are.

I took him straight to the set so he could begin telling László that what he was seeing wasn't worth five million in presales. (Being successful in business, beating down your fellow humans for pennies, must be such a sad, empty way to pass through life).

Arriving at Convocation Hall, I could see Vlad working quickly, grabbing the last of the shots he needed before wrapping the 'Consulate'. He knew that in the cutting room he would need as many editing options as possible, so he was covering everyone's point of view: the Consul looking out the consulate window at Miguel lurking nearby; Miguel looking up at Maddie's window, the Consul entering and leaving, plus shots of demonstrators, all of which he could use — if needed — to pace the movie and to add realism and dramatic tension.

To shoot the beginning of the Cavalcade scene, Vlad had the extras 'demonstrating' as the Consul and Maddie emerged from the 'Consulate'. Nathan had given Vlad a list of revolutionary slogans in Spanish, suggesting they would add 'authenticity' to the scene and so Vlad had asked the art department to make up placards. When the line of black limos drove off, and the small crowd of extras waved their signs angrily and shouted at the second limo, it did look impressive.

I noticed Hardy nearby, watching from behind his sunglasses, his jaw pulverizing a slab of gum.

"Looks real, doesn't it?" I said.

"Who's writing the fucking signs?"

"Why?" I knew Hardy knew.

"It should be done by the writer."

"You didn't write any."

"You didn't ask me. Writing is done by writers. I don't act and actors shouldn't be writing."

"You know Spanish?"

"What's wrong with English? Who do you think is gonna be watching it?"

By early afternoon, we'd wrapped the Consulate exteriors. László took Jeremy off to lunch; the crew grabbed a quick bite; and the unit moved into the studio for the Consulate interiors. I was determined to watch Carey and Nathan act, but didn't want to distract them, so I slipped into the shadows and was looking for a place to sit when I felt Honor's presence hovering beside me. "I haven't received my script yet."

"I'm sorry," I said. "We're having to run more copies. I'll get one to you this afternoon."

"Okay. Is it alright if I stay and watch?"

"Of course."

She nodded politely, and tentatively approached the five director's chairs, sitting carefully in the one furthest from Nathan who, in costume, meditated, vacantly watching Teddy finish lighting the scene. As Carey came onto the soundstage and sat next to Nathan, and Honor gazed at her, I wondered what Honor thought, seeing her Maddie in the flesh. The makeup girl touched up Nathan's cheeks, and I stepped further back into the shadows, finding a riser to sit on. I could barely hear their conversation.

"Do you want a mint?" Carey said, holding the box out to Nathan.

"I just brushed my teeth."

"Good."

"You didn't think I would?"

"I wasn't sure if Hamlet brushed after every meal." Her expression was deadpan.

"You're intimidated by that, aren't you?"

"Of course."

"It's just a play."

"Isn't it the greatest role of all time?"

"Some movie actors, I've heard," Nathan said, "will flatter a newcomer to lull them."

"Really?"

"Yeah. So they can upstage them."

"Really?" Carey said, disingenuously.

"Yeah, they try to shift the blocking so that your back is to the camera."

"Really?"

"But I know a remedy."

"What?"

"Let them do whatever they want in the wide shot ..."

"And ..."

"Kill them in the close-up."

"What happens," Carey asked, "if I shift the blocking in the close-up?"

"Try it."

I knew their banter was their way of establishing a comfortable, almost intimate, working relationship. Nathan was watching her carefully, and she was alert to his every move. I admired them.

I saw Honor get up and approach them, gaping at Carey. "Ms. Lander, I'm Honor Lamprey."

Carey looked at her, puzzled.

"I wrote the book, *The Smoke Pickers*?"

"Oh, of course," said Carey, jumping up and shaking Honor's hand. "How stupid of me. We finally meet. Honor, how lovely. Please call me Carey."

"I'm not disturbing you ..."

"No, no."

"What scene are you doing?"

"It's when Miguel comes to the Consulate. This is Nathan Quill who's playing Miguel."

"Oh. Nice to meet you. You're not quite as I imagined."

Nathan's expression remained stoic. It was clear to me that she hadn't meant it as a criticism, but not as clear to Nathan. "Ditto," he said. "We're just about to shoot."

"Oh, yes of course, well, ah," said Honor, flustered. "Lovely meeting you." Nathan doesn't brook anyone talking to him before he performs and Honor, hearing the slight reprimand in his voice, quickly retreated to the director's chair at the end of the row. I noticed her glancing about, uneasily, trying to look as though she belonged. Her eyes fixed on the chair next to her, she reached across and picked up what I saw, to my dismay, was a script. She stared at the title page, furtively glanced around, put it in her bag, and left.

I saw László and Jeremy enter the studio, and thought to tell László, but knowing he couldn't prevent her from finding out what Hardy had done — what we were *doing* — to her story, I let it go.

On set, Vladimir peered through the camera at the Consulate entry hall door. Looking up, he nodded at David. "Actors please," David said.

Carey and Nathan walked over and stepped onto the set.

"Ah. Ms. Lander, Mr. Quill, it is pleasure to be working with you again."

"The pleasure is all ours, Mr. Pudovkin," Carey said.

"Okay, you can have pleasure. So, now we have important scene to establish deepness of Miguel's love for Maddie, and vicey-versy. The question is, should we shoot rehearsal?"

"I'd like to," Carey said.

"Nathan?"

Nathan nodded.

"Good, I agree. You are brave actors. First, we cover scene in two-shot. This is your mark, Maddie ... and Miguel, you enter door and hit mark here. Alright?"

"Alright."

Glancing at László and Jeremy, Vlad nodded to David.

"Lock it up, everyone," David bellowed. "Picture up."

"Speed."

"Scene 77, take 1."

Vlad paused as everyone settled, then said quietly: "Action."

Nathan stepped catlike through the door and stopped, putting a finger to his lips to silence Carey.

"My husband isn't here," she said. "What do you want?"

"He promised to help us."

"He promised to present your petition to El Presidente."

"Has he?"

"You'll have to ask him."

Nathan paused. "What is your passion?"

"What?" Carey muttered, surprised.

"You heard." Nathan was improvising.

Carey didn't flinch. "My husband will be back in two hours."

"You do not answer my question."

"It was impertinent," Carey said, returning the improv.

Nathan looked about. "You live well. Is this your passion?"

"Now you insult me."

"Do I? You come to my country and you know nothing about it."

"I know that guns do not feed children." That was a line from the script. I recognized it.

"We have no money to buy guns."

"Good, then you can feed the children."

"What do you know about feeding children?"

Surprised by his intensity, and his improv, Carey waited.

Nathan gazed off. "The children in my village die of hunger every day. They lie on the ground in their shacks — none have beds — they grow thin like sticks, lethargic, their bellies swollen, their bodies gaunt, their arms like twigs, bones sticking through skin. Their madres and padres watch, helpless, desperate, they have no food to give them ..."

"Miguel, I ... "

"You will help your husband, and say you have done everything you can. I must do everything I can, even if it means death. We will all fight for our children, our village, our country."

"One continuous war."

"Yes. Poor against rich."

"Not all the rich."

"I do not see any rich helping the poor."

"You must ask the rich."

"No, we will 'eat the rich'."

"Eat the rich?" Carey repeated, startled.

"Rousseau."

Carey smiled. "Ah, how unusual, a revolutionary who quotes Rousseau."

Touché. Carey was holding her own with Nathan who almost smiled.

"Miguel, no one gets saved in a war," Carey said, finding her way back to the script. "In war, people only kill each other. Is that what you want?"

"How else can I help my people?"

"You ... keep ... I don't know ..."

"Help me."

"How?"

"Your husband has a list of 'enemies' of my country, prepared by El Presidente. Get me the list."

Carey crossed to him, laid the back of her hand against his cheek. "Miguel?"

Nathan looked away. Carey leaned in and tentatively kissed him on the mouth. He grabbed her arms and pinned his mouth to hers — both locked together as though they couldn't part, couldn't breathe. I couldn't breathe.

Suddenly, Nathan broke away. "Find the list. I'll be back tonight." He strode quickly away. Carey began to cry.

"Cut! Print. Excellent. Now we do Ms. Lander's closeup."

I realized my fingertips were touching my lips. Their attraction, their intensity, seemed real. Was I jealous? Yes. I could *feel* his lips on hers — and hers on his — and a gnawing sensation in my groin.

Turning away, I noticed László and Jeremy leaving, and Beverly huddled with Vlad, pointing to her script. I assumed she was pointing out that the improvs might be difficult to edit. On any movie, there are usually a few ad-libs, but Nathan was setting a new benchmark and Carey was keeping pace. Almost all producers, and most directors, want the actors to say the lines exactly as written (ad-libbing takes the process out of their control), which is unfortunate, because often an actor will come up with a better line. It's impossible for a writer to be inside every character's head completely, so if an actor, like Nathan — embedded in his character — invents a perfect line, the director would be a fool not to use it. Vlad knew that, and his tacit approval invited Nathan and Carey to nip at the script. Improvs, of course, do not make most writers happy; often they feel threatened. So Hardy, seeing Beverly discussing the script with Vlad, hurried over, and I knew he was complaining about what the actors were doing.

Outside, by the catering table, Jeremy was speaking heatedly to László who, I could see, was not happy. He looked at me. "Jeremy is not impressed with Nathan."

"No?" I said. "That's strange."

"Why 'strange'?" László asked.

"Everyone else is."

"Who's everyone?" Jeremy's tone was mocking.

"The crew. I've noticed that when the crew likes an actor the audience does too. We've been shooting for only two days but I can tell already the crew likes them."

"Them?"

"Carey and Nathan. Haven't you noticed how good they are together?"

Jeremy, who looks as though he would never concede anything to anyone even if his life depended on it, immediately said: "The crew knows diddly-squat."

***

That evening, I picked up Jeremy at his hotel to take him to rushes.

"What time is Madonna showing up?" he asked.

"I asked for eleven."

"I don't have to meet her in the bar or anything?"

"No, she's going to your room."

"Good." He stared out the window at the passing buildings. "So, you think this Nathan guy is hot."

"I do."

"He's no Brando."

"Brando wasn't Brando till he became Brando. I've seen Nathan in the theatre, Jeremy, in Shakespeare. He's amazing."

"Shakespeare does diddly-squat at the box office."

"They haven't seen Nathan as Romeo. I promise you he's hot."

It's not often I can shut down one of these 'hardened criminals,' but Jeremy was silent the rest of the ride, and I didn't bother making conversation. I was excited at the prospect of screening the first day's rushes, the first sighting of the dream that Vlad and I had pushed so hard for.

I'd invited Carey, Martin and Nathan, but Martin had said he was busy (observing the lake?). Nathan was on stage that night at Madbrain. That left Carey, who only watches the first day's rushes to check her performance, and who was sitting by herself at the end of a row. The rest of us — Vlad, László, Hardy (behind his sunglasses), Teddy, Jeremy, David the A.D. and I — were spread out and, when the lights went down and the first shot came on, we gazed at the screen as though we were watching GONE WITH THE WIND. I noted Jeremy looking bored which, I suspected, was to forestall agreeing to the original five million pre-sale, while László, who tries never to reveal his thoughts, regarded the footage warily.

On screen, the intensity between Carey and Nathan was magnified — Vlad's closeups were intimate, almost embarrassingly private. I felt as though I had stopped breathing, then realized I was holding my breath. Movie stars on screen have something the rest of us don't have — people say it's charisma but the truth is that the camera loves some more than others, for no discernible reason.

Teddy's photography was full of crisp shadow — the best work he'd done — as was Vlad's direction. Raising the bar aesthetically had put everyone on their mettle. Martin was commanding — in the footage his quirkiness came across as menace. But of course Nathan and Carey were the real surprise. I glanced over at Carey watching her image on screen as though it wasn't her kissing Nathan.

When the shot of Martin in the Thunderbird watching Maddie and Miguel came on, it ran for three minutes. It was a simple take, and Martin's demeanour, angry, revengeful, regretful — altering slightly every few seconds — chilled us. It was our first encounter with what was to come, three actors bringing (some of) Honor's words vividly to life, and creating their own psychological conflicts on set. When the rushes finished, there was silence. I think László, and even Vlad, were surprised by how elegant and intense the footage was — a step up from our usual efforts.

Carey was out of her seat and striding up the aisle when László said: "Carey, come meet Jeremy who is distributing movie."

She stopped, put on her professional demeanour and shook Jeremy's hand. "Nice to meet you."

"I was sorry," Jeremy said, "to hear about THE BREME FACTOR."

"What about it?" Carey asked.

"The numbers don't look good at all."

Why would you meet a star and proceed to tell her bad news about her new movie? I had seen Jeremy do something like it before and it had puzzled me. Now I understood. It was his 'business' technique. If a star, feeling vulnerable, faltered on our picture, Jeremy could buy up the rights more cheaply — he wasn't buying the performance, after all, he was only interested in the name. It was a negative, fall-back approach, but that's how Jeremy operated, and was probably why he had a bulging bank account and two daughters coming off the rails.

"Really?" said Carey, unfazed. "*I've* heard that it's doing very well in Europe. There's even talk of nominations." She smiled at Jeremy, glanced at me with a wink, then left, leaving an awkward silence.

"Footage looks very good, Teddy," Vlad said.

"It looks fucking great, Teddy," Hardy added from behind the sunglasses.

"It looks good, Laz," Jeremy said.

"It looks very good," László said. "Good work, Teddy, Vlad."

"Confucius say," Teddy said, getting up, "he who make good footage must walk home. See you tomorrow."

"Are there no sex scenes?" Jeremy asked. "I didn't see any in the script."

"Of course. Sarah, when are sex scenes?" László asked innocently.

"We haven't scheduled any yet," I said. "We're keeping them as a rain cover."

I understood why László wasn't telling him about his agreement with Honor. Jeremy expected sex scenes, and László was hoping the quality of the picture without them would, for the moment, keep Jeremy's commitment high. I was sure László still intended to include some — he wouldn't be able to resist, hoping that Honor would be so dazzled at having her book turned into a movie that she'd let it pass (it had happened before); and also hoping that Carey might change her mind about the no-nudity clause. But if that failed, he might try to convince Nathan to perform simulated sex with a body double — he had done that before as well. Then I realized I was thinking like László — and that was distressing.

"I should get back to the hotel," Jeremy said, glancing at his watch.

"Can you catch a cab?" I asked, wanting to savour the moment a while longer. "Just get a receipt."

"Okay. Laz, see you tomorrow, before I go?"

"We have breakfast at hotel. Yes? At seven?"

"Okay, seven. Bye everyone."

Once he'd gone, I wanted to shake them up, to see if they'd realized what we'd achieved. "Vlad, you are a brilliant director, Teddy is a talented cinematographer, Hardy is a superb writer and László is a shrewd producer. THE SMOKE PICKERS is going to be a wonderful, award-winning picture." Surprised, they all looked at me expectantly. Everyone likes a cheerleader.

"It sounds," Vlad said, trying not to smile, "as though you like it."

"Don't you?"

Vlad shrugged. "We have much to do. And always there are potholes on road ahead."

"What potholes?" László asked.

Oddly enough, Hardy jumped in. "Well, for one, everybody's screwing with my dialogue."

"I know, Hardy," Vlad said. "But sometimes when actors improvise it works, and when it doesn't, I can cut in editing. What you are writing is most important. If we get extra from actors, you have no need to be concerned; you will still get single credit."

"You like the writing?"

"Yes, it's good. Actors like it too. You need to think about ending."

"I'm on it," said Hardy, striding to the door.

"So, László," Vlad asked quietly, when just the three of us were left, "is Martin Gage crazy?"

"Why you ask?" László sounded guarded.

"He says he is spy."

"He is not crazy."

"You know this for sure?"

"Yes."

"How?"

"He told us," László said, looking to me for confirmation.

"Yes, I said, "he did tell us he wasn't crazy."

"Ah." Vlad nodded. "That's okay then. Why does he have pistol?"

"Pistol?"

"Marty had pistol in hotel room."

"He is movie star. He needs protection."

"Yesterday, he put pistol in scene where there is no pistol, and told me he is fighting Cold War."

I had forgotten about the pistol, but now I was concerned. "I saw him with a pistol too."

"He's patriotic," László insisted. "He loves his country. Sarah knows this."

"That's what his agent told us."

Vlad didn't smile. "You don't need pistol to love country."

"No, but it helps." László was trying to sidetrack the conversation, so as usual, it was left to me to push for a reality check.

"Carrying a gun has nothing to do with being patriotic. If he's got real ammunition and it goes off, someone could get hurt, or worse. And that could invalidate our insurance."

László sighed. "Nothing is going to happen. How many more days we need Consul?"

Vlad thought. "Six, maybe seven."

"So, we watch him until we have him in can. Then if he wants to shoot someone, he can, right?"

Vlad merely brooded: "Hmmm."

"Besides, he looks good."

"Yes, he looks very good," Vlad said.

"Alright. We say nothing until he is finished."

"As long," Vlad said, "as he is not crazy."

"Martin is not crazy. He told us and I believe him. He's here on official business to check Canadian border for Uncle Sam."

Somehow when Martin Gage said it, it sounded rational, quirky but not insane. Hearing László say it, especially with that defensive tone, I was now having doubts. "How do we know this is true?" I asked.

"Why are you causing trouble? Footage looks good and we only need him few more days."

"If anything happens, it'll cost us."

"Don't I teach you most important job of producer is not to worry? That's your job."

"Footage is looking great," said Vlad, sensing László closing down the discussion. "Maybe Marty get Oscar *and* Golden Globe."

"I think," László said, musing, "Hardy should write scene where Consul and Maddie want to jump on their bones together."

"And," I said, "you could give them guns to fire while they're doing it."

László ignored me. "We need scene to establish why they are together — to make Miguel jealous."

"Carey's contract," I reminded him, "has a clause on nudity."

"We have clause for re-writing."

"Not for nude scenes."

"Why don't you feel her?"

Sometimes László's mangled English stops even me. "You want me to 'feel her *out*?' Is that what you want?"

"Yes."

"Okay. By the way, Honor has a copy of the script."

"I told you not to send her."

"She found one on set."

"Oh-oh, László," Vlad said, "now you will have to kiss Honor's asp."

WHEN CAREY ARRIVED on set the next morning, not wanting to distract her, I asked if I could speak with her that evening.

"Do you want to come to the hotel?" she asked.

"Sure, but it won't be till late."

"I never get to sleep before eleven."

"Okay."

I found a seat in the shadows and, while waiting for Vlad to shoot the Consul and Maddie in the Consulate entry hall, watched Carey and Martin mentally preparing. Vlad was also observing them: Carey was in a muse, focused on a point twenty feet in front of her and Martin, motionless, appeared to be repeatedly scanning the set.

Vlad paused as everyone settled, then said quietly, "Action."

Martin put on his suit jacket.

Carey watched him. "Guy?"

"What?"

"Are you making any progress with the petition?"

Martin stopped. "What do you know about the petition?"

"What you told me."

"I didn't tell you about the petition."

"You did. You told me you were helping the peasants."

"So?"

"Did you?"

"I gave it to El Presidente."

"And ..."

"And what?"

"Is he going to act on it?"

"I don't know. That's his business."

"What if he ignores it?"

"Then he ignores it. What does it have to do with you?"

"Nothing, really. I just think what they're asking for is fair, don't you?"

"No. They're communists."

I held my breath. Vlad was watching Martin intently. The line wasn't in the script. It caught Carey. "Are they?" she responded, tentatively.

"Can't you smell them?"

"Who?"

"The commie rabble."

"They're not rabble, Guy. I've met them."

"Where?"

"In the city. They're just like us except they're poor."

"That's why they're commies. I don't want you associating with them, putting yourself in danger."

"I don't think all the people of Chile are 'commies'."

"No?"

"But the people tell me that El Presidente is a fascist."

"Which people?"

"The people I met in the street. Is he? A fascist?"

"He's a good friend to America."

"I'm told he has a list of enemies."

"Who told you that?"

"The people I met. Is there a list?" I was amazed. Whatever Martin threw at her, Carey responded, and kept weaving back to the script to ensure that the story points were made.

"I can't tell you that."

"Can't or won't?"

"Same thing."

"Guy?"

"Yes."

"Be careful."

"Do you care?"

"Of course I care."

"Be here when I get back," Martin ordered, striding out the door. "Cut. Print."

Carey and Martin had put so much edge on the scene that the crew was respectfully silent as they prepared the next setup. As I was thinking how well Carey had handled Martin's ad-libs, I felt a presence at my elbow. Honor was glaring at me. "I want to see László, now."

"He's tied up at the moment."

"Would he rather talk to my lawyer?"

Her expression was set, determined.

"No. Let's find him."

Hurricane Honor had arrived. In a way, I was relieved. László would be the one to face the brunt of it. Most probably, there would be death and destruction in its wake, but then the skies would clear — I hoped. I led Honor to László's Mercedes, parked just outside the sound stage. He was sitting in the back, speaking quietly on his cell. I opened the rear door.

"I want you to hear this as well," Honor said. The expression on her face wasn't hateful, but it wasn't friendly — it was anguished, hurt, brusque. She was dressed casually and her makeup had run. Obviously, she'd been crying. She climbed in the back with László and I got in the front. I was praying that whatever happened it wouldn't affect the production. I could see her in the rear view mirror. I could hear him on his cell.

"Yes, Eddy, I need two more weeks. Yes."

With Honor sitting beside him, I knew his demeanour wouldn't change — his expression would remain calm, composed. He knew that she had seen the script and so he was expecting her wrath, and had no doubt carefully prepared his response. But she wasn't looking at him. She was staring vacantly out her window, waiting for him to finish his call.

"Okay, Eddy, get back to me." He closed his cell. "Honor, what do you need, what can I do?"

She looked at him. "I trusted you, László. So it's really my fault."

"What is your fault?"

"You destroying my book. Even though I knew better, I still signed a contract with an Hungarian."

"Honor, what are you talking?"

"You really don't understand, do you? Okay, well, in plain language, László, you fucked my book. Do you understand that?"

"We make few changes to help dramatic structure."

"A few changes?"

"If you read contract, only thing I cannot change is to make sex scenes. But to make movie, I can change anything I want."

"You are a sleazy shit-bag, with a breast fetish."

"That is possible, but there is no sex in movie." To maintain the advantage in any negotiation, László never responds to insults, a trait I admired, and tried to emulate.

"It doesn't even resemble my book!"

"It is still love story between Maddie and Miguel."

"*The Smoke Pickers* doesn't take place in Chile; Maddie is not married to the Consul; she's Canadian not American; and Miguel is not a revolutionary."

"Miguel still fights for worker's rights. In movie, there has to be hero who fights, otherwise no one will watch. You want to watch for two hours movie about people who love each other and pick tobacco? Who would buy ticket to see this?"

"It's not my book, László. You've destroyed my work."

"You see, this is problem always with authors. They think they see movie on screen like it is in book. No, it is impossible. Books and movies are not same. In movies, when actors talk, you put audience to sleep. That is why we show men fighting and women having sex. You do not want sex in your movie, so I have to put in revolution to keep audience awake. Now I tell you something. They will cheer for Miguel and they will love Maddie. We have seen footage of Nathan, Carey and Martin and they should all get Oscar. You come tonight and see for yourself."

Staring at him, Honor was silent, conflicted. The script she'd read told her that László had, in fact, "fucked" her book. László was telling her that, not only had he improved the story dramatically, but the 'quality' movie he was making would win at least three Academy Awards. I had much to learn about being a producer — if I wanted to be like László.

"Honor, you are very talented author. Come to rushes and you will see how beautiful Vlad is making movie of your book."

She was uncertain now, his implacability smothering her anger. She gazed at him, confused, opened the door, got out and wandered off. I turned in my seat and faced him.

"This is important lesson for you," László said, coldly. "Do not let authors tell you how to make movie."

"We *did* make some major changes," I said, resisting telling him that we had pretty much destroyed her story.

"She will like Carey and Nathan," he said, as though that would make all the difference.

Honor's anguish, I sensed, had left him feeling vulnerable, so I asked: "Can we talk about Martin?"

"What about him?"

"Do you really think he's not crazy?"

"Martin Gage is okay. He is not crazy."

"Even with what about what he said about coyotes and Somalis?"

"So he thinks they put cameras in coyotes to watch wetbacks, and Somalis are going to invade America."

"And that's not crazy?"

"No, it's not crazy, they're only silly ideas. Even I have silly ideas."

"Like what?"

"Like ... remaking ESCAPE FROM ALCATRAZ with all female cast."

"That is crazy."

"Maybe it's not so crazy."

"So you're not worried."

"No."

"László, Martin Gage is delusional. Ask me how I know."

He stared at me, as though I were about to pee on his leather seat.

"Martin asked me for dossiers on all the picture personnel."

"Dossiers?"

"Bios."

"And you give them to him?"

"Of course. I just assumed he was looking for paparazzi or something. It was no big deal, we have bios on file, so I gave him those, and what I didn't have I made up. But since I was doing 'dossiers' on us, I did one on him. I didn't see any reference to him serving in Viet Nam, but he was in a picture called FLIGHT FROM DA NANG which was set in Viet Nam."

"So?"

"So, there was trouble on set."

"Trouble?"

"He shot the cameraman."

"He killed a cameraman?"

"Just a leg wound. The official report said the gun went off by accident, so I phoned a friend of someone I know in LA. to find out what happened. Ask me why the gun went off."

László was watching me now as though I *had* peed on his seat. "Well?"

"The story I was told was that the cameraman wouldn't recite the Pledge of Allegiance when Martin asked him to. And the reason the cameraman wouldn't recite the Pledge of Allegiance was because he was British and didn't know it, so Martin shot him. Apparently, he didn't intend to, but he's delusional, László. He might even be psychotic."

"All actors are delusional. That is why they are actors. Martin has only few more days. I don't think he will shoot Teddy."

"He could shoot anybody. We need to deal with it."

"No. We need to finish scenes with Consul. We cannot afford·to get new actor."

I knew László was resistant to getting rid of our star because of Martin's low rate, and because there might legal implications — we would be breaking the contract. Also, bringing in a star of similar stature would be expensive; and, by changing stars while shooting, we'd put the movie at risk. Jeremy was still waffling on the pre-sale, which made me think that László might be over-extended. He'd never admit it, of course, but he always tapped his fingers when anxious, and he was now drumming a roll on the armrest that would've put Buddy Rich to shame. Whatever I said at this point wouldn't move him to take action. I'd have to find another way.

"I'm sure it'll all work out," I said.

"Of course. We make wonderful movie."

Honor arrived at rushes that night just as we started, taking a seat at the back under the projection booth. With the author present, the conversation — between Vlad, László, Teddy, Hardy, and me — was constrained. The others hadn't been informed of the tension between Honor and László, but they knew enough to be discreet. When the first take between Carey and Nathan came on, their intensity again drew us all in. Not only did the camera love Carey, it loved Nathan — but it especially loved them together. I knew it was only a movie, but I could see they were made for each other. The age difference (older woman, younger man) only accentuated their passion — the cause, I knew, of that tightening sensation in my chest. I glanced back. Watching the screen intently, Honor was rapt.

When the lights went up, I moved quickly to sit next to her. "They *are* wonderful, aren't they?" I said, surprised to see tears in her eyes. Carey and Nathan's performances had even made her forget that Hardy had shredded her dialogue.

"I love them," she whispered, then slipped away before László could rise from his seat. When he did, I went to him and said quietly: "She loves it."

"Of course."

"It will all be worth it, László."

He tried to appear as though he was unconcerned. "Why wouldn't it?"

***

I don't know what I don't know but always feel as though I'm fumbling to find out what it is I don't know, trying to fathom what I think others know that I don't, and failing; which is how I felt crossing the lobby of Carey's hotel that night to "feel her" on László's behalf. What did I imagine I was doing? I already knew she wouldn't agree to any nude scenes, so why did I go? *Was* I attracted to her? *Intrigued* by her? Yes, of course, but in what way? Was I interested in her only because Nathan was? Watching them together, their 'relationship' — which appeared immediate and intense — left me feeling desolate. Honor's emotional reaction to the footage, a combination of longing *and* regret, was pretty much how I felt. I didn't know *what* I was thinking but, with my imagination working overtime, I had the sensation of wanting to shed my skin.

When she opened the door, Carey, in a thick white bathrobe, was holding a champagne glass, one of those tall, fluted ones. "Champagne?"

"Are you celebrating?"

"Yes."

"What?"

"This is the most fun I've ever had on a picture."

She filled two glasses and we clinked. "To us ... all of us," she said.

Somehow I knew the "us" referred to her and Nathan, and the "all of us" was an afterthought, to include me. Yes, I was jealous, but of whom? She was sharing something deep with Nathan — someone I thought I cared about, but didn't know, not really; and who didn't know who I was. On the other hand, Nathan was sharing something important with her. And I envied him that. But what? I downed the champagne in one swallow.

"Whoa. You're thirsty."

"Sorry."

"That's okay." She refilled my glass. "What's on your mind?"

I almost jumped. "What?"

"You said you needed to talk to me."

"Oh. right. I'm here on behalf of László."

"Okay. I'll be serious," she said, completely deadpan.

It cracked me up. "Stop it."

"Okay, I *will* be serious. What is it?" She was trying not to smile and not succeeding.

"That's not much better. So, László thinks it would heighten the drama if we saw the Consul and Maddie ... ah ..."

"... having passions together." She had László's accent perfectly and it made me laugh.

"Yeah."

"Gosh, that's an intriguing idea," she said with mock innocence. "Maybe they could have sex. I would have thought the audience could guess that they're already physically involved, but I'm sure László's right. Audiences are too stupid; they have to see it. And, of course, watching people have sex always adds dramatic weight to any movie."

"Are you serious?"

"No, I'm just venting."

· Even though I was jealous, I couldn't help liking her because she knew how silly it all was, how stupid and futile — and we could laugh about it.

"Tell László," she said, "that it would destroy the dramatic tension between them, which is what drives Maddie to Miguel and is the reason for their affair. Do you think he knows what dramatic tension is?"

"László's smarter than you think."

"Producers, in my experience, don't have both oars in the water," she said, smiling. "Some aren't even in the boat. László's like most of those I've worked with, aiming for the lowest common denominator, grabbing at the money, with no understanding of story or character, or comedy or dramatic tension, or what actors are about. What they do understand is sex and violence and fill their movies with both to keep grabbing at the money. For the last three days, I've worked in sync with an actor who struggles each day to create an authentic person on screen. Even Martin, for whatever reason, is, as Nathan would say, 'in the moment.' And László can't see that."

Hearing her explain Nathan gave me another jealous twinge.

"Honor came to rushes tonight."

"And?"

"She cried. I almost cried. You and Nathan were pretty amazing."

She refilled our glasses. "To Nathan," she said, clinking my glass again. "I was just about to take a nice long, hot, soapy soak in my luxurious tub. Would you care to join me?"

I was surprised but not startled by the invitation. The champagne had begun to take effect, and champagne is very efficient at dulling inhibitions — like nudophobia. In fact, it's toxic to civilized behaviour. After a few glasses humans often behave quite erratically.

On Felicity's 10th anniversary, László threw a party, serving only French champagne which all the guests drank like water. Many of the high-flyers who attended the party ended up in states of mental unbalance. A well-known impresario drove his Porsche slowly off the street and into a brick wall; a well-known actor went home, fell asleep, woke up ten minutes later to discover he'd peed in his bed, tried to dry the bed with his hairdryer, went out to another engagement and realized on the way that he'd left the hairdryer on. Champagne does that to people. So after two glasses with Carey, I was exhilarated, in love with everything and everyone, even feeling that we shared an attraction to Nathan — we were all connected. "I'd love a bath."

I don't remember much, except that the bathtub, the size of a child's swimming pool, was brimming over with bubbles and deliciously hot; and even though suds covered almost all of her, I could see why men found Carey attractive, and I guess women too.

"Do you think," I asked, "this is how the average person thinks glamourous movie people behave?"

"I don't know; it seems pretty glamourous to me."

"It's my first time."

"First time?"

"Sharing a bath."

"Really?"

"And the first time with a movie star."

"It's my second."

"Are you attracted to him?"

"László?"

László? What was she talking about?

"I'm joking. You want to know if I could go for Nathan. Yes. And you?"

"I just admire him so much."

"Admire?"

"I don't know him all that well." I wasn't about to let her know how much I was attracted to him.

"He's probably a pain to live with, and a lousy lay."

"Would you?" I tried to ask the question off-handedly, as though it were really of no concern.

"That would depend on how much champagne I'd had."

I kept sipping and emptying my glass, and Carey kept refilling it. I knew I was babbling — "Ooops, empty. This is fun. What delicious champagne. It certainly breaks the ice, especially in a tub." I was working hard to sound intelligent but the champagne was having the opposite effect, and I was awed. I was sharing a bubble bath with Robin of Epping. Wow! "Maybe László should negotiate his deals in a tub."

"Maybe he has."

"He's okay, you know, but not terrific like you. I feel like I've known you all my life. You know, I don't think I'm actually gay, not really."

"No? Well, it doesn't matter. It's no big deal — gay is just another way to practice sex."

"I didn't know you had to practice." Champagne also makes you think you're funny when you're not. "Sorry."

"People are attracted to other people of both genders, especially those they admire."

I was astonished. "You admire me?"

"I couldn't do your job."

"I couldn't do yours." I was being sincere. I was no actor. "You want to have sex with me."

"It did occur to me, although I wouldn't put it like that."

"How would you put it?"

"I'm attracted to you."

"I don't know why. I'm not pretty or anything."

Carey laughed. "You really know how to sell yourself."

"I've never thought I was attractive."

"It's in your eyes."

I was overwhelmed, but also timid. I had been intimate with only one other human, in a relationship in which very little happened, sexwise. Then he'd found someone else with whom he could be passionate (or so he told me), which is why I suspected I was asexual. It never occurred to me that *I* would be attractive to another woman — or even attracted to one. "Would you be angry if I said I wasn't sure?"

"Why would I be angry? It's *your* body. Wait until you are sure. Just make sure that you're really not sure until you are sure, if that makes any sense."

"I'm not sure about anything right now, except that I like this champagne. Is there more?"

"I have enough champagne in my fridge to seduce a horse."

I was laughing as she got out to fetch another bottle. Seeing her naked, I hoped that, at 37, I could look like that, and found myself thinking about touching her. Could I?

We drank more champagne, and I jabbered on. She asked about my family. I told her about growing up in a small Ontario town, an only child, shy, fond of books, working hard at school, taught by nuns, tutoring grammar in my spare time to save for university; my dad dying of lung cancer; my mother remarrying and living near a forest with a man who collected butterflies (which I found nauseating). I told her about my father (who had brown eyes like Nathan), how he loved to smoke, making his own foot-long cigarettes on a roller from exotic blends of tobacco, slicing them into regular size ones with a razor blade and placing them in a silver case which my mother had bought for him in New York on their honeymoon. He gave me a love of words — verbal and written — and taught me how to use them wisely. A surveyor by profession, when he retired he bought a small press, and spent his days in our basement printing one-sheets of stories and poems (he loved e.e. cummings); and every Sunday we did the cross-word together. As a child, I had gone with him everywhere — his parental instruction being to *show* me life's lessons, not *tell* me — so, even as a five-year-old, I was always able to relate to adults.

Remembering how everyone loved him, and how much I missed him, I started sobbing. "He had the gift of truth," I told Carey. "He never lied to us" — blah, blah, blah, I was going on, spilling out my emotions;

and in my champagne haze I remember peering at her (the bubbles had long since disappeared), surprised that she was gazing intently at me, listening — really listening. And when I woke, I was in a bed, light was streaming through the curtain and I had no idea of where I was.

When I tried to get up, smashed pottery started banging loudly inside my skull and I had to lie down again. I was naked in a strange bed in a strange room — a hotel room. Was I dreaming — had my nudophobia kicked in? Looking around, I saw the robe on a chair, and remembered the bath. How did I get to the bed? I tried to examine it — two people had slept in it. I fought hard to remember anything, but nothing came back. I found my clothes, put them on and, passing the kitchenette on my way out, saw a note on the table:

Sarah
Orange juice in the fridge.
Coffee on the machine, just turn it on.
Out for my run, back soon.
Carey.

At the bottom, I put:

C.
Early meeting, see you on set.
S.

I had no idea what I was feeling, except panic — I didn't know what had happened, if anything, or what I had done, or felt. Did it matter? I didn't want to offend Carey, but if I had seemed agreeable under the influence of champagne, well, what was I feeling now? Was I attracted to her? Yes. Physically and emotionally she was enticing. And she listened. Did that mean I was gay? Did it matter? No. And Nathan? What about Nathan? Who was he? Who was I? What was I?

15

I HURRIED HOME, showered, and rushed to the set with my aching head and body feeling as though I had been infected with every bird flu in existence. I found the catering table, poured two coffees, added double cream and sugar, and huddled in one of the director's chairs, praying not to have to talk to anyone until I had regained consciousness. But of course 'anyone' in the form of László walked up. "I was telephoning to you last night."

I looked up, unable to speak.

"So?" He was clearly anxious about something.

"So?" I mumbled.

"Did you feel her?"

"What?!"

"Did you feel her?"

"Oh. Yes."

"And?"

"She thinks it would destroy, ah ... the dramatic tension between Maddie and the Consul, which is what drives Maddie to Miguel ... the reason for their affair."

"Sarah, I am not idiot. Why is everybody not want to see sex? Come with me."

"What?"

"I show you how to be producer."

I knew immediately what he intended to do. "László, I don't think this is a good idea ..."

"Come."

László led the way onto the soundstage to the bedroom set just as Vlad was beginning a take, a two-shot favouring Carey sitting on the edge of the bed watching Martin who was standing by the window and peering out every few seconds.

"Action," Vlad said, quietly.

Carey paused. "What are you looking for?"

"The rabble." Martin's improv caught her by surprise.

"Why would they come here?" Carey sighed. It sounded real.

"Because they hate us."

"Why should they hate us?"

"Because we fight for freedom. That's why they want to destroy us."

"They don't want to destroy us. They want to feed their children." I was amazed by Carey — she kept finding her way back to the script.

"Commies don't care about children."

The line stopped her. Then, with barely a pause, she responded. "That's not what JFK said."

The line was so unexpected that Martin glanced at her sharply. He'd been leading the improv parade, but she had just darted ahead. He eyed her warily. "What?"

"President Kennedy. His inaugural address. Don't you remember? 'We all want to cherish our children.' He used the word 'all'."

"The President didn't support commies," Martin said, dismissively. "He stood by the Monroe Doctrine."

"Did he?" Carey asked. Martin had taken the lead again.

"Yeah. Monroe was a great president. Not one of the gutless ones."

"That was a long time ago," Carey stated, tentatively. I sensed she couldn't remember what the Monroe Doctrine was, or when.

"It still applies," Martin said.

"Does it?" Carey said cautiously.

"The fight for freedom is eternal. President Monroe knew that. That's why he told the world to back off the Americas; but commies hate democracy and they'll kill anyone to get their hands on Chile. Well, not on my watch. Tell *that* to your commie friends."

"They're not ... communists, just simple people who want a better life for their children."

"Then they must fight for freedom," Martin said with finality, gazing out past the lights into the dark of the studio, his face set in stone (not unlike a Mt. Rushmore president). Watching him, Carey didn't move, her expression inscrutable.

"Cut. Print," Vlad said, approaching Martin. "That was good, Marty. Where you get Monroe line?"

"It's the truth."

"I liked it," Vlad said.

At that point, László stepped forward. I followed reluctantly. Carey gave me a slight, quizzical smile which I returned, hoping I wasn't revealing my confusion.

"Vlad, Martin, Carey, I've been thinking that maybe we are not seeing enough of Guy and Maddie."

Distracted, all three looked at him.

"What?" Martin said.

"So audience can understand why they are together."

I could see that Vlad and Carey knew what was coming.

"They're married," said Martin, dismissively.

"Yes, but we need to see how they love each other, and how they have passions together."

"Passions?" said Martin, disdainfully, staring at László.

"We need to see their love. Guy realizes they are in danger and how much he loves Maddie. And he wants to show his love to her."

From Martin and Carey's expressions, I could see László was pushing his passions cart uphill. I heard Vlad sigh.

"So he kisses her. And she kisses him and suddenly they are wanting to have each other. Of course, she loves Miguel too but she is caring — and passionate — about her husband. She is vulnerable and wants to give her love to him."

Standing behind László, when Carey glanced at me I shrugged helplessly.

"I don't think," said Carey, "she's ..."

"You think I'm afraid, don't you?" We all looked at Martin. He was eyeing László coldly.

"No ... I ...," muttered László, puzzled.

"I was in Nam. I saw the killing. I know what communists can do to a country."

"You don't think it's important to show ...?"

"They twist everything. They lie. And they desecrate the American flag. We have no time for love-making. We have to save Chile."

"Of course. It was only idea."

Astonished, I saw László signal Vlad to continue. I'd never seen László give way to an actor (unless she was "volumptious"). Was he finally aware of how delicately we were all tip-toeing around our star — how tenuous Martin's grasp on reality was?

"Can we," Vlad asked loudly, "have Ms. Lander's close-up now, please?"

Feeling "like death warmed over" (to quote my late father), and not knowing what to say to Carey, I wanted to be anywhere but on set. I was of no help to Vlad, who was, amazingly, keeping this strange production on schedule, so I returned to the office.

In reception, Liz, the production accountant, was droning on endlessly to Simone about her love life. Her boyfriend's unemployment insurance was about to run out and she was asking Simone if she should dump him, or accompany him to the Turks and Caicos, using the last of her savings to open a crayfish shack. Simone was only vaguely listening; I knew she was waiting for Liz's monologue to end to bring out her wedding pictures. I took refuge in my broom closet, drank a gallon of orange juice and, unable to concentrate on answering emails, was dimly sorting the snail-mail into two piles: the large one, invoices for services and materials on THE SMOKE PICKERS (all arriving daily now in a great heap), and the smaller one, Felicity office expenses.

I knew I was avoiding Carey. I didn't know why. I realized I would have to say something to her, to acknowledge what had happened (whatever that was) and so, after letting it gnaw at me all afternoon, I returned to the studio where they were now shooting the second-to-last scene of the day. Seated at her dressing table, Carey watched Martin in the mirror. He kept peering out the window.

Vlad paused then said, "Action."

"Maddie?" Martin's voice was sharp, commanding.

"Yes."

"I'm waiting for you to tell me."

"Tell you what?"

"That you've been consorting with a commie." Martin was giving a wonderful performance of repressed anger — unless it was real.

"Why would I tell you when you seem to know?"

"He's a communist, for godsake, Maddie."

"He's a young man with ideals. Unlike us, he actually wants to help his people."

"He wants to enslave them."

"Isn't that what we do?"

"I don't want to hear that commie talk."

"What *do* you want to hear?"

"The Pledge of Allegiance," Martin said, abandoning the script altogether.

"What?"

"You heard me."

I stopped breathing. I was seeing Martin shoot the cameraman on DA NANG. Was he carrying his pistol?

Abruptly, he drew back the curtain to glance out the window, as though expecting some menace. At the dresser, Carey sat perfectly still, gazing at him in the mirror. Did she remember the Pledge of Allegiance? And if she didn't?

She hesitated. "Why?"

"So I know you're with me."

"There was a time you knew that without asking." Her ad-lib was amazing. She was staying right with him, no matter what he threw at her.

"I want to hear you say it."

"I haven't said it since high school."

"That's why you need to say it now."

Watching him in the mirror, she collected her thoughts. "I pledge," she said, carefully, "allegiance ... to the flag of Am ... the United States ... of America, and ... to the republic for which it stands, one nation ... with liberty ... no, ah ... one nation *under God, indivisible*, with liberty and justice for all."

"What's the last line?" Martin asked gently.

"... one nation under God, indivisible, with liberty and justice for all."

"Damn fine," said Martin, who crossed to her, kissed the top of her head, put a hand on her shoulder and looked at her tenderly in the mirror. "I knew you could never betray me."

She sat there, staring at the implacable reflection of Consul Hawthorne— the last of liberty's bulwarks against the commie menace.

Carey's unease was palpable. I suspected she didn't know about FLIGHT FROM DA NANG, but clearly she understood she was playing opposite an actor who was unstable; yet she stayed in character, kept the scene going, and remained as close to the script as possible. Watching this verbal tango with Martin, all were mesmerized by the tension; but only Vlad and I knew just how real her apprehension was.

"Cut, print," said Vlad.

Unaware that Martin was edging further from reality, the crew burst into applause.

"Camera is now in wrong place for Mr. Gage's closeup. Ms. Lander and Mr. Gage can take half hour," Vlad said, watching Martin stride from the set.

I needed to talk to Vlad but was anxious about Carey. I caught her outside the studio as she made for her trailer.

"Carey?"

"Sarah."

"Are you okay?"

"Yeah. It's been an interesting day," she said, stepping up into the caravan.

"If you feel uncomfortable at any time ..."

"Actually, he's sharpening my listening skills."

"Can we talk?"

"Of course. Come in."

I had no idea what I was going to say. She was under a lot of pressure, but being amazingly brave. I was afraid of hurting her — and also afraid of losing her. I wanted her to be at ease with me. I wanted her friendship at the very least; I didn't know if there was anything else I wanted. She closed the door and, as we stood there, she seemed, for the first time, fragile. Impulsively, I leaned in and kissed her.

"What?" she asked surprised.

"You seem so vulnerable."

"That's sweet."

"I think you're amazing."

"Why?"

"You're just amazing, that's all."

She was silent.

"That was some bath," I said, awkwardly.

"Yeah."

I didn't know how to ask what I wanted most to know. "Ah, did we ... ah ...?"

Carey looked at me strangely. "Did we what?"

"Did we ... I can't seem to remember ..."

"It's okay. Nothing happened."

"Really?"

"You passed out."

"Ah, that's why I don't remember anything, except the bubbles."

"You were sick first."

"Oh my God, I'm sorry."

"It's okay, I got out in time."

"I'm so sorry."

"No, it was my fault, forcing you to drink champagne." When she smiled, which she didn't often, her warmth was incredibly genuine.

"How did I get to the ... ah ...?"

"Bedroom? I sprayed you down and then helped you walk to the bed, but before I could turn you into a lesbian, you passed out."

"Oh, I'm not saying ..."

"I'm joking."

"Oh. Of course. It's really dangerous."

"What is?"

"Champagne."

"I think that's why people drink it."

"Could we do it again?"

Carey looked surprised. "Again?"

"How about if I buy the champagne — if you promise not to drink so much?"

"Ha!"

"On Sunday, maybe?"

Clearly, I had surprised her.

"Okay."

"Great. Why don't I make dinner at my place?"

She stared at me as though trying to understand something simple. "Okay."

I exhaled as I stepped out of the trailer. I realized that without thinking I had made the next step. I felt excited and anxious at the same time. Where was I going with this? And then it occurred to me that this extraordinary human being was attracted to me. What was my problem?

***

Nathan had been unhappy with the extras we used on our first day at Convocation Hall, but I hadn't acted on his advice. According to him, they didn't resemble authentic Chileans, but conventional movie wisdom was that extras were just bodies and as long as you dressed them appropriately any stiff could fill in the background.

On Tuesday, Nathan had cornered me at the catering table. "Did you call the numbers I gave you?"

"Haven't had a chance."

"You should."

"I will."

"I spoke to one today, a priest who helps refugees," he said. "I think he was in Bosnia. A lot of the people in his church are from South America. They're really poor, and desperate. Many are Chilean."

"You want us to hire them?"

"*I* don't want anything. I'm just suggesting you use real Chileans if you want the movie to be authentic."

"Right."

"Why don't I just take you out there?"

"Sure. Let me see what I can do."

"I'm not shooting Thursday. We could go late afternoon. Do you want me to set it up?"

No wonder he was an amazing actor; he was unstoppable. "Let me ask Vlad first."

I okayed it with Vlad and László, and on the Wednesday made arrangements to drive out there. The pottery had stopped banging in my skull, so after I had seen Carey, I gathered up Nathan and Zoe, put them in the Toyota and set off. I was excited, even though I could tell that Zoe wasn't comfortable being instructed by an actor — their roles reversed — or convinced that *real* Chileans were necessary. Nathan gave me directions, and eventually we found ourselves in a suburban enclave, deep in the West End, driving past ancient, decrepit bungalows and crumbling, low-rise apartment buildings, until eventually we pulled up in front of the plain, yellow-bricked, two-storey Church of St. Clodoald of Nogent.

After Nathan's call, Father Muldoon, the Dublin-born priest, who had taught in Chile for some years, had assembled thirty-seven refugees and immigrants — Chileans as well as a few Peruvians, and a Columbian — in the church hall, poor people who seemed extremely vulnerable.

"This," Father Muldoon said, introducing us to the group, "is Sarah, Zoe and Nathan," and gestured to Nathan to make his pitch.

"Amigos," Nathan said, with the Chileans watching him warily, "we are making a movie about poor Chileans who want to share in Chile's prosperity."

"*Ellos están hacienda,* " said Father Muldoon, "*una pelicula sobre los pobres de Chile, que quieren compartir en la prosperidad de Chile.*" Baffled, the Chileans watched Nathan.

"The Chileans in our movie," Nathan said, "are demanding their rightful place in society, but they will not be making any violence."

"*Los Chilenos,*" Father Muldoon said, "*en la película exigen su lugar que le corresponde en la sociedad. No vamos a hacer ningún tipo de violencia.*"

"We need real Chileans to appear in the movie. For one day's work, we will pay..." Nathan looked at me.

"Seventy-five dollars," I said, having done the calculations in my head on the drive out.

"We will pay you each seventy-five dollars a day."

"*Necesitamos chilenos verdaderos para actuar en nuestra pelicula. Les pagan 75 dólares al dia.*"

Nathan smiled at the group, comprised mostly of men, and a few women (one with a baby), who appeared destitute and fearful but proud. No one moved. I knew that seventy-five dollars wasn't a lot, but that didn't seem to be the reason they weren't coming forward.

"Tell them," I said to Father Muldoon, "that we will also feed them."

"*Van a dar de comer a ustedes.*"

There was a murmur from the group but they remained motionless.

"*¿Por qué no lo quieren hacer?*" Father Muldoon asked.

A man, fiftyish, with a sad, sweet face, stepped forward hesitantly. "*Tenemos miedo que tales personas de Chile nos ven en la película y vendrá hacer daño a nuestras familias,*" he said. "We are afraid," he added, in halting English.

"Gracias, Antonio," Father Muldoon said, turning to us. "This is Antonio. He speaks a little English. I have asked them why they do not want to do this. He told me they are frightened. They think certain people in Chile will see them in the movie and harm will come to their families."

We stared at them, not knowing how to respond. Then Nathan said, "Amigos, we will disguise you, and some can wear masks. No one will know it is you."

Father Muldoon laughed. "*Les van a disfrazar y algunos pueden llevar máscaras. Nadie sabrá que es usted,*" he said.

"*Nadie sabrá que es nosotros,*" Antonio repeated, smiling.

Relieved, the Chileans murmured approval. Almost en masse, they all stepped forward to the table where Zoe took their names.

"*¿Puedo traer a mi perro?*" came a voice from the back of the room.

"This is Alvaro," Antonio explained. "He wants to know if he can bring his dog."

Alvaro, thin, young, the kind of young man who cries out to be mothered, looked at us woefully as did the large German Shepherd beside him. I glanced at Nathan.

"Of course," Nathan said. "Demonstrators have dogs too."

"*Los manifestantes tienen los perros también,*" Antonio said.

"Just make sure he doesn't bite the producer," I said. Alvaro looked at me then to Antonio.

"*Sólo asegúrese de no mordes al productor,*" Father Muldoon said.

All the South Americans stared at me timidly until Father Muldoon laughed. Then they all laughed.

Returning, we dropped Zoe at her condo and I drove Nathan to the theatre. Stopping out front, I said: "It's occurred to me that with the extras disguised it will be hard to tell if they're Chilean."

"You know," he said, ignoring the remark, "it might be worthwhile to hire Antonio as a voice coach. I could use help with my pronunciation and he could be useful in organizing the 'demonstrators'."

"I'll ask László."

"He'll probably think it's a needless expense."

"I'll make sure he doesn't. I thought the way you spoke to those people was amazing."

"No more amazing," he said, looking a homeless man lying in front of the theatre door, "than that guy sleeping on the sidewalk. In fact, what he's doing is more amazing. I couldn't do that. I'm just an actor, trying to live in the moment. He's forced to live in his moment 24/7, and he's better at it than I am."

"What's his secret?"

"I don't think there is one. Acceptance, maybe. He's accepted that he has no choice so he might as well be inside it."

"You're very smart."

"Not really. It's just a matter of choices. What's yours?"

"Choices?"

"He has very few choices, you have many more. Have you thought about what they are?"

"Oh yeah," I said, trying to look as though I thought about it all the time.

"Well ...?"

"Well, I might want to be a producer."

"And ...?"

I could see he wasn't impressed. "Ah ... for a long time, I wanted to be an actor."

"Why aren't you?"

"I wasn't good enough."

"That's horseshit. Everyone's an actor, just not everyone's paid to do it. Look around you. People are acting all the time. They're just not committed enough to do it on stage. If you want to be on stage, your focus has to be total. It has to be your whole life."

He got out of the car but, before closing the door said: "It's like what Rostopovich said about playing the cello. 'Play as though you have a fork in your brain.' See you tomorrow."

He closed the door and strode into the theatre. I felt as though I already had a fork in my brain — from knowing him.

***

Vlad once told me a story he'd heard about Jack Walston, the American actor who was pulled over one night by the Los Angeles Police Department. At the time, Walston was starring in LAPD, a popular cop show on TV. He'd been drinking but, because he was a cop on TV, he hoped he could skate it. When asked for his name he tried to respond clearly: "I'm Jack Walston," and added, "LAPD?" But showing no sign of recognition, the cop arrested him. At the station, the desk sergeant who booked him also didn't seem to know who he was; nor did the officer who put him into a cell with a drunk, who was sleeping it off. In middle of the night, Walston lay awake, reflecting on the vagaries of fame, and was startled when the drunk woke, sat up and stared at him.

"You're Jack Walston," he said.

"Yes," Walston cried, relieved finally to receive any recognition.

"Do you know Suzie Ann Warner?" the drunk asked, referring to an actress who had starred in B pictures in the 1950's.

"Yes?" Walston said, puzzled.

"I fucked her maid," the drunk said, and went back to sleep.

I always think of that story whenever I come up against the obsession we all have with stars — that yearning for a link to fame; our attraction to a thin veneer of lustre that shrouds an elite few, and turns the rest of us into slavish peons. Why do we seek the flimsiest of connections to the gods and goddesses of the screen (any screen these days), or to anyone in the glare of pop culture?

Why do we need to know how the battle sequence was shot, or how the special effects worked, or what star is pregnant and who's screwing whom? What is our endless fascination with an industry of illusion (and its workers) that perpetuates untruths? Do humans really thirst this much for unreality? Yes; and no one seems immune — except possibly the guy asleep on the sidewalk outside Nathan's theatre.

Even I'm susceptible. I was introduced once to a famous movie actress at a Festival party. Still ravishing at 62, she had asked me a simple, make-conversation question, like 'What do you do?' and I had blurted out my entire history in about four and half minutes. I remember her look of bafflement as I went on and on, unable to stop myself. Being next to someone I'd admired on the big screen was overwhelming — because you can reach out and touch this luminous someone, you feel you know them; and you want to ensure that they know *you*. But these celestial bodies have no reason to know us, or to be our friend. Most likely, they couldn't care less about who we are. Our tragedy is that we're still smitten.

All this was running through my head during rushes, and I kept turning to glance back at Honor in her seat under the projection booth, the flickering beam illuminating her rapt expression as she gazed up at Maddie and Guy on screen arguing about 'commie rabble.'

What was she seeing? Having watched Carey and Martin on screen for years, and now having met them in person, was she captivated by their personas, no longer concerned that we — Hardy — had altered her story; or that Carey, Nathan, and Martin were busy improvising a new one? I wondered if, like a mother forced to give up her babies — only to want to be part of their lives later — she had become fixated on these remade characters.

When rushes finished, I caught a glimpse of her dashing out. Was she still angry?

"They're still screwing with my dialogue," Hardy said, rising. The actors' improvs were adding a real tension to the scenes, but he remained concerned that the actors were doing to his work what he'd done to Honor's (except they were better at it).

"Actors give us good lines and make your lines look good," Vlad said, with a withering stare. "You should be thinking about ending."

"I'm working on it," he said, grimly.

"I'd like to speak with you," I said to Vlad.

"Maybe we need drinks," he said, noting my expression.

"I could use a drink," Hardy said.

"I'm afraid I need to speak with Vlad privately."

"What is private?" László asked.

Oh, God — the endless complications of social niceties. "It's personal," I muttered.

"Oh, personal," László said, with a slight mocking tone, as though he never bothered having a personal life. "I will take Hardy for drink."

"Good," Vlad said, "maybe you and Hardy can find ending."

László sighed as though an ending were the last thing we had to worry about.

***

Whenever I needed to clear the brush from whatever path I was on, I would take Vlad — who functioned as my consigliere — to a bar, and pose my problem. He would usually respond with a story, ending with a piece of Russian or Vladian folk wisdom that was often no guidance at all — but just talking to him somehow made the problem seem far less onerous.

Vlad's marriage to Anna (19 years) worked because Anna accepted his occasional need to frequent bars, for Vlad, who will talk to anyone about anything, relaxes completely in one, and probably has his most profound thoughts seated on a bar stool. I have no idea what he gets from me, except unconditional applause. I believe that he's the most decent and interesting human being I've ever met, someone wanting to make a better world, yet wise enough to understand that it's an impossible task but that we must try.

"So," he said, trying to get the bartender's attention, "what is deep philosophical question we need to examine?"

"Before we get to my... ah, question, I need to tell you about FLIGHT FROM DA NANG."

I told Vlad about Martin shooting the cameraman. Vlad looked pensive for a moment, then regretful. "I've been stupid," he said.

"What?"

"He told me he killed little girl."

"What?"

"It is speech from DA NANG movie. I knew I heard it somewhere."

"What does it mean?"

"I am not psychologist but I think he is mixing realities."

"Do you think he's dangerous?"

"I don't think he is having breakdown. He has no reason to — yet. And he is giving great performance. We have three more days maybe before we can wrap Consul. If we don't confront him I think there will be no problem. You agree?"

"It seems risky."

"Life is risky. Sometimes you have to risk bee sting to get honey — is old Russian saying. I don't see other choice."

"We need a plan B."

"What?"

"I don't know."

"There is no Plan B. We have crossed Rubicon."

"Rubicon?"

"When Caesar attacked Rome, once he crossed river — the Rubicon — he could not turn back. Not to worry, most movie stars are psycho. We will finish shooting."

"How can you be sure?"

"Because I am Russian. Now what is your problem?"

I wasn't reassured but he seemed adamant. "It's not *my* problem. There's a young woman I know," I said, lying.

"Do I know her?" he asked, deadpan.

"I don't think so. Anyway, she's at a point in her life where she's trying to decide if she's a certain sex or not."

"You said she was a woman."

"Okay, what I meant was which sex she wants to ... have sex with — if she wants to have sex at all."

"Having sex is okay."

"I think my friend would like to have sex."

"Okey-dokey."

"There's a woman she likes, and there's a man she's attracted to. The woman would like to be intimate with her, and she likes the woman, but the man doesn't know ..."

"... she's attracted to him. I see your problem."

"*Her* problem."

"Excuse me, *her* problem."

"So the question is, is she gay?"

"Hmmmm ... That is deep question. We will need vodka to ponder this. Two large Russian vodkas, please, standing up," said Vlad, catching the bartender's attention, then gazing off pensively. "You know that humans are always trying to make their lives exclusive."

"Exclusive?"

"Samuel Goldwyn once said: 'Include me out.' He was *excluding* himself of course with famous Goldwynism. 'Include me in' would be inclusive, meaning, anyone can join club, no exceptions. When you're exclusive, only certain people, of whom you approve, can join club; rest are *excluded*. Humans want always to make clubs and societies, so they can exclude other people."

"Why?"

"I have no idea."

"What do clubs have to do with sex?"

He held up a finger to let me know he was working it out.

"Sometimes," he said, "a club is entire country or race. In Europe, Nazis and Fascists excluded Jews. In American South, whites excluded Africans — not only that, but Nazis and whites so badly didn't want Jews and Africans to join their clubs, they committed horrible violence on them. The point is all humans want to belong to club so they can exclude other people from joining. Does it make them feel special? I don't know. Now, you know what happens to people who are excluded from club?"

I shook my head.

"They form own club, so they can exclude people. You see how a stupid idea can spread?"

"Are you going anywhere with this?"

"I'm not sure yet," he said, sipping his vodka. "Maybe for thousands of years, people who liked to have sex with their own gender were treated abominably by people who had sex like people in bible. Have you noticed you never read in bible about people having same sex — except maybe Sodom and Gomorrah — but you know people went on having same sex anyway."

"Do you think people are *born* gay?"

"No. I think people are born male and female — and hermaphrodite — and for many reasons some become attracted to their own sex. In Ancient Greece, older men pursued young men with athletic bodies, giving gifts, having lovers. In museum, you see ancient pottery with painting of older man fondling beautiful young man. In Greek culture, it was acceptable to have homosexual acts; it did not mean you did not have wife and children."

"You're saying being homosexual is an act, not a condition?"

"It is condition now. But for years it depended in society where you lived; some acts were permissible, some weren't. All stories in Bible tell of heterosexuals begetting each other. Maybe it was then — maybe people who wanted to make homosexual acts formed secret clubs to have same sex: Gay clubs, lesbian clubs, transvestite clubs — bisexual, transsexual, intersexual — every kind of sexual forming own club. You know, for long time I thought bisexual was having sex once every two weeks."

When I don't respond to Vlad's jokes, he presses on. "So this went on for two thousand years, and is still going on, but now is out in open with homosexual bars, cafes, even marriage because there are many more who join clubs."

"People don't want to be excluded."

"That too. But mostly it's business."

"Business?"

"Business loves clubs. You could be a Mason, a golfer, a gay, a Shriner, a Rotarian, a lesbian, a Republican, an Elk, a Liberal, a cowboy, a bowler, a dominatrix ... and some smiling businessman will run up, shake your hand, and try to sell you costumes and props — every club wants costumes and props so they can be noticed — which is attraction to join club, people love to dress up and act out. They love to party and parade. So, my point — if I have one — is that to join club to have sex, you have to buy costumes and props, and pay dues, when you don't have to be member and can have sex with anybody you like. And the money you save not buying costumes, props and paying dues, you can use to buy next round."

I sat there, mulling this over. "You could have just said you don't need to be gay to have gay sex."

"I wanted to explore historical background. It was more interesting, don't you think?"

I'd heard what he'd said. Why then was I so anxious? Was I afraid of making a decision? Did I need to make one? Or had I already made it?

ON THE FRIDAY, the crew moved to the Valparaíso street that Eve had built on the lot behind the studio. Behind the set, a large green screen had been erected to allow us to insert (by computer) Valparaíso's hillside slums. Even the garbage (Coke cans, candy wrappers) scattered about in front of the Chilean shop fronts added realism. Somehow, the movie story — generating its own 'authenticity' — was now out of anyone's control, Vlad having compared directing Nathan, Carey and Martin to herding orang-utans through a crosswalk. It seemed a miracle that he was holding it together and, standing in the 'street', enveloped in the movie magic, I felt hopeful again until I turned and saw Vlad gaping at me.

"What's wrong?" I said.

"Are you in scene?" he asked.

"No?"

"You can be in shot if you want but I don't think László will pay associate producer to be extra."

"Sorry," I murmured, dashing behind the camera.

Vlad was beaming. I don't think he'd ever shot such a superbly detailed set and he paused to delight in it before nodding at David.

"Lock it up, people," David said. "Picture up."

"Speed."

"Scene 12, take 1."

"Action," Vlad shouted.

Entering the street, Carey wandered toward the camera, frowning at the garbage, the aging shop fronts and the shoddy goods in the windows. Behind her, ten Chilean extras crossed back and forth, padding out the background.

Prompted by Nathan, Vlad and I had managed to convince László to allow Nathan and the Chileans to speak Spanish. It would add authenticity, we insisted, especially with subtitles. László was against subtitles (an extra expense) and wanted Nathan to speak English only. We pointed out that, if Nathan's Spanish didn't work, we could always dub it into English in post-production (another cost). He was resistant, but with Vlad and I pushing for it, he gave in. Nathan then, of course, quickly supplied the Spanish translations for the scenes with the Chileans, which brought no joy to Hardy.

He had also discovered that one of the Chileans, Felipe, muscular and mean in appearance (even his smile was ominous), could act. Felipe had been helping tutor Nathan in Spanish, which is why Nathan had suggested him as the gang leader to Vlad.

Looking up from a shop window, Maddie noticed four burly men following her. She sped up. They did as well. She walked faster, the camera following until Felipe and another Chilean man abruptly stepped out from a shop front, blocking her way, grinning at her menacingly. Realizing she was trapped, Maddie affected a look of nonchalance.

Felipe said nothing for some seconds. Carey glanced behind her at the men blocking her escape.

"*Señora, ¿has perdido tu camino?*" (Madam, did you lose your way?). Maddie remained silent.

"*Señora, ¿no habla español?* It's okay," Felipe said. "I spoke English. You give money."

"*Amigos,*" a voice said from the alleyway, "*¿ustedes tienen algo a hacer?*" (You have something to do?)

"*Vete* (Go away), *Miguel,*" Felipe said threateningly.

Nathan ambled towards the group. "*Creo que va a dejar la mujer en paz. Ella es mi huésped.*" (I think you will let the lady be. She is my guest.)

"*Ha,*" Felipe replied, "*pero ella no se conoce.*" (She does not even know you.)

"*Si,*" Miguel said, "*pero lo hará. Ahora nos perdonará quizás.*" (Yes. But she will. Now perhaps you will excuse us.)

Caught between wanting to rob Maddie and the quiet threat in Miguel's voice, the men hesitated.

"*Amigos,*" Nathan said. "*No creo que quieren hacer maldades para la revolución, ¿verdad?*" (I don't think you want to make trouble for the revolution, do you?)

"*No, no, Miguel. Buenos días.*"

The men vanished. Maddie was watching Miguel, uncertain as to whether to be grateful or apprehensive.

"You do not need to be afraid," Nathan said.

"I am not afraid."

"Good, but you should not be here."

"I am the wife of ..."

"I know who you are. Why are you here?"

"I was only observing. I want to know your country better."

"There is only poverty here, nothing you want to see. You must know that these people do not welcome the wife of an American official."

"Are you a revolutionary?"

"What you ask is dangerous."

"Why?"

"The people of Chile might think the American woman is a spy."

"Do you?"

"No, because I know who you are, and who your husband is."

"If you know so much," Carey said, "it must mean you want to be my friend."

"I am your friend. I have already prevented violence on your person."

"Is it not a Chilean custom to invite a friend for coffee?"

Carey's ad-lib stopped Nathan, momentarily. "I do not have time to drink coffee with an American woman who is at ends with herself."

"You speak interesting English. I would like to converse with a real Chilean."

Nathan sighed. "We will drink coffee, then you must leave."

"Agreed."

"Cut. Print." Vlad looked at Carey, thoughtfully. "Interesting line, Ms. Lander."

"It just came out."

"I like it. Ms. Lander's closeup, please."

Liking the 'coffee' ad-lib, Vlad decided to improvise a scene using dialogue from the book that Hardy had discarded. So after he shot Carey's closeup, the crew moved to a hastily-erected courtyard set assembled by Eve, with a rickety table under a pergola of vines, with three squawking chickens in a pen, quickly provided by Paddy Props.

An hour later, Carey and Nathan sat at the table, waiting. I was close by, with Honor's book open in my lap. Vlad was fearless. I knew that he felt that Hardy had discarded too much of the Maddie-Miguel relationship from the novel, and so he was about to let Carey and Nathan (who had now read the book) rebuild it with an improvised scene.

An old woman, conscripted from the crowd of South American extras, waited patiently near the table, holding a dented coffeepot.

"Action." Vlad nodded to the old woman who stepped forward, poured coffee into two cups and put out buns. Carey picked up one of the buns and took a bite. Nathan sipped his coffee, and looked at her. "Is the Consul's wife a good cook?"

"You know so much about me and you don't know that?"

"I am not perfect."

"Neither am I. I can't cook."

"Why did the Consul choose you as his wife?"

"Because I am beautiful, intelligent and charming," Carey said, sardonically.

"Is that all?" Nathan asked.

"Isn't that enough?"

"It's enough to get you a coffee in the poor section of Valparaíso," said Nathan, deadpan.

"What do you do, Miguel?"

"Nothing. There are no jobs. Everyone must scavenge to stay alive."

"What do you scavenge?"

"Ideas." He was off again.

Carey gazed at him. "What kind of ideas?"

He shrugged. "Crazy ones."

"Such as?"

"Such as ... children should go to school. They should not be forced to work in the fields and factories. All Chileans should have enough to eat, clean water to drink, and a place to live. The people of Chile should decide what happens in Chile, not some foreign power, or corrupt government official. But in my country many consider these ideas strange."

"Some would say they're the ideas of a communist."

"They should use care."

"Why are you not a politician?"

"Politicians with such ideas do not live long."

"You hate Americans."

"I do not hate Americans," he said, "especially when they are so beautiful and intelligent and charming."

"Whom do you hate then?"

"I hate no one. Ah, but *what* do I hate?" Nathan spat out the ad-lib. "Injustice. Corruption. Stupid money."

"Stupid money?"

"Money used to hurt people and Mother Earth."

"There will always be 'stupid' money."

"And I will always fight it."

"It is human nature. It has been with us since the beginning."

"Ah, a philosopher."

"My major at university."

"Bryn Mawr."

"How do you know so much about me?"

"It is my business to know. Now you must go."

"May I see your house?"

"Why?"

"So I will know," Carey said, manoeuvring them back to the book, "how real Chileans live."

"If you promise not to come again."

"You don't like me."

"I don't know you."

"I would still like to see where you live."

Gazing at her, considering, he shrugged.

"Cut. Print."

I hadn't realized Honor was on set until she walked up to Vlad. "Was that from my book?" she asked, tentatively.

Vlad nodded. "Yes, but I let actors improvise. Sometimes you strike vein of gold. You approve?"

"Oh, yes, it's very good," she said, staring wistfully across the sound stage at Nathan and Carey. "They're very good." As she walked off, I hoped that she was taking some pride in knowing that some of her story had been salvaged.

In the studio, the art department had created the interior of Miguel's hut, a squalid, earth-floored abode, not dissimilar to the bunkhouse in Honor's novel where Maddie visits the migrant workers.

I had begun to notice that crew members were deferential to Carey and Nathan as a couple. They did look like they fit together. Were they? Is that what was giving their scenes such intensity?

Vlad waited for stillness. "Action," he said quietly.

Nathan allowed Carey to enter first through the squeaking,

shattered wood door, Carey affecting surprise at the room's extreme poverty — bits of broken furniture, cracked windows, stained walls.

"You see now," Nathan said, "where I live."

"Yes."

"You pity me?"

"No."

"I see it in your eyes."

"I did not know."

"You did not look." That was not in the script. It was Nathan adding conflict to their relationship.

"I have *looked* now," Carey said, fiercely. "Do you think I am without compassion." Carey's retort was also improvised, and the crew, I noted, was listening intently.

Nathan led her to an alcove where a little girl, quite thin, lay still, silent, her eyes closed. "This is Iris."

"Is she ill?"

"Hepatitis."

Carey was horrified. "Has she been given medicine?"

"Only the rich have medicines."

"There must be something we can do."

"We?"

"I am your friend, Miguel. I will do what I can."

"We will see."

"I will see," Carey said emphatically. "I will go now."

She took a last piteous look at the girl, and hurried from the shack.

"Cut. Print. Excellent. Miss Lander's closeup now, please."

One set-up, and an hour later, Carey stood outside the door. Nathan sat by the little girl.

Vlad waited for David, who had stepped forward quickly to close the door, then said quietly, "Action."

At the sound of a knock, Nathan jumped up and approached the door cautiously, then flung it open. Carey, standing with a man, stared at Nathan.

"Who is he?" Nathan demanded, tensely.

"This is Dr. Marcos. May he look at your sister?"

"Why?"

"May he look?"

Nathan glanced at 'Iris' lying on the cot then, without looking at the actor playing Dr. Marcos — a Toronto Italian who played any role requiring an olive-skinned complexion, shrugged. Dr. Marcos hurried to the bedside, took out his stethoscope and examined the little girl. "It's as I suspected," he said. He opened his bag and took out a vial. "This," he said, "is a new serum for hepatitis. It is still being tested, but we have no other medicine for this strain of the disease. Have I your permission to try it?"

"Does she have a choice?" Nathan said, mordantly, staring at 'Iris'.

Dr. Marcos injected the little girl. "It will take a few hours to see if it has any effect. I will return."

"Gracias," Nathan said.

'Dr. Marcos' slipped from the abode.

"I will make maté." Nathan, having studied the biography of the revolutionary, Che Guevara, like him was consuming gallons of the Paraguayan tea.

"She will be well, Miguel."

"Of course she will," Nathan said, hopelessly.

"Cut. Print."

After lunch, Carey, holding a cracked cup, sat on a stool beside Nathan 'asleep' in his chair.

"Action."

Carey sipped from her cup, then gently took Nathan's hand, and examined it. Nathan woke. "How is she?"

"Nothing yet."

"You should not stay. You will be missed."

"It is not important."

Nathan laid his head on the back of the chair. "I wanted to go to America when I was young."

"Why didn't you?"

"I needed to pay for something else."

"Iris?"

"Is America beautiful?"

"Sometimes. Sometimes it can be ugly, like anywhere."

"It would be very beautiful if you were there," he said.

"You are one smooth-talking Romeo." Carey's ad-lib caught Nathan off-guard. I had told her about his performance in the play.

"What is 'Romeo'?"

"It is curious the English words you understand and those you do not."

Nathan nodded sadly. "Yes, they are hard to understand, even when spoken by a beautiful woman."

"This," Carey said, "is the same in English as in Spanish," and pushed his chair so it tipped and threw him to the floor. Her action was so unexpected that we were all startled, Nathan most of all. He started laughing, which caused Carey to laugh. I thought the scene had been ruined, but Carey, still in the moment, bent down and touched Nathan's cheek with her lips. Suddenly the laughing stopped. They looked at each other. Slowly, tentatively, she kissed Nathan. Nathan didn't respond.

"You don't like me," Carey said, returning to the script.

"You are married."

'Yes, and you are not." She kissed him again. He resisted for a moment then kissed her passionately.

"Cut! Print! Excellent! Thank you!"

Laughing, the crew burst into applause. Suddenly, László was there. "Vlad," he said quietly but firmly, taking him aside, "we are adding extra scene."

Vlad's brows began to converge. "What scene?"

I walked over. I had never seen László so tense. "What's the problem?"

"It is not problem. We need to see how much Maddie cares for Miguel."

I suddenly felt very weary. "Didn't we just see that?"

"László thinks we need extra scene to show this," Vlad said flatly, staring off.

"What would that be?" I asked.

He sighed, as though everyone were against him. "We need to see them having connubial relations."

"Why?" I said.

"When they have connubial relations, she is breaking marriage vow, and he is having much suffering because he is Catholic. This is giving dramatic tension to audience."

The Lászlós of this world are unremitting and will push and push forever.

"Why don't we ask them?"

"Who?"

"The actors — the ones who'll have to play it. Vlad?"

"Yes," he agreed, understanding my intent, "good idea."

László stared at me, warily. He sensed — rightly — he was being led into a trap. "Alright," he said. "We will ask opinion."

I walked over to where Carey and Nathan were waiting. "László would like to shoot another scene. Could we discuss it?"

I could see Carey's expression harden. She and Nathan followed me into the shadows beside the set.

"We need more," László said, looking at Carey and Nathan earnestly.

"More what?" Nathan asked.

"More passion."

"More?"

"When they are having connubial relations, she is breaking marriage vow, and Miguel is suffering because he is Catholic. This is what gives dramatic tension. Audience must see this."

I looked at Carey. Stone-faced, she was gazing off.

"László," Vlad said, "when you see it on big screen you will see passion."

"It is not enough," László said.

"What you're saying is that you want to see sex," Nathan said matter-of-factly, as though László were discussing the plumbing (which, in a way, he was).

"Yes."

"There is difference," Vlad said, "between passion and sex. I have passion for cinema, but I do not want to have sex with camera."

László ignored the joke. "Audience wants to see connubial relations."

"Why?" Nathan didn't sound angry, just baffled.

László — unable to exert his authority — was clearly frustrated. "So they can enjoy movie."

"László," Vlad said, "we have made two pictures together, and we have never had two actors who are passionate on screen like these two. There is so much passion going on between them, I cannot get it all in camera. There is old Russian expression: 'Do you need to buy goose eggs when you have duck?'"

"Why does everybody fight producer? You want to make movie that no one wants to watch? Audience wants to see passions."

"Body functions," explained Nathan, "are boring. Watching people ejaculate is like watching somebody take a shit. Would you want to watch a movie with two people taking a shit? I wouldn't. All the drama — all the interesting stuff — happens before and after. So why would you want to watch two people engaged in basic hydraulics?"

László stared at Nathan, bewildered. He had no idea what he was talking about.

"Humping," Nathan clarified, "is interesting only to the humper and the humpee."

"May I remind everyone" — Carey's tone was final — "that my contract specifies no nudity. Any request for nude scenes requires my express permission, which I haven't given, and will not give. End of discussion." She turned and walked back outside.

Eggs had been broken. Angry, László left, and I knew from his expression that Vlad and I had reason for concern. We were getting marvellous footage but László's obsession to insert sex could easily destroy this fragile process.

In the late afternoon, Vlad prepared to shoot Nathan and Martin's first scene together. If I'd thought with László gone, the tension would lessen, I was mistaken. When Martin finally arrived on set, he seemed on edge. "I'm a fan," said Nathan, approaching him. "I've been looking forward to working with you."

He sounded respectful but Martin, not expecting compliments from someone resembling Che Guevara, eyed him cautiously, and I noticed that Vlad, as he blocked out their movements, took care to keep them separated.

Vlad took a final look through the lens, and nodded at David.

"Lock it up, folks," David shouted. "Picture up."

"Speed."

"Scene 50, take 1."

Vlad paused, took a deep breath and exhaled. "Action," he shouted.

Martin emerged from back of one of the storefronts and, as he made his cautious approach down the street, put his hand inside his jacket, and I remembered the pistol — was he gripping it now?

Inside the 'Bobinados Bodega' café front, Carey sat at a table at the front. Nathan, beside her, glanced out the window and, seeing the Consul, stepped out to intercept him.

In Hardy's script, both were to pretend that Miguel and Maddie weren't having an affair, and the scene — with both males claiming

Maddie's devotion — would end with her going home with the Consul. At Vlad's suggestion, I had one eye on my script to see if I could connect any improvs to what Hardy had written.

Martin had entered the store front just behind Bobinados, then seconds later emerged, turned towards the bodega and noticed Nathan standing in front, waiting.

"Consul Hawthorne," Nathan said.

"Who are you?"

"I am the 'friend' of your wife."

"Where is she?"

"She's here."

"What's she doing?"

"She has come to see where the people live."

"Tell her I'm here."

"She knows."

Both actors so far were following the script. I was surprised.

"Have you spoken," Nathan asked, "with El Presidente?"

"I speak with him frequently."

"About what?"

"Topics of mutual interest," Martin ad-libbed, "like fighting communism."

"I thought it was dead."

"You know damn well it's not dead."

"Are you referring to the list?"

"What list?"

"I am not stupid, Consul Hawthorne."

"Trying to overthrow the government is stupid."

"We do not want to overthrow the government, amigo."

Martin pulled his hand from his jacket and I tensed, expecting to see the pistol, but he formed his hand into a pistol shape, and pointed it at Nathan. "I'm not your amigo, commie."

"You do not have to be my enemy."

"That's your decision."

"No, *you* decided that, when you came to my country and my people starved. Now you are angry when we Chileans call you *ladrón* — thieves — and say that you are not our friends."

"That's communist talk."

"Is it communist to want freedom to speak against oppression? Didn't Americans fight British for freedom? Does that mean Americans are communists?" Both actors had left the script and were wandering through a battlefield strewn with dead political clichés. I noticed the crew watching intently.

"We are friends of Chile. We invested in your country."

"You invested in our corrupt politicians."

"We brought you free enterprise."

"There is nothing free about free enterprise, amigo. It is paid for by the poor and by the workers."

Martin smiled, sardonically. "Where would Chile be without the Coca-Cola Company? You'd be out of work *and* thirsty."

"You think that Chileans do not know how to make sugared water? We are not stupid. We would make jobs and do what we need to do to feed all our people, not just the rich."

"Your country would die."

"It is dying already, amigo, thanks to your generosity."

Martin was stumped. "Where's my wife?"

"Cut! Print!"

Teddy, nodding at Vlad who returned the nod, began resetting the lights and camera for Martin's close-up.

"Excellent, Marty," Vlad said, walking Martin to his trailer. "You are frightening even me."

"You liked it."

"It was very good."

"It needs more, I think."

"Yes, you can add more in closeup."

The take had real tension, but would it fit into the movie? Vlad hurried back to huddle with Beverly, Hardy and me.

"Why can't they," Hardy moaned, chomping on his gum, "just say the goddamn lines?"

"Hardy," Vlad said, "usually director has to light firecracker under actors' asses to get emotion. We have so much emotion with these actors, I am not going to bridle them; but we must know if we need to explain improvs. See what story points are missing before I shoot Marty's close-up."

Sensing that Martin's clock was ticking down, Vlad was grabbing what he could with two-shots favouring Nathan and then focusing on Martin's close-up. If he could shoot at least two angles, he hoped in editing to keep the story moving.

Like boxers, Martin and Nathan had retreated to their corners, refreshed themselves and were now facing each other again for Martin's close-up. I wondered where the script would meander to this time, and noticed Martin eyeing Nathan, guardedly.

Taking a final glance at Martin, Vlad stepped away, paused, and said, "Action."

"Ah," Nathan said. "Consul Hawthorne."

"Who are you?"

"I am friends with your wife."

"Where is she?"

"She is here."

"Tell her I want to see her."

"She knows."

"Why isn't she coming out?"

"Have you spoken," Nathan asked, "with El Presidente?"

"What do you know about El Presidente?"

"I know he could do more to help the people of Chile."

"I don't speak about El Presidente to commies," Martin said, pulling out his pistol.

I almost gasped.

"Are you going to torture me or kill me, amigo?"

I realized that Nathan didn't know that the pistol Martin held was not a prop, and prayed that it wasn't loaded with real bullets.

"Americans don't torture."

"Has El Presidente told you to kill me?"

"I'm an American diplomat, not a hired assassin."

"Same thing, no?"

"Shut up. One thing I hate about commies is that they lie about America. Well, let me tell you, my little friend, America's a great country, and many brave Americans have died for it."

"Which ones?"

"What?"

"Which Americans died for their country? Poor workers or fat capitalists?"

"Shut up. You commies are always insulting America. We bring democracy to countries all over the globe and to Chile, and are you grateful? No, you steal our factories. You shout your stupid slogans and say that America's a fascist country. You're ungrateful. You oppose us with your monolithic and ruthless conspiracy. All you want is to enslave free societies, and expand your evil totalitarianism everywhere. Well, Amigo, the buck stops here."

As Martin's speech time-travelled back to the Cold War, each sentence taking him further from reality, no one moved, or seemed to breathe. I kept willing Nathan not to speak. Then Martin paused and Nathan, knowing where the scene had to end, said: "Consul Hawthorne, would you like to see your wife?"

"What?"

"Your wife, amigo, shall I tell her you're here?"

"What have you done with her?" Martin demanded.

"My sister is very sick. Your wife has been kind enough to find a doctor. All Americans should be like Mrs. Hawthorne."

Confused now, Martin's eyes darted back and forth, as though he was not longer certain of who the enemy was. "Get my wife."

"Cut! Print!" Vlad cried, then hurried over to Martin, who appeared dazed. "Marty, that was excellent."

Martin gazed at him, his expression bewildered. "Did I miss any lines?"

"Marty, I hope you are not superstitious, but I think you have Oscar in bag."

"You liked it?"

"You frightened me it was so good. You are wrapped. Now you must get rest for tomorrow."

Martin's assured manner returned. "I think we had a good day."

"We did. Marty?"

"Yeah?"

"You can put pistol away now."

"Right."

Martin put his gun back in his jacket and walked off, I rushed over to Vlad. "Well?"

"László is right. We have no choice."

"We have to do *something*."

"What? Do you want to tell Marty he is cuckoo? We must not confront him. As long as he is acting, he is not shooting anyone. You agree?"

"I don't know." I was no psychologist but even I knew that confronting people with delusions might set them off.

"I will try to shoot Marty's scenes by Monday so we can wrap him. You warn Nathan about pistol."

I went looking for Nathan and spotted him sitting with Carey on the 'bodega' steps, going through the script. Carey had her arm around him. Their intimacy and intensity was apparent. I felt my stomach lurch (I used to think that 'stomachs lurching' was a terrible cliché but my belly at that moment was lurching about like a canoe in a hurricane). I wasn't imagining it — you could see how good they were together. It was obvious that I'd have to let go. Not knowing what to do, I walked off — forgetting that I was supposed to warn Nathan.

***

That night, Honor arrived as rushes began. As the scenes of Martin and Carey played out, I glimpsed her gaping up at the screen, completely absorbed by the intensity of their performances. Vlad no longer had control of Carey, Nathan or Martin, all putting into the camera what was left of her novel, Hardy's script, and their own personalities. Maddie, Guy and Miguel had changed and so had the story and dialogue, which is why I thought Honor was entranced — I was entranced. I'd worked only on small, genre pictures where the actors spoke their lines exactly, so watching actors take command of the narrative and flesh it out was exciting, like an adventure — no, more like a revelation.

When rushes ended, I ran after her as she dashed out the door, and caught her putting on her coat in reception.

"Honor?"

She stopped and looked at me, as though expecting something ominous.

"Would you like to go for a drink?"

She seemed surprised. "Alright," she said.

In the bar, we ordered two wines and sat quietly staring at our reflections in the mirror behind the bottles. "What did you want to talk about?" she asked.

I had to choose my words carefully. "Nothing really. I know this whole movie 'thing' has probably been overwhelming for you, and I just wanted to make sure you were okay."

"You needn't worry. You can tell László I won't be suing him."

"It has nothing to do with László, although I'd like to say that I'm personally sorry that we didn't remain faithful to your novel."

"I noticed that."

"But I am curious."

"About what?"

"About the way you seem to be enthralled in the lives of three fictional, on-screen characters."

She stared thoughtfully at her reflection. "It is curious. I always become involved with the characters in my books, but I've never done *this* before. I've admired movies and been affected by stars and performances; but this one's different. I feel I know the characters so well — even though it's not my story anymore. But every night I'm caught up in Maddie's pain, Miguel's struggle, Guy's rage. What I'm seeing isn't even a movie, just bits of scenes, so how can it fascinate me? And yet, each night, I want to know — I must know — what's happening to them. I've tried not coming — obviously I have no reason to — but then I find myself in my car, driving into the city to see an hour's worth of footage. And oddly enough, when I drive home, I feel serene, relaxed — and hopeful — because I've seen them." She smiled, wistfully. "I suppose I'm like a teenybopper, without the screaming."

I didn't know what to say. Especially as that was the way I felt myself, although I had two sets of realities to deal with: being captivated by Maddie, Miguel and Guy on screen; yet caught in the real life adventures of Carey, Nathan and Martin on set. It was almost as though six people had invaded my life.

"Is that how you feel?" Honor asked.

"Yes."

"In a funny way, I find it satisfying."

"Is it?" I didn't feel satisfied. I was overwhelmed with confusion, jealousy, envy, fright, agitation and, fleetingly, hope. Life-defining moments were jostling for my attention, and I had no idea which ones needed attending to — or if I should attend to any. I went home to bed and slept badly, with images of Carey and Nathan holding tightly to each other pinging around in my brain like steel orbs in a pinball machine.

17

I WAS PHYSICALLY depleted on that bright, crisp, sunny autumn Saturday morning, driving onto the R.C. Harris Filtration Plant grounds. I'd barely slept all week and was hoping to revive on the Sunday, even though I knew I'd be spending it with Carey. The thought of seeing her again was causing me anxiety until I realized it wasn't supposed to — I mean, I *was* attracted to her. Then, just beyond the rooftops, the sparkling, tundra blue waters of Lake Ontario came into view and took my breath away. I took it as an omen — a good one — and felt hopeful again.

Why wouldn't I be? We had an hour's worth of stunning footage in the can, we were on schedule and only slightly over budget (according to Jean-Paul). We could wrap Martin on Monday after completing his four remaining scenes, and almost relax during the final eighteen days shooting Maddie, Miguel and the revolution. I knew that László would continue to try to insert "connubial relations" into the movie, but that Vlad and I could restrain his influence. And, best of all, the disapproving voices of Sister Fiona and the nuns had fallen silent, probably because I hadn't had to hire any nude actresses to simulate "flicky-flicky."

The R.C. Harris, a stunning set of elegant Art Deco buildings — having served in previous movies as a police headquarters, a prison, an asylum, a think tank, a futuristic corporate HQ, a brewery, and a centre for the criminally insane — Eve had dressed as Chile's Presidential Palace for the Cavalcade scene.

The R.C. Harris bore no resemblance to the large,

neo-Moorish pile in Santiago, the home of Chile's leader, but constructing an exterior that large would have cost as much as our entire movie; and László didn't care. Nor did he care that the Presidential Palace was 80 kilometres inland at Santiago and not at Valparaíso, overlooking the ocean — Lake Ontario standing in for the Pacific. (All week Vlad had been referring to the R.C. Harris as "El Presidente's *summer* palace"). "Only people of Chile know difference," László told Vlad, "and Chile is quarter one percent world movie market." I wasn't concerned either, it's what movies are supposed to do — alter reality.

Teddy and Vlad were getting great footage, but László appeared increasingly dour. Vlad had informed him that for the Cavalcade scene, he'd be shooting the "world's longest dolly shot" which impressed László (it gave his movie prestige), but frightened him as well. We'd hired two green screens, seventy-five extras, seven limos and additional production staff and crew to assist with the coordination, the lighting, and the two-camera setups. When Vlad suggested having a helicopter gunship roar over the procession, László gave him a Magyar stare and the helicopter gunship fell from the sky. Even without it, today's shooting would be Felicity's costliest.

Of course, we still didn't have an ending. In Honor's novel, Maddie's husband dies of a heart attack in the fields after catching Maddie and Miguel *in flagrante delicto* among the tobacco leaves. But having the Consul die of a heart attack seemed anti-climactic, especially during a revolution.

Hardy had written two: a CASABLANCA-type finale ("Here's looking at you, kid") in which Guy, having witnessed Miguel's torture, has a change of heart and tells Maddie that her work with Miguel is too important, before returning to America alone — a speech which, in his condition, Martin was unlikely to make.

Or — more of a downer — Miguel, presented with the opportunity to kill Guy, and refusing to do so. Guy then kills him, leaving Maddie kneeling in front of El Presidente's Palace with Miguel's bloody head on her lap. Hardy was keen on this ending, with a bloodbath leading up to it. Having Martin 'kill' anyone was risky (and not terribly original), so we were still searching for a suitable finish while time, as they say, was running out.

After parking, I stood admiring our ant colony as they prepped the site: the art department erecting signs in Spanish, and making final adjustments to the newly-built guardhouses, metal barricades, and piles of sandbags; the grips laying dolly track beside the main building; and Teddy setting lights with his gaffer and sparkies, and placing the cameras with his operator and loader. I was starting to feel revved again when my cell rang.

"Yes, Martin."

"Come right away."

"Where are you?"

"Here." He hung up.

Looking around, I saw him peer out from behind his trailer door, and beckon to me.

Quickly I walked over and stepped inside. It *was* a shabby trailer, with a bed, a miniature toilet, a tiny kitchen and a dining table on which sat his laptop, wired to the telescope now pointed through the window at the lake.

"Good morning, Martin, it's a beautiful day."

Martin didn't respond. Sitting at the table, he seemed older and more tightly-wound than usual. He hadn't been to makeup yet. Carefully, he lifted the faded curtain with his finger.

"Who are they?"

"Who?"

"Those people."

"Which people?" I looked through the window to where he was pointing. He was indicating the extras. "You mean those people?"

"Yeah."

"They're extras."

"I know they're extras," he said, curtly. "Where're they from?"

"Chile mostly."

"You're sure?"

"Yes."

"How do you know?"

"I went to their church. Why?"

"They're all from Chile?"

"Most are. Some are from Columbia and Peru."

"No Somalis?"

"No."

'What do you know about them?"

I shrugged. "Not much. Most are having difficulty settling in to their new country."

"Did you run a check?"

"A check?"

"A security check."

"We don't run security checks on extras."

"You don't?"

"No."

"I see."

Silently, he stared out the window.

"We could run a check I suppose," I said, making it up, "if you're anxious about them."

"Don't say I'm anxious. I'm not anxious. What about the dog?"

"What dog?"

Martin pointed at Alvaro's German Shepherd sitting on its haunches beside Alvaro near the catering table. The dog was staring at the trailer. "That dog."

"What about it?" I asked.

"It's been watching the trailer for the last hour."

"Watching the trailer?" I remembered his story about the coyote with the camera implant.

"Yes."

"It belongs to one of the extras. I can have someone remove it if it's bothering you."

"Don't say it's bothering me. It's not bothering me. It's a guard dog?"

"No, just a pet, I think."

"From Chile?"

"I don't know, I think so."

"Find out."

"Of course."

Silence. We gazed out the window. Then quietly he said: "I'm not afraid to die."

I didn't know what to say. He was showing me a vulnerability I hadn't seen. "I know that," I said.

He didn't move, his eyes fixed on the extras.

"But if you were," I offered, tentatively, "that would be okay. I mean, everybody is, even me." I felt stupid saying it, but I wanted to comfort him somehow.

He stared out the window, motionless, as though I weren't there. I stood waiting until I realized I'd been dismissed.

"I'll check on the dog then," I said. "If you need anything else, just call me." As I left, he was still staring out the window.

I found Vlad at lake's edge, leaning on the guardrail, watching the crew lay the dolly track.

"I've just seen Martin."

Vlad cocked an eye at me.

"He seemed worried about the extras. Then he said: 'I'm not afraid to die.' What do you think he meant?"

Vlad's eyes lit with recognition. "How did he say it?"

"How? Quietly."

He nodded. "It's from DA NANG."

"What?"

"It's just before Marty attack Viet Cong."

"Really?" I was trying to understand the extent of his delusion.

"You think maybe," said Vlad, "he is thinking he is going to attack Viet Cong?"

"I don't know. What should we do?"

Vlad shrugged. "I am open to ideas."

"He needs help."

"Do *you* want to tell him?"

I could see his point. Until Martin acknowledged he had a problem, he had no problem, as far as he was concerned.

"I suggest we try to finish before he does. Not to worry," said Vlad, noting my concern. "It is why we make movies — for unbearable excitement. I have asked David — if we wrap Cavalcade early — to have Consul interrogation scene on standby, so we will have only two scenes to shoot on Monday: meeting with El Presidente, and ending — whatever that is. Then Marty will go back to Hollywood. So you see, pas de problem." He smiled, and squeezed my shoulder reassuringly.

I found Alvaro near the costume truck, where Nadia and two assistants were fitting the extras with accessories.

"Alvaro?"

Alvaro was alarmed until he saw it was me — why did the extras always seem so fearful? Then I remembered that they were from a country which had suffered under military rule.

"What's your dog's name?" I said slowly. Alvaro looked puzzled. I pointed at him and said, "Ah, your name ... Alvaro." I waved my finger at the dog. "Ah ... dog ... chien? Name ...?"

"*Ah, si,*" Alvaro said, "dog ... name Che."

"Che?" I repeated. I tried to imagine Martin's reaction to a dog named Che. "Signor Gage has problem ... oh what's the word ... Antonio, can you help?" Antonio had stepped out from the costume truck. "Please explain to Alvaro that Mr. Gage is allergic to dogs."

"*Ah, si. Alvaro, Gage señor es alérgica al perro.*"

"Ask him please to keep Che away from Mr. Gage."

"*Si. Puedes por favor, tenga Che lejos de Gage señor.*"

"*Si* ... okay," Alvaro said.

I went looking for David to check in with him, passing a group of extras dressed as Chilean army personnel near the two ancient army trucks in the parking lot. Nearby, Nathan and Antonio were drilling the 'revolutionaries' and 'students,' shouting out Spanish slogans beneath the green screen erected on the mound onto which we would digitally insert Valparaíso's shanty town.

Nathan's voice rang out above the noise of the movie set: "*¡Hasta la victoria siempre!*" (Until victory always!). Antonio had been with us just two days, but Nathan's Spanish accent sounded, to my ears, quite real.

"*Hasta la victoria siempre,*" repeated the extras enthusiastically.

"*¡No pasaran!*" (They shall not pass) he shouted to another group.

"*¡No pasaran!*" they repeated loudly.

"*Venceremos,*" he shouted to a third group. "We will overcome."

"*¡Venceremos!*" shouted the extras, wildly. "*¡Venceremos!*"

While I had been searching for David, László, accompanied by a young, nubile, strawberry blonde dressed in faded army fatigues, her open shirt flashing mounds of cleavage, had approached Nathan.

"*Buenos días,*" Nathan said.

Startled, László said, "What?"

"*Buenos días, amigo,*" Nathan said.

"Nathan, this is Samantha. She is revolutionary who is in love with Miguel."

"What page is that on?"

"It is re-write."

"Where are the new pages?"

"They are coming. Meantime, you will show Samantha how to act... like revolutionary." László smiled at her and walked off.

Nathan gazed at Samantha. She was staring at him with gawky blue eyes. She didn't look like a revolutionary, or even Chilean, more like a Playboy centrefold. "What do you want me to do?" she asked.

"Shout. You are angry at El Presidente."

"Who?"

"The President of Chile."

"Why am I angry?"

"He is corrupt."

"What do I say?"

"Antonio? Can you help me?" Nathan was trying to avoid staring at Samantha's cleavage which, he realized, was being keenly admired by all the Chilean men. "Just repeat after Antonio, in Spanish."

"Spanish?"

"Yes, the language of Chile."

"I don't know that."

"Antonio will teach you. Just repeat what he says."

"Okay."

"*¡Obrer!*" Antonio shouted. "*¡Campesinos! Estudiantes! Preparemos para la victoria!*" (Workers! Peasants! Students! Prepare for victory!)

"*¡Obrer!*" shouted Nathan and all the extras. "*¡Campesinos! Estudiantes! Preparemos para la victoria!*"

"Order," Samantha shouted. "Campers-all you aunties ... ah ..."

"*¡Preparemos,*" Antonio said, "*para la victoria!*"

"Pair a moose, pair a victoria!"

Nathan was wondering where in the crowd he might hide Samantha when he saw Vlad gesture to him.

"Wait here a moment," he said to Samantha, and rushed over to Vlad.

"We have problem," Vlad said.

"*¿Qué problema, amigo?*" asked Nathan.

"Producer is nervous. Distributor wants sexy movie, otherwise he will not commit. But we cannot put sex in movie because author of book has contract with no sex, and leading lady has contract with no nudity, so producer is thinking he will not get financing. I work with László before. He is okay guy, but is obsessed always to make shots of women's breasts and flicky-flicky-bang-bang because he thinks this is how to sell movie. This is best film I ever make because I am working with three fine actors — one of whom is whack-fuck star. Did Sarah mention pistol he carries is his?"

"Are you serious?"

"Yes, I would suggest you not disturb his thinking."

"The one he had yesterday?"

Vlad nodded.

"Was it loaded?"

"We don't know."

"Well, find out. I'm not working with a loaded gun. I don't fuck with ordnance."

"We don't know for certain if gun is loaded."

"Why don't you ask him?"

"What will he tell me?" Vlad said. "'Yes'?"

"You could take his gun away."

"*You* could ask him for gun."

"It's the *director's* responsibility to ensure that all the actors are safe." Nathan's expression was implacable.

"Of course," Vlad said. "You are right. I will ask. Now to problem. To finish picture we need to calm producer who wants leading man — that is you — to make sexy scene with Samantha who is going to undress and embrace leading actor — which is also you. Now I know you will not want to do this ..."

"What do you mean by 'sexy'?"

"To have some ... groping with her."

"Just groping?"

"Unless you want to make penetration. I don't think producer will object."

"No, no, no. We shouldn't even be groping. It has nothing to do with the story."

"It has everything to do with story. We have to calm producer if we want to finish picture *we* want to make. So I suggest we shoot scene but maybe Teddy's lighting is too dark; or maybe angle we shoot is not good, or maybe you go crazy and we have to cut scene from picture. But we need to shoot it to keep producer sweet — unless you have better idea."

"Go crazy?"

"Imagine you are like, ah ... giant steam engine."

Nathan stared at Vlad. "You want me to play the scene like a steam engine?"

"No, like actor imagining he is giant steam engine."

"You give interesting direction."

"I know. At Leningrad Film Academy I spend two years shooting tractors. By the by, László will be 'directing' so you must be convincing. This is strictly *entre nous*. No one else must know."

Still searching for David, I wandered by the trucks a second time, and recognized Samantha who was being admired by the male extras. László had cast her in KISS MY ASP as the stripper who dies from snakebite at the end with the camera lingering on her nude body under the credits, so I knew he was up to something.

I found Nathan sitting on the rise. Eve Guiliani was standing nearby, smoking and eyeing him.

"What's up?" I asked.

"I'm about to do my first 'sex' scene," he said with no emotion.

Something fluttered and died inside me. "What?"

"I'm about to do my first 'sex' scene."

"What sex scene?"

"It's a rewrite."

"There is no re-write."

My tone was emphatic and Eve, taking a drag on her cigarette, glanced at me with a look of pity.

"It's alright," Nathan said. "She's not hard to look at, so it might even be fun."

"Who?" I asked, even though I already knew.

"Samantha."

"Fun? Fun?" I looked closely at his expression. It was deadpan. Was he putting me on?

"I think," said Eve, in her heavily Italian-accented English, gazing at Nathan, "for your first time you should have someone older." Her face remained expressionless but I could see her eyes telegraphing him invites.

"I'll be okay. If either of you'd like to watch, ask Vlad. It's okay by me."

"I'm not a watcher," Eve said, meaningfully.

I didn't know that Vlad had talked to Nathan so I was astonished. "Why would I want to watch? I can't believe this doesn't upset you."

"Why would it?"

I stared at the little shit, angry for having misjudged him. Obviously, he was no different than other men — I had created a fantasy Nathan. I didn't know who was making me angrier: Nathan, for destroying my illusions of him; or László, for sneaking a stupid sex scene into the movie I'd worked so hard to keep pure. "Well, if you don't know, I certainly don't," I said.

I went to find Vlad. He was watching Teddy film silent hand-held shots of Samantha joking with the 'revolutionary' extras by the trucks. László was standing on the back of one of the trucks, directing. "All revolutionaries are all wanting to have you, but you are telling them that you are Miguel's woman."

Samantha pouted and giggled, playfully chastising the Chilean men. I fought hard to keep from yelling, or worse; yet there was nothing I could do to keep our elegant movie from mutating into another Felicity "flicky-flicky-bang-bang". I stared angrily at Vlad who was pointedly ignoring me.

"Alright, now we shoot scene with Miguel," said László, extending a hand to Samantha.

The Chilean men rushed forward to lift her up into the back of the truck while László continued giving her 'direction'. "Miguel is strong leader. You are hungry for him. It is not healthy to be thinking always of revolution, so you must give yourself to him to save Chile."

Our camera operator, Gundar, was sitting in the back of the truck on a grip box. Strapped into his Steadicam harness, the camera resting on his lap, he waited patiently for László to finish. How many times, I wondered, had Gundar watched László direct starlets?

"You take Miguel by hand," said László demonstrating, "and pull him into truck. He wants to think about revolution, but you want him so badly you tear off pants and shirt."

"When do I take my clothes off?"

"When you are taking his off."

"How can I do both?"

"You are *crazy* with desire. Remember," László said, "he is strong revolutionary, so you must fight like tiger to make him stop having revolution to have you."

I strode down to the lake. Why was Nathan doing it? I'd believed in him, in his integrity. I stared out over the water, angry, helpless, staring vacantly at a speedboat anchored just offshore with Salmo on the back deck. I was so upset that it didn't register.

I could hear Vlad and the crew start the take.

"Lock it up, please," David shouted from the back of the truck. "Picture up."

"Speed."

"Scene 127a, Take 1."

"Action," Vlad said.

Minutes went by. I tried not to imagine what Samantha was doing to him. Then I heard loud moaning coming from under the truck's canvas cover. Nathan?

Turning, I saw members of the crew gathered by the tailgate, listening. The moaning grew louder.

Later, Vlad told me what had happened. When Samantha pulled

Nathan into the back of the truck and began to undress, touch and 'arouse' him, he started 'lusting' after her. He moaned as she began to remove his shirt; then, breathing heavily (like a steam engine, Vlad said) started groping her. Vlad, who was keeping one eye on the lovers and one on László, said that László, nodding encouragingly, kept motioning to Samantha to intensify her 'lovemaking.'

Nathan increased his puffing, pawing Samantha as she tried to remove his shirt. As Nathan's groping (which, Vlad said, bore no resemblance to 'arousing') became more intense, he began grunting, wheezing, and whimpering. Samantha, unsure now of who — or what — she was trying to seduce, bravely tried to remove his trousers, which was when he started licking her. Alarmed, she stepped back, glancing helplessly at László who, waving his hands, signalled her to intensify her 'passions.' Again, she reached out and tried to caress Nathan who was salivating over her. He pulled her to the floor — she was now resisting — and began to lick her face. He cried out: "Lamerme, lamerme" — and when she stopped moving, he growled: "Lick me, lick me." Panicking, Samantha tried to push him away while, László waved his hands and cried out: "Kiss him, kiss him!" But she only pushed harder, and began to cry.

Realizing he'd gone too far, Nathan stopped, staring helplessly at Samantha who, sobbing, had rolled up into a foetal ball on the floor of the truck. Vlad saw Nathan look up at him and remember, too late, that their ruse was secret. Glancing at László, Vlad saw that he had caught the look.

After Vlad said: "Cut," Nathan knelt beside Samantha and whispered: "It's alright, it's alright, it's only a movie." By stroking her hair; he calmed her and slowly helped her up, putting her shirt back on. Tenderly, he hugged her — Vlad was surprised she let him. Possibly she was so distressed that any comfort was welcome.

Looking up, Vlad saw László gaping at him — he had guessed what had happened. And that's when I saw László climb down from the truck and stalk off.

I hurried back. Mac was helping the Steadicam operator down from the truck as Nathan and Samantha dressed. I found Vlad instructing Teddy. When Teddy went off, Vlad said quietly, "Sometimes when I am clever, I am too stupid. You would think I would know this by now."

"What?"

"You cannot take away a man's dignity."

"László?"

"I forget he is *not* stupid man. I have gone too far. He will not forgive this."

"What?"

"I tell you later. You know where he went?"

"Try his car."

Vlad found the Mercedes parked at the end of the cavernous space between the buildings. As he told me later, it was a long walk to the car, knowing that László was watching him make every step. Reaching it, he opened the rear door. László was on his cell, and as Vlad slid into the back seat, he barely glanced at him.

"So what are you offering, Jeremy? Right. Let's make it 2½, I know you will make profit on that. I will come to New York with test print and we will talk about release. We will have to do something different, more classy. No, Jeremy, we can do it. Send me agreement so I can finalize with Simon. Bye."

László closed his cell. Vlad noted that he didn't seem angry. What was he thinking? Usually he could read László but at the moment he was inscrutable.

"Vlad," László said after a pause, "I have made new deal with Jeremy. He will put up less money for picture without sex. We will have to cut scenes and reduce salaries to complete picture, but I think we will finish. No one wants to see sex in movie — not author, Sarah or you or actors, so I think maybe God is talking to me. I decide we do it your way, and hope that picture is strong to sell without sex. But, I am sorry to say after SMOKE PICKERS we will not require your services."

Knowing he had no possible response, Vlad remained silent.

"You are talented man, and I have enjoyed working with you. I know you will have much success."

At that moment, Brahms' Hungarian Dance No. Five blared out from László's cell. I was on the other end, informing him that Vlad was required for the next scene. "He is coming now," László said and hung up.

Humbled, Vlad managed to say, "László, I ... I want to thank you for opportunity to work with you, and for all your kindnesses to Anna and to me."

"Give her my regard, and look after her."

Vlad stepped out of the Mercedes and, stunned, wandered down to the lake. He stood at the railing, staring out at the horizon as the crew finished setting the lights. All the neurochemicals in the synaptic pathways of his brain were flooding his neurons as he tried to make sense of this sudden swerve in his existence. He was so distressed that seeing Bruce on the speedboat anchored just off the jetty didn't register.

Glancing back at the set, Vlad noticed Martin striding over to him.

"Vlad, we need to talk."

"Yes, Marty."

"You lied to me, Vlad."

Vlad gazed off. "It's possible. Sometimes I tell truth and sometimes lies. It's hard for me to keep straight."

"You *were* a member of the Communist Party."

"What?"

"You were a member of the Communist Party."

"Yes."

"Yes?"

"How you know this?"

"I ran a check."

"You investigated me?"

"I run a check on everyone."

"Why?"

"Why?" Martin looked perplexed.

"Why?"

"For security."

"Ah. So what you learn from check?"

"You lied to me."

"No, Marty. I did not lie. You asked was I communist and I said no, and I wasn't; but I was member of Communist Party."

"What's the difference?"

"Marty, I thought you were smart but now you act dumb. Do you not know why people joined Communist Party?"

Martin looked uneasy. "Why?" he asked.

"To eat, Marty, to eat. You are American. Americans have always plenty to eat, but if you were born in Soviet Union, and you were not in Party, you were born hungry; so if you wanted to eat, you joined Communist Party. If I had not joined Communist Party, I would not have gone to Leningrad Film Academy and would not be here today to direct famous movie star in Oscar-nominated role."

Martin looked confused. "Only nominated?"

Vlad suddenly recognized the man on the boat. "Marty, is that Bruce on boat?"

"Yes."

"What is Bruce doing on boat?"

"That's my boat."

"What you need boat for?"

Martin pointed across the lake. "Do you know what that is?"

"Lake."

"Beyond the lake."

"Other side of lake."

"Not just the other side, Vlad, that's New York State."

"I know that."

"That's America, and this body of water is all that stands between freedom and totalitarianism."

"What kind 'ism'?"

"Totalitarianism."

"Marty, that word is too big for me. What you trying to say?"

"That lake is an unguarded border."

"So?"

"So, anyone could sneak into America."

"Who Marty, who?"

"Somalis, Vlad. Mexican wetbacks, radical Muslims with explosives up their gauchies, Iranians with nuclear devices, Iraqi bombers, Afghans, Uzbekistanis, Syrians, Nicaraguans, Guatemalans, Cubans, North Koreans, the Burmese, the Chinese — do you know there's almost a billion commies in China? — America's enemies, Vlad, that's who; desperate people who'll stop at nothing to infiltrate our way of life. Do you think a lake is going to stop them?"

"And you are going to stop them with boat?" Irritated, Vlad forced himself to remember that Marty had a gun. Did he have it on him now?

"Have you forgotten Dunkirk?" Martin asked.

"What about it?"

"It all started with one boat."

"Ah." Trying to visualize Martin Gage standing on the prow of his speedboat, pistol in hand, cruising out into Lake Ontario, leading a flotilla of tiny boats to guard America, made Vlad laugh which he covered with a cough.

"I'm sorry I called you a communist," Martin said.

"It's not worst I been called." Vlad knew he'd been taking out his self-anger on someone who was delusional. He forced himself to remember that he admired Martin. He needed to like him — having misjudged László, he didn't want to risk setting Marty off. His only objective now was to complete his 'quality' movie. It was his only hope. "You are ready for next shot?"

"I'm always ready, Vlad."

"Good. This is important, Marty. It is big scene leading to ending which we need to get right. We are small company and cannot afford to spend days making coverage."

"Gotcha."

"So we need to make strong, clean master shot."

"I got it."

"May I give you direction now?"

"Hit me."

"First, is no need for pistol."

Martin's eyes betrayed a slight apprehension. "No gun?"

"No. Consul is not coming to *rescue* El Presidente, he is only coming to *speak* to him. Demonstrators do not have weapons, they are only ... demonstrating. But most important, Consul does not want to *show* pistol to demonstrators, and do you know why?"

Anxiously, Martin's eyes flitted across the horizon as his mind searched for the answer. "Why?"

"Because he is Vince Brody, and pistol is secret."

"Right. That's sharp, Vlad. What do I do?"

"You stare at demonstrators. You have scorn in your eyes, but you are also dignified Consul, representative of United States of America. You know America wants to be Chile's friend, so you do not want to hurt demonstrators; they are only angry and misguided. I was raised in Soviet Union; and I can tell you these are not real communists."

"Not real communists?" Martin repeated, trying to understand.

"No, they are only poor people who want to have decent life like Americans."

"Then why do they make trouble?"

"They do not 'make trouble,' Marty. In your Constitution, people have right of assembly, do they not? Is it not American to demonstrate?"

Martin was hesitant. "Sometimes ..."

"You, being American, sympathize with demonstrators who are protesting."

"I do?"

"Well, they are only expressing their desire for freedom; isn't that American?"

"None of them are wetbacks?"

"No, if you were Chilean wetback you would have to swim to China."

"Somalis?" Martin's eyes were now vigorously scanning the crowd of extras.

"No," Vlad said, desperately praying that Martin was absorbing this.

"Then who's the enemy?"

"We are." As soon as he'd said it, Vlad knew he'd made a mistake. His quip was too subtle, too sardonic for his star to grasp — in Martin's world there were only heroes and villains.

"Are you saying America's the enemy?" Martin's expression had hardened.

"No, Marty. What I am saying is that we must not think people are enemies when they are only crying out for freedom to feed their families."

It was too late. Vlad had lost him.

"Freedom's a tricky thing, Vlad. The commies used to say they were free."

"I know. I was there. They lied."

"That's why we have to be careful. We can't let our guard down. The commies have probably infiltrated the demonstrators."

"No, Marty, we had security check."

"By who?"

"I can't tell you that."

"I have the highest clearance."

"I still can't tell you."

Martin stared at Vlad. His look of trust had vanished, replaced by a cold wariness. "It's okay, Vlad. I know how to handle this."

Watching Martin walk back to his trailer, Vlad knew that he had just lit a fuse. How was Marty going to "handle this"? What could he do?

He could fire his gun, that's what he could do. So what should he, Vlad, do? Stop the shoot? What reason would he give? He couldn't ask Jean-Paul to write: 'Shooting stopped, leading man delusional' on the production report. László wouldn't allow it, and they would think Vlad was crazy. Too much was riding on completing the picture. Stopping production would not only bankrupt Felicity, but almost certainly ignite Marty who was clearly psychologically unstable, believing on some level that he *was* the American Consul. So there was no way of knowing what might happen if they tried to stop him from 'saving Chile' — undoubtedly, it would set him off. Nor could Vlad imagine trying to disarm him.

On the other hand, there was nothing in the Cavalcade shot to provoke Martin. It was only a drive-up. Martin had no lines; all he had to do was arrive in the limo, get out with Carey and walk into the building. It could be done in one take. Simple. Marty could do that — he was a star, and walking into buildings was what stars did best. Nathan would be in the crowd, behind the barricades, some distance away.

It was the scene following, with the Consul 'observing' the two soldiers interrogate Miguel in secret that might be a problem. How could he keep Marty and Nathan separate on set? He couldn't; so there would be less risk if, after shooting the scene with El Presidente and the ending (whatever that was going to be), it was Martin's final scene. He would ask David to reschedule the interrogation scene for late Monday, and ask Hardy to write an ending that would cushion Martin's delusion.

"David," he said quietly, into his walkie-talkie. "Find Hardy. Ask him to stand by. I need to speak to him and you after shot."

Then he made his way to the camera.

***

By 3:00 o'clock, Vlad had rehearsed the camera and car moves with the stand-ins, and was ready to shoot. The actors, the crew, and the extras were in position, waiting silently, expectantly. David stilled the set with his bullhorn and, watching Vlad, waited for his signal. Vlad took a last look at the setup and nodded.

"Lock it up, everyone," David bellowed through the bullhorn. "Picture up."

"Speed."

"Scene 101, take 1." Mac's voice echoed against the building.

Vlad paused, then shouted: "Action."

"Start Cavalcade," David whispered into his walkie-talkie.

Vlad was shooting on a long lens, so the black limos, advancing down the hill, immense and menacing, American flags fluttering on their front fenders, filled the screen. Magisterially, they rounded the curve, and headed for the main building. Reaching it, the camera began to dolly alongside the second limo, close on Martin who gazed out his window, his expression set in stone. Vlad told me later it was the most exciting shot of his career.

Finally, the Cavalcade reached the far corner of the building and turned into the parking lot. As it drew near the entrance, throngs of chanting demonstrators — the Chilean refugees, led by Nathan, some with bandanas pulled up over their faces — shouted and surged against the barricades, while 'army' personnel banged on the barricades with their riot sticks.

"*¡Hasta la victoria siempre!*" Nathan shouted.

"*¡Hasta la victoria siempre!*" repeated the extras.

"*¡No pasaran!*"

"*¡No pasaran!*" they repeated.

"*Venceremos.*"

"*Venceremos,*" shouted the extras, enthusiastically. "*¡Venceremos!*"

"*¡Obrer!*" Nathan shouted. "*¡Campesinos! Estudiantes! Preparemos para la victoria!*" "*¡Obrer!*" shouted the extras. "*¡Campesinos! Estudiantes! Preparemos para la victoria!*"

The Cavalcade stopped near the building and four soldiers stepped to the second limo to escort Carey and Martin to the entrance. The driver opened the rear door and slowly Martin got out, stared at the building, then dramatically turned and faced the crowd. With his stony gaze fixed on the extras, the chanting died out. Silence. No one moved.

Vlad told me later that this was the moment he knew "it was all going to go for shit."

Martin gazed at the 'demonstrators' fearlessly. "Amigos," he said loudly, breaking the silence, and I knew at once that his delusion had taken charge. Vlad, beside the camera, muttered: "Marty, shut up and go inside," as though he could will him to walk into the building. But Martin remained motionless, a lone man valorously facing the crowd.

"America is your friend," Martin announced, breaking the silence. "I have come to fight for your freedom. I will speak to El Presidente and let him know how much Americans want the people of Chile to be free."

"Chileans want to eat," Nathan shouted, stepping forward.

I stopped breathing. Nathan, shut up. I was ten feet behind the camera and noticed Vlad trying to catch his attention.

"People of Chile," Martin cried, "you have been infiltrated by communists."

"Chileans want jobs," Nathan shouted, as the extras chanted: "*¡Venceremos. ¡Obrer! Campesinos! Estudiantes! Preparemos para la victoria!*"

"Chileans want education," Nathan yelled.

Martin pulled his gun from inside his jacket. "Arrest the communists!" he shouted. The extras stopped chanting.

Seeing the gun paralyzed me. I knew then that it would go off and someone would get hurt — or killed. But Martin held the gun at his side.

"*¡Hasta la victoria siempre!*" Nathan shouted.

"*¡Hasta la victoria siempre!*" Haltingly, the chanting started up again.

Observing Martin's eyes fixed upon him, Nathan suddenly understood that something wasn't right at the same moment that Martin raised the gun slightly and fired into the ground to quell the chanting. It sounded like a bullet ricocheting. The chanting stopped.

I could see Nathan glancing at Vlad now. But Vlad was watching

Martin who, behind the limo, gripped Carey's arm with one hand, waved the gun with the other, and shouted to the soldiers: "Move to the barricades!"

Vlad gestured at Nathan, pointing frantically at the ground. Nathan understood, and quickly pulled down his mask, motioning with his hands: "Amigos, sit. Lay down your signs and sit! Sit!"

"*Establecen los signos, sentarse,*" Antonio shouted, waving at everyone to sit. "*Establecen los signos. Sentarse, sentarse.*"

The extras, gazing at Nathan and then at Martin, slowly sat on the ground. Martin, backed by the four 'soldiers,' had stopped and was staring at Nathan and the extras. Glancing at Vlad, I was astonished to see the camera still running. He explained later that he didn't know what else to do. He was hoping the tension would de-escalate so that when he did yell 'cut' Marty's delusion would evaporate.

Martin took Carey's hand and, pointing the gun at Nathan, led her forward, past the barricade, picking a path through the extras sitting on the pavement who hurriedly shuffled aside for him.

"Amigos," said Martin, loudly, as he made his way to Nathan, "you are good friends to America. We will not forget your courage, or your fight for freedom."

Puzzled and uneasy, the extras kept their eyes on Martin, sensing that something unplanned — possibly dangerous — was happening. Triumphantly, Martin stepped up to Nathan.

"Do I shoot him now, Maddie?" he asked Carey.

"No Guy," she said, watching him carefully. Surprisingly, she seemed composed.

"You'll stand by me?"

"I've always stood by you ... even when you thought I wasn't."

Martin paused, keeping his eyes on Nathan. "What about that Cuban in Panama?"

I was stupefied. What movie was that from? I was behind the camera, ten feet away from Carey, but I could see wonderment cross her expression. Later she told me that, in that instant of improvised insanity, she felt as though she and Martin were children, crawling into a balloon basket, which floated lazily up into the sky. "What about your Puerto Rican secretary?" she asked.

Martin glanced at her. "None of that matters now, Maddie. It's always been you. You know that."

Carey hoped to distract Martin, even though the overzealous gleam in his eyes was ominous. But before she could respond, he took hold of his delusion again (it was *his* after all), his voice booming out, "Amigos, I will take this communist to America to be tried for crimes against the Chilean people."

Watching intently, Vlad struggled to determine when to yell 'cut,' his hands steepled together as though praying.

"Chile," Martin shouted, "is free again! Long live Chile!"

Silence.

"Chile," Martin repeated, louder, "is free again! Long live Chile!"

A few extras murmured, "Long live Chile!"

"Cut," yelled Vlad.

"Long live Chile," Martin urged, even louder.

"Long live Chile," Nathan shouted, hope to defuse the tension.

"Long live Chile," shouted the extras.

"Long live Chile," Nathan shouted again.

"Shut up," Martin yelled, prodding Nathan toward the jetty with his pistol. "Move."

"Cut," Vlad cried.

My heart wasn't beating — it was shouting. I understood now what the boat was for. Escape — and he was taking Nathan. But to where? Without thinking, I rushed past the camera and pushed my way through the extras.

"Cut, cut, print!" Vlad bellowed.

Martin wasn't listening. With one hand griping Carey's arm, he nudged Nathan forward with the barrel of the pistol.

"Martin!" I yelled, hurrying to catch them. He stopped, pointed the gun at me, warily watching my approach. I had no idea what I would do and, without thinking, took out my cell and handed it to him. "You'll need clearance. 416-973-6436."

Martin stopped, his eyes searching my expression, and said: "I *have* clearance."

I have no idea where it came from, but I heard myself saying: "You know the password?"

His eyes flickered. He was working it out. "You dial it."

I noticed Carey and Nathan gaping at me. As I was dialling, in the midst of my fear (and adrenalin rush), it did occur to me that he could shoot *me* (which, oddly enough, wasn't frightening). What was more amazing, at that moment, was that I was thinking how good my improv was — how supercilious is the human brain?

"Who're you calling?" Martin demanded.

"RCMP."

"RCMP?"

"Our FBI."

It started ringing, and I held out the phone to Martin. Taking it carefully, he put it to his ear. "That's not it," he said, suspiciously.

"Are you getting a recorded message?"

"Yeah."

"Does it say Telefilm Canada?"

"Yeah."

"That's the right number. It's a front. Wait for the prompt."

"What?"

"'Special projects' or Micheline Duras."

"Who's she?"

"Chief of Counter-intelligence." Wow! How did I think of that?

"A woman?"

"Why not? Would you suspect a woman of being chief spymaster? What're you hearing?"

"Nothing."

"Press zero."

Martin didn't answer. He was listening intently — still with his gun on Nathan, his eyes constantly scanning the crowd. I knew that, when he moved his gun hand to press zero, I would have one chance to grab the gun — no, not the gun, his arm. If I could push his arm away, it would deflect the gun from Nathan. After that I had no idea what would happen. It was daring, but what choice did I have? Maybe luck would be with me and I'd knock it from his hand.

Carey was watching me intently. She knew I was up to something, but what? It was madness but I didn't know what else to do. Martin was wholly inside his delusion, and wouldn't be returning to the real world any time soon.

In the silence, I was aware of someone sobbing, "*¿Por qué?*" We all heard it. Looking around I saw Alvaro, walking though the crowd, carrying Che, limp in his arms, crying, "*¿Por qué? Por qué mataste a mi perro?*" I didn't realize then that he was lamenting, "Why? Why did you kill my dog ?"

Distracted, Martin stared at him, confused, and at that moment, I dove at his wrist, grabbing it with both hands and pushing downward, praying that, if the gun went off, it would fire into the ground. The gun did go off, and I felt a searing pain in my left leg. "Yeeeooow-wwwwww!" I cried, clinging tightly to his arm.

The sharp crack of the gun going off and my scream broke the silence. Panicked, the extras jumped up and ran off in all directions.

"Back off, get off," Martin shouted, trying to free his arm as Nathan and Carey now gripped his gun arm as well, rigidly hanging on (all of us resembling, I'm sure, a free-for-all tag-team wrestling match).

Martin let go of the pistol, wrested his arm free, and ran for the jetty. He was in amazing shape for a man his age, sprinting with the stride of someone twenty years younger. I slumped to the ground, trying to understand my pain. I didn't see what happened, but apparently

Salmo had pulled the boat up to the jetty and, as Martin jumped on board, gunned the engine and roared off. The boat sped straight out into lake, and in two minutes was a speck on the far horizon — a classic Hollywood ending.

"You alright?" Nathan was kneeling beside me, with his hand tentatively on my shoulder.

"Of course. Why do you ask?" I said, disbelievingly.

"You're bleeding."

"A lot?"

"No ... well, actually, yeah."

"My leg hurts," I said. The pain was intense, and I wondered if I might be paralyzed — but then if I were paralyzed, would I be able to feel the pain in my leg? Would they have to amputate? Then Vlad was beside me, shouting to everyone, "Call 911, get ambulance," easing me onto my back, putting his jacket under my neck, and making a tourniquet with his belt. David immediately called 911, then tried to staunch the bleeding with large compresses from the first aid kit.

Over the hubbub of harried voices, I could hear Alvaro's plaintive sobbing: "¿Por qué mataste Che. Por qué?"

The pain in my leg was throbbing now — which I think is why everything from that moment is etched in my memory. I lay there trying to get inside the pain to control it. Vlad was cinching the tourniquet; Nathan was on the other side, his hand gently grasping my arm, caressing my shoulder. What was he doing? Did he imagine he was infusing me with his energy; or that rubbing would help my circulation — or (more likely) was he working out bits of business for future doctor roles? Carey stared down at me, looking distraught. Why was everyone reacting like this? I wasn't dead. It was only a leg wound, wasn't it? A shadow crossed over me and when I glanced up, László was gazing down at me. He said, encouragingly: "You are always making complications. Do not spend too much time in hospital, we need to finish picture." Then he walked off.

Even though my leg was throbbing fiercely, I thought, he's right. We need to finish the picture. I know this sounds crazy, but the mind reacts strangely when the body's been compromised. I had concentrated so hard on gettting THE SMOKE PICKERS made, that I was now programmed to keep making it. But how? Martin would be arrested, and without Martin there was no picture. How would we finish his scenes? We'd have to explain why he shot me, and what he was doing with a gun loaded with real bullets, just like FLIGHT FROM DA NANG. Wait! That was it — it was just like DA NANG — an accident. A movie set perfect storm, not really his fault. We *could* finish the picture. After all, FLIGHT FROM DA NANG was finished. It was possible. Everyone knows movies are enormously complicated — things go wrong all the time. Yes, and everyone likes Martin, so he'll be forgiven. Obviously, shooting me was an accident. Maybe we hadn't crossed the Rubicon.

"Vlad, listen," I whispered.

"What?" Vlad asked, leaning in.

"Tell Martin the gun went off accidentally."

"What?" Vlad said, astonished.

"Like DA NANG. The gun went off accidentally."

"Martin is gone."

"Gone?"

"He run away."

Oh my God. Where would he go? Not far, obviously. He was probably back at the hotel. It wasn't like he was a criminal.

"Well, find him and tell him the gun went off accidentally. Right?" Vlad, Nathan, Carey and David were all gaping at me, as though I had been shot in the *head*.

"The gun went off accidentally. Do you understand?" I said emphatically, looking at each one in turn to make sure they grasped what I was saying. "The gun went off *accidentally*."

Vlad glanced at Nathan, Carey and David. "We understand," he said, smiling. "It was accident."

"The gun went off accidentally," Carey said nodding.

"Yeah," said Nathan, "that's what happened."

David nodded. "That's what I saw."

The way they looked at me was eerie, as though *I* was the delusional one.

"Alright," Vlad said, "now close eyes, relax. Ambulance is coming. Doctors will give you nice drugs to make dreams — almost as good as movies."

AFTER THE MEDICS put me in the ambulance and we raced off, Teddy slipped up to Vlad and whispered, "Confucius say: 'Hard to catch camera when it is still running.'" Vlad looked at him then at the main camera, and saw the red light flickering. Teddy had kept filming, capturing the gun going off and Martin's escape — he was even shooting additional footage with a handheld camera.

"Keep footage separate," Vlad said quietly. "Do not tell anyone. I will ask friend at lab to process."

So before all the drama unfolded — the police sirening in, cordoning off the area, questioning everyone — Teddy and Vlad had the camera assistants remove the exposed film from the two cameras and hide it; one of the assistants was now recording everything with a small digital camera; and Vlad had quietly instructed Rob, our soundman, to keep running his recorder.

In the ambulance, the medic pumped me with Demerol, deadening all pain. I gaped up at Carey sitting beside the gurney, holding my hand, watching me and gazing out through the rear window at the street receding (she reminded me of Greta Garbo in the last shot of ANNA KARENINA). As we sped to the hospital, with the siren wailing, the visions began — I was kissing her passionately on the steps of the R.C. Harris while Teddy filmed Samantha and Nathan writhing naked on the grass with snakes, as László, Vlad and the extras chanted: "*¡Obrer! Campesinos! Estudiantes! Preparemos para la victoria!*"

18

Fluorescent ceiling lights whizzed by as the gurney careened down hospital corridors. A doctor's masked face flashed into view above me. "Don't worry, Ginger. We'll have you up and whirling about with Fred again before you know it." Then 'whoosh,' the gurney rammed through the swinging doors into the frigid air of the O.R., and I was swarmed by hooded 'gowns', one of whom placed a mask over my face.

I awoke fogged and thirsty, dimly perceiving a nurse replacing my IV drip. She assured me I was fine and that Doctor Gilbert would be in to see me shortly. I fell back inside the morphine, waking from a dream — Martin and I running down a street in Valparaíso, firing guns at fleeing Chileans — to find Dr. Gilbert (a cliché of the tall, handsome doctor) sitting beside the bed, eyeing me.

"Ms. Fielding, you're feeling better?"

The voice was the same as the one with the Fred & Ginger crack. I nodded.

"Your leg will be fine."

"Will it?"

"Yes."

"Will I be able to dance?" I always joke to ward off bad news.

"I don't see why not. The bullet only chipped the bone. It'll depend on how you heal, but most likely you'll have a very slight limp. Not even noticeable. You'll be able to tango."

"That's great, 'cause I don't now."

Those first drugged-days were timeless, dozing and waking at all hours to find the aged, frail Indian woman in the bed next to me, sitting up, her mattress cranked at a 80° angle, sleeping or staring at the 24-hour Cooking Channel flaring on her TV.

Thanks to the Demerol, morphine and other narcotics they were feeding me, I felt little discomfort, but the dreams never ended: László and my father pacing and chain-smoking in the hospital waiting room; Carey sitting at my bedside, confiding that she thought my mum was sexy; me naked on the gurney, trying to cover myself, leered at by a grinning Dr. Gilbert — and other fragmented visions.

Sometime during that post-op time, peering up from the valley of drug-sleep through the mist of unconsciousness, I was aware of a foreboding sensation. I opened my eyes to see two uniforms on either side of the bed — Metropolitan Toronto Police — one containing a middle-aged male, sporting salt-and-pepper Brylcreemed hair and a Molson pot; and the other, a stocky, young woman who in profile resembled a bloodhound. They were polite, but definitely sniffing around. They looked down on me with that reserved, accusatory expression that all police affect, and I knew I was facing the first hurdle to save the picture.

"Are you feeling better?" asked the bloodhound.

"Yes, but I'm quite drugged. Legal drugs, of course," I said jokingly.

Their lugubrious expressions didn't change — not even the hint of a smile.

"We have a few questions."

"Sure."

"On the day you were shot, did you know," Molson Pot said, "that Mr. Gage was in possession of a firearm?"

"I assumed it was a prop."

"Even though he threatened the other actors?" the Bloodhound asked, her tone suspicious.

"He was acting."

"Acting?"

"Yes."

"There's nothing in the script," Molson Pot said.

I was surprised. "You read the script?"

"Yes."

I tried to imagine a cop reading the script. "He was improvising."

"Improvising?"

"Yes."

Molson Pot gazed at me dubiously. "What do you mean 'improvising'?"

"Making it up. Actors sometimes call it 'living in the moment'."

Both officers thought about this. Molson Pot said: "I must tell you, Ms. Fielding, I've worked on a few movies — I've even been on camera a few times — and I've never seen any actor 'improvising'."

"It is unusual — which is why it was so surprising."

"Surprising?"

"All three actors had been improvising all week, adding enormously to the scenes."

They stared at me, bewildered.

"You're the associate producer?"

"That's right."

"Were you in the scene?"

"Which scene?"

"When the gun went off."

"No. I was waiting with the actors to see if Vlad wanted another take. It was a complicated shot."

"So why did Mr. Gage shoot you?"

"It was an accident. He was giving me back my cell."

"Your cell?"

"Yes. I'd asked him to call Telefilm." I knew the police would check my cell for numbers.

"Telefilm?"

"A government funding organization."

"Why?"

"It was a joke. In retrospect, it wasn't funny."

"It's no joke. You've been shot and a dog has been killed."

"A dog?" I remembered Alvaro sobbing, carrying the dog in his arms. "Che?"

"Che?" Molson Pot looked puzzled.

"Alvaro's dog?"

"Yes."

"But there were only two shots."

"The first one ricocheted off the asphalt and struck the dog in the head."

"Oh my God." Martin killed Che. Was I right to protect him?

"We're trying to find out why Mr. Gage was using a real gun. You didn't know it was his?"

"No." That was a lie, and I prayed Sister Fiona wasn't listening.

"Why did he shoot you?"

"It was an accident. I tripped and grabbed his arm as I fell, so somehow I must have caused him to pull the trigger." Another lie. I hoped the nuns would absolve me.

"What did you trip on?"

"I'm not sure, possibly a cable."

"Why wasn't he using a prop gun?"

"I don't know."

"And the first shot, what was he firing at?"

"The ground."

"Why?"

"Again, he was ... acting. He was trying to quell the demonstrators."

"Demonstrators?"

"It was a scene with people protesting."

"You say he was 'acting' with a *real* gun?" The bloodhound's tone and wide-legged stance suggested she'd seen too many cop shows.

"We didn't know it was real."

"But he must've known."

"Possibly, but he might have done it before. As you know, Americans are quite ... ah, casual about using guns."

"This isn't America," the Bloodhound said.

"When did you know it was real?" Molson Pot was obviously playing 'good cop.'

"When I felt the pain in my leg."

Both of them gazed at me, working out the next question. "Was his behaviour normal?" Molson Pot asked.

"No. He behaved like a movie star — it was normal behaviour for a movie star."

At that point, the Bloodhound came in for the coup de grâce. "So where is he?"

"At his hotel?"

"No. You don't know where he is?"

"No."

Seeing the officers glance at each other, I had no idea what they knew or what they were thinking. "Alright, Ms. Fielding, we may need to question you further so please don't leave the city without contacting us. We'll also need your cell. It'll be returned to you tomorrow. If Mr. Gage contacts you, please tell him to call us."

"He won't contact me."

"How do you know?"

"You have my cell."

They paused, imperceptibly. "Thanks for your time."

Molson Pot handed me his card and they left.

***

When next I woke and found Carey holding my hand, and Vlad sitting next to her, I wasn't sure they were real until Vlad handed me a bouquet of yellow roses and a book entitled *Как к фильму Тракторы* (*How to Film Tractors*); and pulled three tiny airline bottles of vodka from his pocket, handing one to each of us.

"That was bravest deed I have seen anywhere."

"It was brave," Carey said, watching me fondly.

"We drink to long life of finest associate producer. Nazdrovia," he said, downing his vodka.

"What's happening? Where's Martin?"

"Marty," Vlad said, downing my vodka, "is 'sought' by American authorities. Water Police search lake and find boat near Gananoque; OPP find Bruce in pool hall in Kingston. Did you know Bruce's real name is Salmo? What kind name is that? Bruce/Salmo told police Marty swim to America in scuba suit. This means — irony is too much to bear — Marty is now 'wetback.' American police have 'warrant to apprehend'."

"Shit."

"What?" Vlad asked.

"Martin."

"What about him?"

"How are we going to finish the picture?"

Stupefied, Vlad and Carey stared at me, then burst out laughing.

"What's so funny?"

"You," Vlad said. "This is why you are finest associate producer. You are ...ah ..."

"Relentless," Carey said.

"Yes," Vlad said, "like Russian soldiers at Stalingrad."

"That's why they won."

"We don't know where Marty is, or if he will go to prison for heinous crime of shooting associate producer but, most important, we cannot finish picture when you are still in hospital."

"In other words," Carey said, "it's dead."

"Movie is kaput."

They watched me as I silently mourned THE SMOKE PICKERS. Having wanted it so badly, I was unable to let go, even though I knew that, without Martin — even if what we shot could be cut together — we had no ending. Our insurance company wouldn't pay to complete the picture — it would cost too much to hire another star to re-shoot Martin's scenes. They would find a way to void the agreement; and if it was discovered that we — László — had known Martin was delusional, they might even sue us.

I imagined Martin hiding, frightened. "Do you think he's alright?"

Vlad shrugged. "He is Martin Gage."

"I don't understand how he got the gun past security at the airport," I whispered, suspecting the hospital room might be bugged.

"I think he get gun from Bruce."

"Did the police talk to you?"

"We all see same thing," Vlad said. "Pistol went off accidentally. Cops want to look at footage, and I show them scene with Martin improvising, which I cut before gun going off." Vlad placed his finger against his nose, and lowered his voice. "Cops don't know we have other footage."

"You did tell them it was an accident?"

"Of course, but when you run away, it looks suspicious."

I suppose I'd been expecting this moment. I felt enormously depressed. "Couldn't we shoot around him? Rewrite the story? We still have Carey and Nathan."

"We are missing three important scenes, four counting ending. I try to work out compromise, but cannot see way to finish picture with what we have." I didn't know then that Vlad's mind was already at work on salvaging the wreckage.

"Why doesn't God want us to make a good picture?" I moaned, crying out to the nuns.

"She works in mysterious ways," Carey said. "The sad thing is that they'll probably throw the book at Martin."

She was right. Martin would be slammed into jail. I felt selfish. I had been thinking about the picture and not about him. I couldn't stand the thought of him suffering. Why should he? He wasn't a criminal. I understood then what I had to do, and that the nuns wouldn't like it — I'd have to lie; but I would be practicing the Golden Rule. I'd be doing unto others, namely Martin.

"How's László?"

"He is László. You know how broody Hungarians are. He is tense about insurance."

László might be tense, but I knew he'd be fine. He was a survivor. It was Martin who was in danger. He was deluded, yes, but that was why he was more vulnerable. He wasn't mean or crazy, just a man dealing with psychological difficulties. I had no doubt that because he was Martin Gage the legal and media jackals would pounce. I kept seeing him in handcuffs, being led to prison or, worse, an institution. The thought was unbearable. No one wanted that, we *all* liked him. He was one of us — one of the ant colony. And he *was* Martin Gage — bigger than life. He'd enfolded us in his mystique.

A day later, he was tracked down to a Holiday Inn in Rochester, taken into custody, and held for questioning. His lawyer in L.A., Jonathan O'Toole, was on the case immediately and managed to have him flown back to L.A. where he was put under house arrest, pending possible extradition to Canada. Shortly thereafter, O'Toole's office contacted me at the hospital. I suggested a conference call with the others which I hoped would be cryptic. I'd forgotten that 'cryptic' is what lawyers do best.

"Before we begin, you must understand," O'Toole said over the phone, his granite voice weighted with caution, "that, if asked, I am obligated, as an officer of the court, to reveal any information pertinent to the case which I may have acquired." (Translation: I don't want to know).

"We understand," I said.

Vlad, Nathan, Carey, David and I re-affirmed that the gun had gone off accidentally. I told my story first, so that the others would 'discover' that we were all in agreement with what had 'occurred' — including the call to Telefilm. Fortunately, Vlad, Nathan, David and Carey had given the police very little detail. We were *all* trying to shield Martin.

***

While I was in hospital, László waited anxiously for a decision from CinemAssurance, our guarantor: would they indemnify our investors, or cover the cost of re-shooting Martin's scenes with a new star? When the police concluded that both shootings (my leg and the death of Che) were accidental, he was relieved; but then distressed when the prosecutor's office charged Martin with possession of an unlicensed firearm, negligence in discharging a firearm, and leaving the scene of an accident. This gave the insurance company the excuse to reject our claim, pointing out a clause in the fine print that instructed us to take 'reasonable precautions to protect the safety of all personnel,' citing Martin's pistol as evidence. László knew taking them to court would be futile. You never win with insurance companies — they're surrounded by a moat of corporate lawyers.

A few weeks after I left the hospital, with Martin under house arrest in L.A., O'Toole flew up to instruct the Toronto barrister he had retained to represent Martin in court. We arranged to meet, and of course I brought Vlad.

"Let me remind you that I am obliged," repeated O'Toole, a hefty man in a deep brown suit set against his long silver hair, "as an officer of the court, to reveal any pertinent information to the case which I may have acquired."

O'Toole's manner was so precise, so cosy and self-protective, it almost made me homesick for the law. Vlad, familiar with the concept of conversations on many levels, nodded knowingly.

"We understand," I said. "Any information which comes your way you are required to reveal to the court."

"If asked," he repeated, sipping his coffee.

"Right," I said. "So, is Martin okay?"

"He wanted to appear in court," said O'Toole said, carefully, "but he needs to rest. At the moment, he's at a special 'spa' which caters to over-worked entertainment professionals."

"It is good that Marty is taking rest," said Vlad, disingenuously, "I think he worked too hard. I hope I am not to blame."

"The charges are serious so we'll need to show that, while there was some negligence, what occurred was a series of compounded mistakes. Ms. Fielding, I'd like you to testify."

"Of course."

"You will need me?" Vlad asked.

"I might, but in my experience it's better to keep it as simple as possible."

In court, O'Toole was allowed to read out Martin's deposition in which Martin stated that he had acquired the gun — which he needed for protection — in Canada but had neglected to register it. He'd had no intention of using it but was so compelled by the intensity of the scene that he fired, although he'd been careful to fire into the ground. When the gun had gone off the second time by accident, he'd panicked as a result of having been in 'Viet Nam' (neither the prosecutor nor the judge questioned what that meant), and fled.

I was then called to the stand, and told my version of events, led by O'Toole's barrister. Then, Mr. Blanchard, the prosecutor, a heavy-set man in an ill-fitting grey suit, who habitually ran his hand over a rapidly-receding hairline, rose slowly and approached the witness box. With Vlad in the front row watching, I felt as though I were in a TV drama.

"Why was Mr. Gage in possession of a firearm?" he asked.

"I don't know. I know that many Americans insist on carrying guns."

"This isn't America. You *have* hired American performers before, have you not?"

"Yes."

"Did any of *them* bring guns into Canada?"

"Not to my knowledge. It would be difficult, I think, to get one through airport security."

"You are aware that for an American to possess a firearm in Canada would require a Canadian permit?"

"Yes."

"And yet, he didn't have one."

"Apparently."

"So the first time you saw the gun was in Mr. Gage's hotel room?"

"Mr. Gage didn't show me his gun there." That much was true, Martin had tried to hide it.

"Who else was present?"

"A man named Salmo."

"What was he doing?"

"I understood that he was Martin's assistant, someone who ... fetched things."

"Did this Salmo handle Mr. Gage's gun?"

"Salmo was on the boat. He wasn't anywhere near the gun." How stupid does he think I am?

"I meant in the hotel room."

"I don't know. As I said, Mr. Gage didn't show me the gun there." I knew that if I had 'seen' the gun in his room, I would have difficulty explaining why we didn't try to prevent Martin from using it.

"You're sure?"

"Yes." Considering this was a quasi-lie, I was remarkably composed and guilt-free, although I doubted that the nuns would have appreciated that. "But I was part of a conversation with Mr. Pudovkin and Mr. Kovacs in which Mr. Pudovkin said that *he* had seen Mr. Gage with a gun."

Mr. Blanchard seemed surprised. "And what was your reaction?"

"I said that if Mr. Gage did have a real gun — it might have been a prop — we'd better make sure that he was licensed."

"So did you?"

"Did I what?"

"Make sure he was licensed?"

"No, and I take full responsibility."

Mr. Blanchard gazed thoughtfully at the empty jury box. "So the first time you saw the 'real' gun was when he threatened the actors."

"Yes, but because he'd been improvising I didn't know it was a real gun."

Mr. Blanchard paused. "Improvising?"

"Yes."

"*Improvising*? With a pistol loaded with live ammunition?"

"As I said, I didn't know that at the time."

"You must have known that a gun wasn't scheduled on the call sheet." I was impressed. He'd done his homework.

"Quite often an actor or director will ask for a prop on set. I had no way of knowing whether Martin — Mr. Gage — had. Movie-making is a collaborative process, and when actors and directors are in sync they often improvise. And because so many people are involved, all at the same time, it's hard for any one person to know everything that's going on on-set at any given moment."

The prosecutor looked confused. "Improvise?" he repeated.

"Yes, over the first week of shooting our actors had built a rapport."

"Rapport?"

"Trust. Improvisation is built on trust, and all three actors, Nathan, Carey and Martin, were very good at it." This was only a partial lie. Martin didn't trust Nathan. He wanted to shoot him.

The prosecutor gazed at me doubtfully. "So, Mr. Gage was — as you put it — *improvising*?"

"All three were."

He paused, pondering his next question. "You were the associate producer, is that correct?"

"Yes."

"And yet you were *in* the scene."

"Which scene?"

"The one in which the gun went off."

"No, I was waiting with the actors to see if Vlad — Mr. Pudovkin — wanted another take."

"So why did Mr. Gage fire his gun? Was he '*improvising*'?"

"It was an accident."

"An accident?"

"I'd asked him to call Telefilm on my cell."

"Why?"

"I thought having a star like Martin Gage call the chief executive might impress her. It was a silly idea."

"What happened then?"

"When I reached out to take my cell back, I tripped and grabbed Martin's arm to steady myself which must have caused him to pull the trigger. So really, it was my fault."

"That was the second shot?"

"Yes."

"And when he fired the gun the first time, he was... *improvising*, is that correct?" The more he paused before saying the word, the more ridiculous it sounded.

I sighed. "Yes."

"Did you know then it was a real gun?"

"No."

"When did you know it was a real gun?"

"When I felt the pain in my leg."

"Not when he shot the dog?"

"I didn't know he'd shot the dog—then. I'm sure he didn't intend to."

"So after the first shot you still didn't know he was using a real gun?"

"No."

"You didn't hear a bullet ricochet?"

"No. There was a lot going on." Another lie.

"So why did he run away? Was he ... '*improvising*' then as well?"

"Your Honour?" protested the Toronto barrister.

The judge gazed down at the prosecutor. "May I remind the prosecutor that the witness is not hostile."

"Thank you, Your Honour," the prosecutor said, unfazed. "Why did he run away?"

"I assume he panicked, fearing some attack on his person."

"Was that likely?"

This was what I'd hoped for. Lying in my hospital bed I had been thinking about little else, working out a rationale to excuse Martin's actions.

"Movie stars," I said, "aren't like you and me. They tend, as one once told me, 'to stick out.' They're vulnerable. Martin had been threatened in the past. Possibly he over-reacted, and escaping on the boat was, in his mind, a necessary precaution."

"How many crew were on set that day?"

"Fifty-five or so."

"So, surrounded by a crew of fifty-five, some of them quite hefty men, he still felt 'vulnerable'?"

"Stars aren't like the rest of us. People come at them all the time, from everywhere, asking for autographs, favours, money, photos, interviews, endorsements, their time, jobs, recognition, anything — many want to be their friend, and the paparazzi constantly hound them. Sometimes they're even threatened — many feel as though they're being besieged. So those stars who've spent twenty or thirty years dealing with notoriety become tenacious in protecting their privacy and, as a result, are — I won't say 'flighty' but — extremely wary. So if that were me — if I didn't feel I had control of the situation, that I might be in danger — I'd probably run away too. Running away would be a conditioned response. I wouldn't call it normal, but I also wouldn't call it irrational. Martin Gage was not unlike other movie stars I've met."

The prosecutor gazed at me, not sure how to pick his way through what he'd just heard. I could count the seconds ticking by.

"Mr. Blanchard?" the judge said.

"That's all, Ms. Fielding, thank you. Prosecution rests Your Honour."

In his summation, Martin's barrister suggested that, to Mr. Gage, leaving the set was a rational response to perceived danger. It didn't matter that the danger didn't exist; Martin Gage was convinced that it did.

It was curious that no one asked why Martin had a boat standing by.

We had to wait a week for the Judge's decision. The shooting of Che and my leg were ruled as accidents, and O'Toole's and the Toronto barrister's handling of the case got Martin off with a fine for possession of a firearm without a license. Given a suspended sentence for having left the scene, he was ordered to pay Alvaro one thousand dollars for the loss of his dog; and to contribute another five thousand dollars to the Canadian Actors' Fund. The Judge also recommended that Martin undergo therapy. O'Toole told me later that Martin's presence in court would have involved additional legal risk, but as it was — even though his punishment was lighter than expected — it was unlikely he would be making other pictures here or anywhere else in the near future.

It looked as though THE SMOKE PICKERS would be the iceberg that sank the Felicity — without a sudden influx of new 'Canadian Tire money,' László would lose everything, the company would fold, and he'd have to start again, find new investors and reinvent himself. He was, apparently, unlike his true, fearless Magyar self, wallowing in a deep dark funk.

When Vlad had gone to him a few days after the shooting to explain that he and Teddy had captured everything on film, László's response had been stupefied anger — he had just received the lab bill for processing (keeping the cameras running had exposed a lot of film) and he didn't understand what Vlad was trying to tell him — that he might be able to salvage something from the footage.

Vlad had been thinking about it since that fatal Saturday and, knowing what he had shot, had glimpsed the possibility of a documentary-comedy — THE UNMAKING OF THE SMOKE PICKERS — but he needed László's permission to try. László couldn't visualize what Vlad was describing but having any picture to sell — even a documentary — was better than nothing. So, on condition that Vlad do the editing for free and cover any additional costs, he agreed.

Lying in a hospital bed for ten days can induce intense introspection and, in a wide-awake, three a.m. revelation, just before I was released, I understood that THE SMOKE PICKERS catastrophe would be the cause of Felicity's demise. László would be forced to let me go, and I'd have to find other work. What would I do? I had no intention going back to law. Then I remembered I'd been trying to get to Europe, and that I had enough money saved to buy me a few months there. Why couldn't I just go? Having worked day in and day out at Felicity for three years, I was now free!

I went from depression to elation, imagining all the wonderful possibilities, (the drugs might've helped). I could spend Christmas in England — I cherished my mom but the thought of being cooped up in her tiny farmhouse in snowy rural Ontario with her new husband and his dead butterfly collection was depressing.

I had secretly hoped Nathan might've dropped by the hospital, or phoned, or sent flowers, but he hadn't. So I had to assume the worst — that I didn't mean anything to him. Or more likely, that he and Carey had gone wherever couples go. Then Carey dropped by, just before returning to L.A.

"I came to say goodbye."

"I'll miss you."

"I brought champagne," she said, holding up a half bottle and opening it.

"Wow," I said, when she handed me a glass, "you movie stars really *do* consume it."

"It's mandatory." Carey lifted her glass. "What'll we drink to?"

"You and Nathan."

"Nathan?"

"And your future."

"He's not my future."

"He's not going with you?"

She seemed puzzled. "No, why would he?"

"I don't know. You two seemed ..."

"I'm supposed to be gay, remember?"

"I'm confused."

"Obviously. You need a holiday. Why not come visit me in L.A.?"

"It's not really my kind of city."

"No?"

"No, it's too ... I don't know ... fake?"

"It grows on you."

"I don't think it would grow on me."

"I have a hot tub bigger than a bath."

"Does it have bubbles?"

"If you come I'll get some."

"Maybe when I return from Europe."

"Europe?"

"I'm going to London and Paris to see theatre."

She was silent for a moment. "I have some time off coming up. What if I joined you there?"

I was startled. Then I realized that I *was* emotionally attached to her, and that I was excited at the thought of seeing Paris and London through her eyes as well. Those green eyes were saying: 'You're an interesting and vital human being and I want to hold you.' I wanted to hold her. It seemed so easy. For once in my life, I could sail close to the wind and go with whatever would happen. Maybe I wasn't an amoeba — maybe I was a gazelle.

"Are you sure?" I asked.

"I'm not sure about anything, but wouldn't it be fun to try."

I could see the openness in her eyes. "Yes, it would. I'd like that."

She kissed me. And I liked that too.

***

Instead of lying around my apartment after being released from hospital, I hobbled in the park, and exercised continually, all to strengthen my gimp leg. Wanting to let László know that I wouldn't be returning right away, a week later I limped into his office. At the time, he was trying to avoid selling his building to pay off the company's debts and, while I couldn't know that, I could tell he was putting on a brave face.

"There is nothing to do for you. I must try to find new investors, so it is best you do something until I can produce new movie."

"You don't need me?"

"You are finest associate producer I have worked with, but there is nothing to produce."

He was quite gracious, considering he was in the midst of immense money problems caused indirectly by his HQD.

"Maybe you should have holiday."

"I'm thinking of going to Europe."

"What you want to see in Europe?"

"All those people having sex you talk about."

László laughed — I'd never heard him laugh out loud before. He told me that once he had new financing he would call me. He suggested, mysteriously, that I stop by the editing room. I did, and was surprised to find Vlad at the Steenbeck, viewing footage from THE SMOKE PICKERS with Honor sitting beside him, scribbling in an exercise book.

He didn't elaborate on what he was up to, but he did wish me a safe trip. "When you get to London, don't forget to kiss Blarney Stone."

"That's in Ireland."

"Same thing."

When Honor left the room for a moment, I asked: "You're not using Hardy?"

"He is not right for what I am trying to do. Honor has better instinct."

Once the court case had been settled, I bought airline tickets, booked a (relatively) cheap flat in London, gave notice on my apartment, applied for a passport, walked my wonky leg every day in the park, and hung out in cafes, surfing the theatre news from London and Paris. I emailed Carey to let her know where I would be staying and when, so I had everything organized but something kept niggling at me. When I saw the ad in the paper announcing the last two days of Madbrain's Essential Shakespeare season, I realized I hadn't seen Nathan's Hamlet. Or Nathan. And I wanted to see him one last time, at least on stage.

The buzz on Nathan's Hamlet was strong and, it being the second last night, the 'mattress depot' was so packed I had to stand at the back. Even though my leg throbbed, I stood for two hours, mesmerized. Nathan's Hamlet — with all his intensity — was unlike anything I'd ever seen. At the beginning of the 'get thee to a nunnery scene' in Act III, he reached cruising speed, his Hamlet fighting so desperately to restrain his madness that the audience was breathless.

"Thus conscience doth make cowards of us all;
And thus the native hue of resolution
Is sicklied o'er with the great pale cast of thought,
And enterprises of great pith and moment
With this regard their currents turn awry,
And lose the name of action. Soft you now!
The fair Ophelia! Nymph, in thy orisons
Be all my sins remembered."

Nancy entered. They had performed this scene twenty times since the cell phone incident; and Nathan's Hamlet, pushing against sanity's constraints, terrified her (as she told me later), her initial puzzlement turning to fear in each performance. I had never heard an audience so still.

When, with a standing ovation, the performance ended, a voice kept telling me not to go backstage, but I wasn't listening.

"Hi," I said, waving at Nancy as I peered through the door of the packed, unisex dressing room. "You were amazing."

"Thank you," she said. "He's just behind you."

I turned and there he was with a towel, wiping off his makeup.

"Oh, it's you," Nathan said, his fellow actors squeezing by him. "How's your leg?"

"It's fine. You didn't come see me."

"No time."

No time? Didn't the little shit remember that I'd probably saved his life? "I came to say goodbye."

"Goodbye?"

"That was boss, Nathan," a passing fan said.

He gazed at me, puzzled. "Goodbye? Where're you going?"

"I'm off to France."

"France?"

"To audition for the Comédie Français."

He looked as though I had just smacked him. Finally, I'd gotten his attention. "I'm joking, I'm taking a holiday."

"Oh."

"I'm going to London and Paris to spend a couple of months seeing theatre. I'm meeting Carey there."

He looked baffled. "Carey?"

"Yeah."

"Oh."

"I've been learning French."

"What about your job?"

"I've left it."

"Oh. When are you going?"

"Wednesday."

"Wednesday," he repeated, appearing distracted. "Wednesday? You're going Wednesday?"

"Yes."

"This Wednesday?"

"Yes, Wednesday."

"You'll be safe?" he asked abruptly.

"Safe? Yeah ...? Why wouldn't I be?"

"I don't know."

"Why would you mention it then?"

"Well, is it the best time to go?"

"I don't know. What's the best time?"

"I don't think now is a good time."

"No?"

"No."

"Why not?"

"I heard something about the theatres being closed."

"What?"

"Three people are ill, I think. I don't know if anyone's died."

"Died? How?"

"Some kind of flu epidemic."

"Flu?"

"I think that's why they closed the theatres."

"Are you serious?"

"You haven't seen the papers?"

"No."

"I wouldn't go now."

"Are they cancelling flights?"

"I think so."

"They didn't say anything at the agency. Are you sure?"

"I'm not sure."

"I can't believe this." I was confused.

"It reminds me of the Plague."

"The Plague?" Was I hearing correctly?

"Why don't you go in the Spring?"

"How can it be the Plague?"

"I'm sure it's not the Plague."

"No?"

"It's probably some chicken flu."

"Flu? The flu's not like the plague."

"I wouldn't know."

"Are you saying I shouldn't go?"

"Can I make a suggestion?"

"Sure."

"I'm going in the spring. Why don't you go then? We could go together."

"What?"

"You could come with me in the spring."

"I've already booked everything." What was he thinking? Why was he asking me to go with him? Which was when I clued in, remembering that I hadn't seen anything on the internet about a flu or theatres closing. "There is no flu, is there?"

"I'm sure I heard something on the news. It might have been somewhere else though." The little shit was good at deadpan.

"How many theatres are closed?"

"I don't know."

"And how many people have died?"

"I'm not sure."

I was angry. "This is very cruel."

"What is?"

"Don't you think?"

"I was serious. You should wait till the spring. We could go together."

"Why would I go with you?"

"I know all the plays."

"Do you speak French?"

"You can get a tour guide to speak French."

"In the theatre — during the performance?"

"I know all the French plays too."

"In French?"

"No ..."

"So why would I want you to come with me?"

"I thought you were coming with me."

I was dumbstruck. What game was he playing?

"Why don't we have dinner," he said, "and discuss it."

"When?"

"How about tomorrow."

"How about now?"

"Now? It's late, isn't it?"

"No."

As we made our way to the Monacle, with me limping, him bab-bling, it occurred to me that he seemed nervous. This wasn't the Nathan I knew. He was genuinely curious about what had happened to the movie, and to Martin, but mostly about my not returning to Felicity.

Although Barney had closed the kitchen, he brought us two roast beef sandwiches, some coleslaw and beer. That was when Nathan told me that the other actors in Madbrain had offered him the position of Artistic Director of the Company. He'd taken it, and was busy plan-ning the spring season.

"What we need now," he said, expansively, "is a Managing Direc-tor — someone to free up the Artistic Director from the business end so I can concentrate on the plays. What do you think?"

"That's probably a good idea."

"So you'll take it?"

"What? Take it? No, no. I'm going to Europe."

"You should become Managing Director. We can save up our money and go later."

"I've saved up my money. I'm going Wednesday."

"We *could* go together." He sounded uncertain.

"Why would I take you?"

"What do you mean 'why'? You like me, don't you?"

"You don't like me."

"Why would you say that?"

"You didn't come see me in the hospital."

He was silent. "No," he said quietly, "I didn't."

"Why?"

"We were in rehearsals — yeah, I know. That's no excuse — I guess I wasn't sure what you thought."

"Thought about what?"

"About me."

"What about you?"

"Well, I didn't know if you and Carey were ..."

"Did she say something?"

"No, no. I just didn't know."

I watched him. He stared at his beer for the longest time, then looked up. "I didn't know if you liked me."

I laughed. "You mean you didn't come see me because you didn't know if I liked you?"

"Yeah."

"That seems rather narcissistic, doesn't it?"

"I am narcissistic. I know that."

"I admire you," I said. "but I don't know you."

"I guess I don't know you either, but I do admire you."

We sat there, admiring and not knowing each other. "So what do you think we should do?"

"Well," he said, pausing, "maybe we should get to know each other. We could go to Europe together, in the spring. We'd get to know each other even better then."

"Why not now?"

"We're still in rehearsal."

"Right."

"Another reason for you to take the job."

"Which job?"

"Managing Director."

"You want me to be your donkey."

"No," he said, emphatically. "You'd be Madbrain's Managing Director."

"Same thing."

He laughed. "Yes, same thing, but the donkey would have a voice."

"A voice?"

"A vote, same as all the other members."

"You mean like deciding which plays get mounted?"

"Among other things. By the way, if you take it, you'll need to apply for a grant to pay yourself."

"What?"

"You'll need to apply for a grant to cover your salary."

I gaped at him, not knowing whether to be angry or amused. He wasn't being sly. Because he loved what he was doing, he assumed everyone would — anyone would be honoured to be Managing Director of an impoverished theatre company because they would, and should (in his view), be motivated by their love of the stunning work they would all do together.

I had no intention, however, of being in one of those relationships where one side — me — does all the work. On the other hand, he was, I thought, being up front about it.

"I think we'd be good together," he said.

What? Had I heard correctly? I'd imagined him saying those words but never expected it. Why now? "Would we 'be good together' if I *didn't* become managing director?"

"I don't know," he said, carefully watching my expression, "but I'd ... I'd be willing to try."

I stared at him, as though I was trying to decide — which I was — and then found myself saying, "Okay."

"Okay what?"

"Okay, you can pick up the cheque."

"That's it?"

"No."

"What else?"

"You can kiss me."

His gaze was intensely direct. "How's your breath?" he asked, deadpan. It was the first time he made me laugh.

***

Becoming Managing Director of Madbrain was not the smartest thing I ever did. I had to manage *everything:* the building, the company, writing up the grant applications, advertising, hiring and firing, contracts, coffee-making, bagel-fetching, props-buying, ticket-taking, and poster mounting. I refused, however, to be bookkeeper, which we farmed out.

In essence, I was Nathan's girl Friday for less money than I made as László's; and, to begin with, I had to keep slicing off a portion of the box office receipts to cover my expenses until we received the grant to pay my salary. The difference was that now I was, along with the actors, part of the company; part of the decision-making process (even able to have an opinion on the plays that Madbrain presented). Finally, I felt as though I were doing something that mattered. And I didn't have to drive to the airport or fetch coffee or, most importantly, hire nude actresses.

I called Vlad during that period. He was having the best time of his life. As he explained, THE UNMAKING OF THE SMOKE PICKERS would be a new kind of cinema, a collage — part documentary, part comedy, part romance, documenting the production as it unravelled. He'd convinced Honor, after a vodka-filled evening in a bar, to narrate and co-write it. The film made full use of her descriptive abilities and his Slavic wit. He used all the footage available, even stock footage of the R.C. Harris Filtration Plant, as well as documentary footage of real Chilean demonstrators, inter-cut with Nathan and our extras demonstrating (our extras looking quite authentic of course). He interviewed the major players to relate those parts of the story he didn't have on film. I was the only person who didn't appear in THE UNMAKING OF THE SMOKE PICKERS. I supported his project, but had a difficult time convincing Vlad that I wanted to tell the story from my point of view in a book, even though I had never written anything before (as you can probably tell). In the end, he understood.

After he had assembled a fine cut, he asked László (who of course asked me) to send out invitations to a test screening for crew and friends, to get some sense of whether or not it worked.

The screening was thrilling. It seemed as though all Vlad's talents, experience and instinct were in sync, and what emerged was quirky, charming and enthralling. All the scenes shot for THE SMOKE PICKERS worked just as they would in a real movie: Carey and Nathan touched the audience when they came on screen; Martin was terrifying; and the Cavalcade scene was electric; Honor's narration was witty and self-deprecating — even the Hungarian Prince had his own special charm:

"This was big question for movie. Do we show Maddie and Miguel having sex? I am thinking it is important. Sex is everywhere; insects in the gardens are having sex, demonstrators in Chile are having sex; you cannot hide it — it is unhealthy to forbid it; it is part of life."

Vlad had followed that with a shot of Nathan licking Samantha who was squirming to escape. The audience roared.

There was a positive buzz in the crowd. I was certain that Vlad and Honor had pulled it off. THE UNMAKING OF THE SMOKE PICKERS wasn't spectacular but played like a real movie, illustrating the pathos and humour of humans trying to impose their will on fate. It also demonstrated how a movie comes together, and how easily it could fall apart. Vlad had been proud that night to present it to László.

As I left the theatre, László was standing by the door, his expression almost lugubrious. I was puzzled.

"Well," I said, "you have a happy ending, a quality picture."

"Maybe," he replied, "but this is only crew." I could hear that insecure tone in his voice.

"If it makes the crew laugh, it'll make audiences laugh. You know that."

"We will see."

Given the response, I couldn't understand why he was pensive. No doubt it was the financial stress. Anyway, it was no longer my affair, my responsibility or my job. I let it go.

Two months later, I heard that he had made a deal with a Canadian distributor and, three months after that, Vlad phoned to tell me the movie was opening at a suburban theatre. On opening day, he took Honor and me to see it.

Our first disquieting moment came as we approached the theatre, the poster screaming out the new title RAUNCHY REVOLUTIONARIES, set boldly above images of Carey, Nathan, Martin *and* Samantha appearing — through the magic of Photoshopping — as though they were in the midst of an orgy; and just below that, the cut line — WHEN THE REVOLUTION COMES, SO DOES EVERYONE!

We took seats in the back, noting only seven other patrons in the theatre, and gaped up at the screen as the movie came on. Martin driving the Thunderbird up to the Consulate, then cutting to Maddie in the street meeting Miguel, and the two having sex in Miguel's hovel. I was stunned. The Maddie-Miguel scenes were the same, but there was footage I didn't recognize: close-ups of naked bodies, doubles for Carey and Nathan simulating sex, inserted into the intimate Maddie and Miguel shots. László had ravaged Vlad's stunning work.

László had also awkwardly inter-cut the Maddie-Miguel sequences with the Maddie-Guy scenes but again used body doubles for Martin and Carey, inserted to show Maddie and Guy 'having each other.'

Periodically, we were jolted by the inexplicable inclusion of revolutionaries firing guns (stock footage?) coming on screen, with no intelligible connection to the storyline.

In the midst of all these sequences, he introduced Samantha, first seen pouting in closeup against a brick wall, staring intently off-camera, inter-cut with shots of Martin and Carey leaving the Consulate past the demonstrators — suggesting that Samantha was sexually stalking Martin.

Then came the shots of Samantha flirting with the 'revolutionaries' near the army trucks, followed by the scene of Samantha undressing Nathan, him licking her, and closeup shots of her breasts, to establish their 'affair.'

After the goodbye scene between Carey and Nathan, László inserted the shot of Martin striding from the Consulate and, passing the columns, pulling out his pistol, rushing to the Thunderbird, jumping in and roaring off. Then he cut to the Martin and Nathan scene — now reworked — having removed most of the political dialogue.

"Consul Hawthorne," Nathan said, emerging from the cafe.

"Who are you?"

"I am the 'friend' of your wife."

"Why isn't she coming out?"

"She has come to see where the people live. Have you spoken," Nathan asked, "with El Presidente?"

"What do you know about El Presidente?" Martin said, pulling his pistol from inside his jacket.

"Has El Presidente told you to kill me?"

"I'm an American diplomat."

"I am not stupid, Consul Hawthorne."

"Trying to overthrow the government is stupid."

"We do not want to overthrow the government, amigo."

"I am not your amigo."

"You do not have to be my enemy."

"That's your decision. We are friends of Chile. We invested in your country. We brought you free enterprise. Where would Chile be without the Coca-Cola Company? America's a great country. We bring democracy to countries all over the globe."

At this point, László had inserted the first shot we'd taken of Martin driving up to the Consulate and rushing in. Then cut to Samantha alone in the Consul's bedroom set (had László been planning this during the shoot?) badly-lit, inter-cut with shots of the demonstrators yelling outside the consulate. Then a shot of Martin by the bedroom window staring out.

Standing by the bed, Samantha asks: "Oh please, Consul Hawthorne. Help me. I'll do whatever you ask."

Shot of Martin turning his gaze from the window to just off camera (suggesting he was looking at Samantha).

Samantha pouting, removing her blouse. "Won't you protect me?"

"I'm waiting for you to tell me." The line was from Martin's scene with Carey.

"Why should I tell you?" she said plaintively, stepping out of her skirt.

"I want to hear you say it."

"What?"

"That you've been consorting with a commie."

"I didn't want to, but he forced me," she said.

"Do you care?"

"Of course I care," said Samantha, using Carey's line.

"You need to say it now."

Samantha smiled raffishly. "He's not half the man you are," she said, getting into bed in her bra and panties.

Shot of Martin, watching her.

"I can show you what he did to me," she simpered, holding out her arms.

László had Martin staring sternly off-camera, then cut to the bed as Martin's body double entered the shot, quickly undressed down to his briefs, and crawled under the covers. Samantha hugged him. The double lay beside her, his back to the camera.

"You don't have to be so diplomatic, Mr. Consul. You can search me if you like. I'm not afraid. Ohhh, you've found my hiding place. Oh, you're so strong ... and big," she said breathlessly. And so on, ad nauseam.

For the climax, László had assembled a sequence of shots: Martin arriving in the Cavalcade, inter-cut with Teddy's hand-held shots of the extras; Martin staring down the 'demonstrators,' and firing his gun into the ground, forcing the extras to sit.

Finally, Martin proclaimed: "Amigos, we will not forget your courage, or your fight for freedom."

RAUNCHY REVOLUTIONARIES ended with a hand-held shot of Samantha by the truck, hugging two soldiers, then cut to a shot of Martin in front of the R.C Harris, also staring just off-camera (suggesting he was looking at Samantha), then a final shot of her in front of the army truck, revealing all that lovely cleavage, smiling past the camera as Martin's double entered the frame and hugged her — happy ending complete.

Even more baffling, over the entire film, László had added festive Latin American music (circa 1950 — Prez Prado style), sounding as though it had been recorded on a Casio in a back-lane garage.

The screen went to black and the end credits rolled. I noticed two directors listed: Vlad and the rodent-like director from HALLOWEEN HOODOO. The lights came up. We sat there speechless.

László had completely re-cut the movie by discarding large chunks of Hardy's script, showing the Consul as the good guy who gets the girl. Honor's story, now twice removed, didn't even exist in name, and what was on screen bore no resemblance to her novel.

We sat motionless, unable to comprehend what we'd just seen.

Vlad shook his head. "I never learn."

"What?"

"It is second time I insult László."

"How?"

"When I use footage of Samantha and Nathan after clip of him talking about sex — you remember, it got big laugh? — I embarrass him."

I remembered. László's clip was no longer in the film, nor any of Vlad's interviews. Honor's narration was cut, all documentary shots were taken out — all Vlad and Honor's hard work to create something witty, ironic and intelligent from the wreckage had been eradicated. With all meaning and intent removed, the movie was incoherent, almost a self-parody.

"It's a travesty," I said. "Both of you worked hard for no money to salvage something from the wreckage, so that all that work wouldn't be lost. And this is how he repays you."

"László is László. You cannot ask camel to change humps. You live and learn."

"What do you learn — how to let people fuck up your work?" I never swear but I was livid. I felt violated on their behalf, and probably not a little guilty because of Honor who, I imagined was feeling much worse than I. But no, she was staring off reflectively.

"László," she said, "must have seen THE UNMAKING OF THE SMOKE PICKERS as a slight. My limited experience with Hungarians is that they're very proud. They take things literally, and often find it hard to laugh at themselves. He wouldn't have wanted the film made public — he didn't understand the irony."

They were telling me it was time to move on. For Vlad, there would be no opportunity to resurrect his relationship with László. Nor, obviously, would László change. Our attempt to make a 'quality' picture at Felicity had been our swan song. RAUNCHY REVOLUTIONARIES lasted less than a week in theatres before ending up in DVD sale bins. (I bought a copy for $2.99 to show Nathan, who still hadn't seen himself on film, and who was angered by the body double sex scenes.)

While writing the narration, Honor had viewed the footage many times; and, watching Vlad, she had become utterly engaged in what they were creating, so when László mutilated their sly, witty and, in some places, moving docu-comedy, he broke her heart a second time. Both she and Vlad sued him to have their names removed from the credits; and she's suing him now for the remainder of her money for the rights to the book, which László claims he doesn't owe because the film was never completed — all of which is helping two lawyers add to their retirement fund.

Honor never spoke to László again, nor did she want to talk to me for this book. (Why me? I can't take all blame, can I?). She's also refused to let any of her novels be filmed, although there's talk of letting Vlad direct one.

I walk now with an imperceptible limp, but Nathan says that it's the most beautiful limp in the world — I had no idea he could be that corny. He's even suggested we take up ballroom dancing. I won't say more about us because, like Nathan, I believe that people have a private life, which is not all that interesting to see on screen — or to read about in a book. Nor would I ever want to be eligible for the Bad Sex Writing Award, but I can tell you — as I told Vlad when he asked if Nathan and I had 'consummated our relationship in the biblical sense' — we are, at present, sharing his walk-up apartment on College Street.

And something else quite wonderful has happened. At the 'mattress depot' this Spring, we're running a series called Madbrain's Essential Shaw; and the others are permitting me to perform. At present, I'm playing the Parlour Maid in *You Never Can Tell*, and I have four lines. Coming on stage every night and saying: "Beg pardon, ma'am ... I'm waiting for Mr. Valentine. I have a message for him," has rekindled my desire to act. Some nights, I even get laughs.

And, I've made an empowering discovery. According to Nancy, I'm the only one who has ever made Nathan corpse (break up on stage). On the fifth night, before going on, we'd had a heated discussion (about what I can't remember), so on stage a desire to shake him up came over me and after I'd delivered my line: "The landlord, sir, wishes to speak to you before you go out," I turned my back on the audience, crossed my eyes, stuck out my tongue and wiggled it at him.

He had started to say: "Oh, tell him I have four patients ..." stopped, stared at me incredulously, then turned quickly away, struggling to keep from laughing.

"If ... if ... ah, he wouldn't ... ah, ah, mind ..." he sputtered, trying to get the line out, and to appear as though he'd intended to deliver it upstage. Finally, he composed himself, turned back to face the audience, and me — I could see the anger in his eyes — and said sternly: "Say I'm busy, but that I want to see him."

"Yes sir," I said, thrilled to discover that I had some power over the little shit.

When the curtain came down, he said nothing; but at home that night he gave me a severe lecture about being 'unprofessional.' I've only done it twice and only when he's irritated me, but I'm thrilled to know that it works. I doubt he'll ever cast me in anything again, but you never know; after all, the Managing Director does have some clout. I was also asked to understudy the role of Dolly, played by Nancy, so maybe one night she'll be sick (and who knows what could happen then).

I have no idea about the future. Nathan insists that he lives in the present but, when he's not promoting the company, he spends much of his day planning a tour of the world's capitals for Madbrain — a tour which will take place only if *I* find the funding.

Frank Hodge has tried to send him on auditions for movie parts, but RAUNCHY REVOLUTIONARIES seems to have soured Nathan on film, and he now refers to movie producers as 'turkey turds.'

Shortly after Nathan and I became involved, I worked up the courage to phone Carey, to let her know that I wouldn't be in Europe till summer — but more importantly, why.

"Hi," I said, trying to sound cheerful.

"Hi. How are you?"

"I'm good. How are you?"

"I'm by the pool, and it's a lovely L.A. evening, not too much smog. It's too bad you're not here. What's up?"

"I've had to postpone my trip to England."

"Oh?"

"Something's come up."

"What?"

"Nathan."

She started to laugh.

"What's so funny?"

"Sorry. I wondered when you two would figure out that you were meant to torture each other."

"I'm so sorry."

"Don't be. You made a smart choice."

"You think?"

"We would have had fun, but eventually you'd have figured out you weren't gay."

"Is it that obvious?"

"Who knows — who cares, as long you're happy. Anyway, if you and the kid ever get to L.A. you have a place to stay."

"Wow. Thanks."

"Good luck. Send me a postcard from wherever."

Part of me regrets not having had the Carey experience. I've told Nathan she'd make a wonderful Lady Macbeth if he ever stages the Scottish play; and believe it or not, he's actually thinking about it (he likes the idea of Lady MacBeth as an older woman). Maybe I'll get to play one of the witches.

Recently, Vlad told me that László has established a new company, Bellaire Pictures, and is again making low budget genre movies, like the ones Felicity made. I ran into him at a screening not long ago. He was with a svelte redhead, thirtyish, whom he introduced as Giselle, his new Head of Quality Development.

"What're you up to?" I asked.

"We are making new quality picture, Sexy Poets Society. And you?"

"Running a theatre."

"Ah, actors still talking."

I told Vlad about seeing László and that he was back making movies.

"It is good to know," he said, "that he is still fighting to free women's breasts."

Vlad wants me to work with him on THE MOOSE IN THE LOOK-ING-GLASS, a picture based on one of Honor's earlier books; but I've been focused on Madbrain and getting to England, hoping to take the Queen Mary to Southampton. Nathan, of course, wants to take a freighter so that we'll have an *authentic* sea voyage, so it's possible I might never get there.

He also hasn't learned any French even though I've tried to share my lessons with him. I've told him that if I'm conversant in French and he's not by the time we get to Paris, I might "dormir avec un acteur français merveilleusement sexy, n'est pas?" Then I crossed my eyes and stuck out my tongue. To which he had no reply — ha!

I still feel like an amoeba — we protozoa never get past that sensation — struggling forward as we do single-mindedly (in my case, with a limp). I know now that we're not sexless (or 'sexy'), but we are the foundation of all life. Some of us are even parasites. They say we one-celled creatures respond to every stimuli, unlike the higher forms of being who are more selective; but we've been here since the beginning of life on earth and we have a force, a purpose; and though we frequently change shape, we remain centred.

Some nights, standing in the lights downstage, waiting for my cue, listening to the audience breathe — like a large mammal — I feel connected to all species, and to all four billion years of the earth's past; and, beyond that, to a vast, complicated universe, full of possibility.

And how, I ask myself, could it get any better?

ABOUT THE AUTHOR

During the 1970s and 80s, Barry Healey wrote television variety for such performers as Milton Berle, Arte Johnson, Soupy Sales, Bob Crane, Andy Griffith, Sally Kellerman, Jackie Mason, Henry Mancini, Van Johnson and others. His motion picture credits include the award-winning shorts: OUTTAKES (1978) writer/director/producer; THE NIGHT BEFORE THE MORNING AFTER (1979) writer/director; and the feature films: THE GREY FOX (1982) co-producer; ONE MAGIC CHRISTMAS (1985) writer; BIG DEAL (1985) director; HOLLYWOOD NORTH (2003) writer. *The Sex Life of the Amoeba* is his first novel. Barry lives in Toronto.

Printed in August 2014
by Gauvin Press,
Gatineau, Québec